TO FIND A
KILLER

a natural state murder mystery

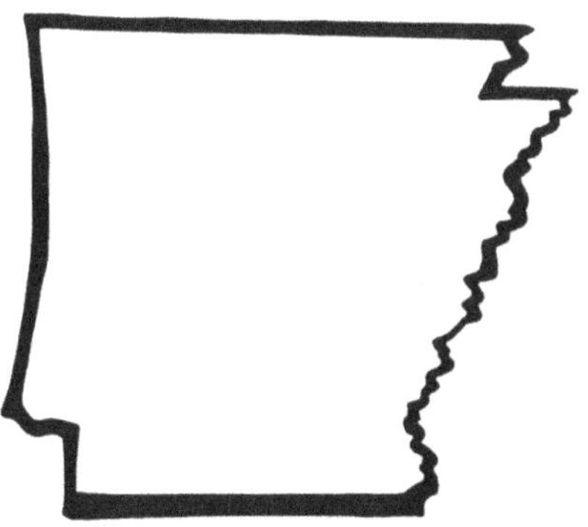

leah brewer

dedication

In memory of my late sister-in-law, Tammy. She loved fiercely, protected those who couldn't protect themselves, and held nothing back. She also welcomed me into the family with open arms. She is missed and loved by so many.

chapter one

IF THERE WAS ONE thing Tammy Gail Sharp had learned over the past ten years as an Atlanta homicide detective, it was never to hesitate when facing a killer. Then what would cause her to stand there like a fool instead of pulling the trigger? Because Chip Reeker looked young enough to be her child. The child she'd never have.

The basement in the home Chip shared with his grandmother reminded Tammy of the sauna she frequented at the gym – tiny and hot enough to melt a bucket of Rocky Road ice cream in seconds. Sweat clung to her scalp, and she had no doubt her chestnut hair looked as greasy as Chip's bleached blonde locks.

His right hand shook as it clung to the pistol. His open-mouth breathing caused his chest to move up and down. Despite his bloodshot eyes, Chip's round face almost looked angelic as his finger twitched on the trigger of the 22-caliber pistol in his short, plump hand.

"There's no need for anyone to get hurt," Tammy said, her eyes working to align with Chip's. "Your grandmother asked me to stop by to talk to her."

A tendon in Chip's neck twitched before he adjusted his view downward. "She was going to fill your head with lies." The bulge of his throat rippled with every swallow.

She didn't want to believe he'd shoot her. He hadn't even been on her radar as a suspect in his father's murder. Not with his solid alibi. Now that they'd made an arrest, what could be the reason? And where was his grandmother?

The scent of too many animals and dirty bodies in a small space assaulted Tammy's nostrils as she continued her stare-off with the manchild. Teeny meows broke the silence, followed by loud purrs from a cardboard box at the end of the worn brown sofa. A black cat poked its head out of the box, meowed, and disappeared.

As Tammy gripped her Glock 19, she considered ways to diffuse the situation. "Chip, please put the gun down. I told you I'm just here to speak to your grandmother. That's all."

Chip's gaze darted to the box of cats and lingered there momentarily. His brows softened, and the hand holding the weapon slackened until it dropped to his side.

Relief twirled inside Tammy. Her gaze left Chip, and she took inventory of the room. Three computer monitors sat on an L-shaped desk. A massive TV screen hung on the wall above the desk. A plush black office chair and gaming consoles completed the space. Bright images of a virtual world kept flashing on the screens.

The only door in the room creaked open a few inches. A dim light shined on a pedestal sink. Tammy froze. Miss Reeker peeked out from around the bottom of the door. Dried blood caked around her nose. She moaned and struggled to sit up.

A burst of panic lit Chip's eyes right before he thundered toward Tammy.

In the blink of an eye, Tammy whirled about and advanced on Chip. Using the butt of her gun, she struck him across the head. He fell to his knees. Tilting his head, he glared at Tammy. Tears pooled on his lashes.

Tammy anchored her gaze to his right before a bullet tore through her chest. Her back hit the wall, but she didn't feel it. Her legs buckled. She crumbled to the floor.

Chip didn't spare her a glance as he escaped up the stairs.

She should've disarmed him. Because of her reluctance to shoot, she could meet the same fate Daddy had all those years ago.

What a stupid rookie mistake.

It couldn't have been more than a minute before Tammy's partner, Thomas Riggs, yelled for her to stay with him. Where had he been anyway? Outside on the phone. That's right. He must've heard the gunshot. His face seemed to jump around as he leaned over her. He pressed something on her chest as he yelled into his radio, "Officer down!"

A sweet chocolate scent reached her nose as Thomas's breath tickled her cheek. He must've been in the candy stash she thought she'd hidden. She groaned. What an odd thing to think about. Shouldn't her life be flashing through her mind?

Another officer leaned on Tammy's other side. She pointed at Miss Reeker. It seemed to take every ounce of strength to speak, but she had to. "Help her," she moaned and pinched her eyelids tight.

Thomas moved close to Tammy's ear. "I'm so sorry. I shouldn't have ever let you come in alone."

Let? Did he say he shouldn't have let her come in? They'd been partners for almost five years – surely, he knew no one let Tammy Gail Sharp do anything.

"You're one of the strongest people I know, Tammy. Stay with me!"

Tammy wanted to live, but she couldn't find the will to open her eyes. She tried to tell him it was okay. If only her mouth would cooperate.

As darkness loomed, she wondered how she'd greet Daddy on the other side.

chapter two

Even though a week had passed, Tammy could still smell the gunpowder like the day Chip Reeker shot her. A mist of cold sweat coated her body. She'd almost died. How had she been so stupid? Because they'd already made an arrest. She never would've dreamed that Chip was an unstable gaming addict.

Luckily for Tammy, the low-caliber handgun he used had struck the strap on her leather gun holster before entering her chest. No major organs had sustained life-threatening damage. Dr. Gable seemed to think her emotional state would be more problematic to get past than the physical.

The stiff hospital gown clung to her legs like she had a heavy curtain draped over her body, stifling her movement. She took a breath and hit the call button.

Julie, her nurse, poked her head inside the door. The edges of her mouth spread into a grin, deepening the wrinkles around her compassionate brown eyes. The few times Julie had been Tammy's nurse, she'd brought joy into the hospital room.

"Good to see you're awake." She checked the beeping monitors and turned to Tammy. "What can I do for you, honey?"

Tammy licked her dry lips and closed her eyes. "I'm thirsty."

"I'll be back in a New York minute with a can of your favorite drink."

Tammy couldn't help but smile when Julie nearly floated out of the room. She swallowed past her dry throat and looked beyond the half-opened blind at the rooftop to the next building. So much had happened while Tammy had been out of it. She still couldn't believe Uncle Ellis had drowned a few days back. A sob gurgled as she thought of how much Chip Reeker had cost her.

"Knock knock," Mama said as she strolled into the room.

"Hi, Mama." Seeing her caused the tears to flow even harder.

Mama wiped the moisture from Tammy's cheeks with a tissue. She grasped Tammy's hand and held it close to her chest. "Mama's here now. I'm so sorry I had to leave you."

"It's okay, Mama." Tammy shifted her backside, ignoring the muscle cramp traveling up her calf. "You've not been gone that long."

"I just can't believe Ellis drowned," Mama said as she moved to the window. "He was just here a few days ago."

"It's hard to grasp, that's for sure." Tammy's stomach bunched into a knot that matched the cramp in her leg as tears continued to wet her cheeks. "I just hate I had to miss his memorial."

Mama's tears spilled down her face, leaving tracks behind in her makeup. "Ellis would've understood. It's not like you could travel after what you've been through."

Julie drifted near the bed with a can of Sprite. Her face softened with sympathy. "Here you go." She poured the drink into a cup and patted Mama's hand. "Ruby, it's good to see you're back. I was so sorry to hear of your brother's passing. He seemed like such a nice man the day he was here."

"Yes, he was." Mama's face flashed with pain. "Thank you. I appreciate you all taking care of my Tammy Gail."

"She's a good patient, so it's been easy."

Tammy snorted. "Now, Miss Julie, I know I haven't been the best patient." She closed her eyes when the tightness in her calf softened.

Julie planted her hands on her hips. "I said good, not the best." A gentle puff of a laugh left her. "And you haven't slapped me yet, now, have you?"

A wag of her head said no. "Of course, I haven't slapped you."

"A patient popped me right in the eye a few months ago. I had to hide the bruise with my tinted cream for almost two weeks, so you're one of the better ones." She tucked the cover around Tammy's legs. "I'm going to let you two visit, but I'll be back in a few minutes with a fresh gown."

"Thank you."

After another week of poking and prodding, the day Tammy had been waiting for arrived. Julie buzzed into the room. "I bet you're ready to get checked out." She glanced at her watch. "Your release papers are done, so it shouldn't be too long."

If Tammy could, she'd jump up and down. "Even though you've been a wonderful nurse, I'm ready to get home."

A smile so big it almost broke Julie's face appeared. "I wish you the best, Detective Sharp."

An hour later, Tammy stepped out of the wheelchair and climbed into the back of the cab beside Mama. The driver took off toward Peachtree Park, the suburb of Atlanta where Tammy lived.

Mama's legs bounced and she nipped at her bottom lip. Tammy's nerves seemed to dump a bucket of lead in her stomach. She had no doubt Mama had something to say. Something Tammy most likely wouldn't want to hear.

A sad frown etched the side of Mama's mouth. "Tammy Gail, I have to ask, whatever possessed you to go to that house without a bulletproof vest?"

Cars passed in a blur as the driver sped down the Atlanta highway. "I was going to see a little ole granny, so I didn't think it was necessary."

"You may be in your forties, but that better be the last time you go without one when you're on duty. You hear me?" Her lips drew into a hard line, and Tammy had no doubt Mama meant business.

"Yes, Mama."

Yes, Mama? What was she, twelve years old again?

"I don't know if I could survive losing you, too." Mama studied Tammy's face like she needed to memorize every detail.

"I promise I'll be careful." Tammy leaned across the back seat and took Mama's hand. "I promise."

"Why were you there in the first place?" Mama continued to stare at Tammy.

"I just had to speak to Miss Reeker about her son's recent murder."

"How was he murdered?"

"Somebody stabbed him outside a bar a few blocks away from where he lived."

"Did you find out who it was?"

"Yes, it turned out to be a man he'd gotten into a fight with at the bar."

"Then what caused that boy to shoot you?" Mama held onto the back headrest when the driver swerved. "I'm just shocked you didn't take him down before he got the chance."

Tammy's lashes fluttered closed. "He was a kid. I kept thinking about how he could've been my child. I know it was stupid."

A short, loud horn blast and shouts from the driver made Tammy regret not driving them home herself. Thomas had offered, but she'd declined because she didn't want Mama interrogating him. She'd know better next time—not that there would be a next time.

"But why did he do it?" Mama asked, ignoring the scene coming from the front seat.

After craning her neck to make sure they were good, Tammy sighed. "Chip and his grandmother had been arguing about a new game he wanted. He lost his temper and attacked her right before I got there."

"So, it was poor timing?"

"I guess. For me, anyway. But Miss Reeker is alive because we showed up when we did." Tammy bit her bottom lip, her head swimming with heaviness. "I'd say things worked out how they were supposed to."

"Why can't you do something behind the scenes?" Mama raised a perfectly formed eyebrow the same color as her flaxen blonde hair. "Your daddy wouldn't want to see you die like he did. He'd be fighting mad if he knew your chosen career."

Tammy bristled. She scooted closer to the door on her side. The ache in her chest lurked behind her ribs, making her forget about her head for a moment. "I disagree. I think he'd be proud."

"You're wrong. He's rolling over in his grave. I can promise you that."

"How could you say that?" The ache behind her ribs intensified, rattling her pounding heart.

"Because it's the truth." Pain and anger stirred behind Mama's eyes. "After graduating college, you never came home. Instead, you immersed yourself in a dangerous job."

"What's that supposed to mean?" Tammy dug her nails into her palms.

The taxi driver glanced in the rearview mirror when Tammy's voice rose.

Mama didn't seem to notice or care. "I spent many years praying for you not to get killed. You have no idea how it hurt when Thomas called to tell me you'd been shot."

Mama's words caused Tammy's heart to pound. "You think I don't regret my choices?"

She rubbed her fingers across her forehead. "I imagine you do, Tammy Gail."

"Sybil has offered to stay with me for the next few days. Why don't you book the next flight out? I'll be fine without you." Sybil was Thomas's wife and Tammy's closest friend.

A shocked look crossed Mama's features. "Fine by me. I just thought you needed me."

Tammy lowered her gaze with shame. "Mama, I will always need you. I'm doing good, though, and figured it would be easier for Sybil since she's right here."

Mama blinked back tears, the hurt evident on her face. "I'll book the next flight out." She turned toward the window, her shoulders heaving up and down.

The cab driver shot Tammy a dirty look before turning the music up. Great.

"I'm sorry, Mama," Tammy said as she placed her hand on Mama's knee.

"I'm sorry, too. What I said was unnecessary. I can't help but worry about you with this job." Mama placed her hand on top of Tammy's.

"You don't have to leave."

The music lowered, and the cab driver nodded approvingly in Tammy's direction. She couldn't help but grin at him.

"No, it's fine." Mama took a breath and let it out in a swoosh. "It may be best I go home and see to Ellis's affairs. That is if Sybil really did offer to stay."

"She did. I hope you're not mad at me."

"No, honey, I'm not. This has been a hard month for both of us."

A bubble gum wrapper lodged underneath the floormat stole Tammy's attention for a moment. She locked her eyes on the wrapper as thoughts of Uncle Ellis's last moment overtook her. She couldn't shake the feeling that his death had been no accident. There was no way he would've been fishing while Tammy lay in the hospital. No way.

Her jaw muscles locked shut as resolve grabbed her. She needed to figure out what really happened. If it turned out she had the most personal murder of her life to solve, she would do whatever it took to find Uncle Ellis's killer.

chapter three

Thick streams of rain hammered the windshield of Tammy's hunter-green and white 1973 Ford Bronco as she traveled down Interstate 55 toward Pocahontas, Arkansas.

After taking a bullet, she guessed she should be thankful things hadn't turned out worse. Who knows, the leave of absence from the Atlanta Police Force may be the best medicine she could get. She needed time to mourn. Not only the person she'd been before the shooting but time to mourn losing Uncle Ellis. That and to figure out what happened to him.

Her stomach churned as she considered surprising Mama with an unannounced visit. How would she deal with being back in Pocahontas without Uncle Ellis? Tammy prayed she would find the willpower to give Mama the comfort and support she needed. Poor thing had been put through it over the past few weeks. First, with Tammy getting shot in the chest and then her brother's death.

The moment of weakness in Chip's basement had cost Tammy more than she'd ever imagined. Iron shackles tightened across her chest, and she swallowed the tears that threatened to flow.

Castle, her three-year-old brindle pitbull, whined. Tammy reached over and patted his side. "I'm sorry, boy. I know you feed off my emotions. I'll try to do better."

A big truck passed, going way too fast. Sheets of water covered the Bronco, temporarily blinding Tammy in the already dark night. She jerked her hand off Castle and gripped the steering wheel. He licked her elbow, and she felt his expressive brown eyes on her.

She tipped her chin in his direction. "Quit being a baby. I can't keep petting you and drive in this storm."

They passed the first Trumann exit. Good. They had an hour to go before reaching Tammy's childhood home. She hit a bump in the road, and Castle grunted.

"Don't gripe at me. I'd like to see you try to drive in this weather," Tammy said.

Castle turned his head like she hadn't spoken. Mad again. Ignoring her must be his favorite way to let her know how he felt. She'd spent two days apologizing to him with meaty treats after she'd been released from the hospital. Thomas and Sybil told her Castle had stood at the door every night she'd spent away from him, watching and waiting.

Her stomach rumbled, and she groaned. If memory served, Trumann boasted several fast-food joints that stayed open late.

A few minutes later, she balanced a soft taco on one knee and shoved a bite of chicken enchilada into her mouth. With a grin, Castle dove into his bowl of dog food.

Hot sauce drizzled down her hand, and she held it out. Castle licked it off and tried to climb onto her lap. She nudged him over to the passenger seat with her elbow. "Oh no, you don't. Get yourself back to your bowl."

When she pulled into Mama's driveway a few minutes after midnight, she yawned. The dim porch light shined enough that Tammy could tell the house looked more modern since she'd been here last. The white brick, deep brown wood shutters, and matching front door stood out. Her gaze lingered on Uncle Ellis's house for a few minutes. She wiped the mist from her eyes, got out, and motioned for Castle to follow. "Come on, boy, let's get going."

He leaped out of the car and followed Tammy up the front steps. She cracked a grin when she glanced at the porch swing. The sea green paint color looked good. A low, deep growl echoed from Castle's chest when they reached the door.

Something had to be out of place. Castle had never steered her wrong.

She twisted the doorknob. The door didn't budge, which made sense. It wouldn't make sense for Mama to keep the door unlocked, even in a small town like this one. Despite his obvious discomfort, Castle stood still and on high alert while Tammy fished in her purse for her set of house keys.

The door slid open without a sound. The place stood dark and silent. A noise must have caused Castle to react that way. Her heart slowed to its normal rhythm until she flipped the light on.

She unholstered her weapon as she took inventory of the living area. Couch cushions lay scattered on the floor, drawers had been pulled out, and plants turned over. Mama would never allow her home to get in this shape. Had the person who killed Uncle Ellis come for Mama?

Tammy's heart tripled in speed. Please let Mama be all right. She barreled down the hallway with Castle on her heels. "Mama!"

Castle's body shook with slight tremors when they reached Mama's bedroom. She pushed the door open with her foot, poised to rush into the room.

Only to meet the end of a rather large gun.

chapter four

JACE EUBANKS POURED A black coffee and settled onto the sofa. His gaze landed on the painting of his great-grandfather standing proud with colorful feathers in his long, dark hair, paint on his face, and a bow and arrow in his hand. Pulling his jet-black hair into a ponytail, he imagined what it would've been like to live as a traditional Native American.

He glanced at the clock. Almost midnight without a wink of sleep. His mind raced as he thumbed through a stack of old newspaper articles on the town of Old Davidsonville. His instinct led to several stories in his years as an investigative journalist. And right now, his gut told him his late landlord and neighbor, Ellis Martin, lost his life over rumors of gold and jewels said to be buried in or around the town of Old Davidsonville.

Since the police had ruled Ellis's death an accident, that left Jace to figure out what happened. He thought back to the day Ellis called, convinced he'd stumbled upon a story that needed to be told. Jace agreed to move into one of Ellis's rental houses long enough to help Ellis investigate.

Over the years, Jace learned to step away from investigations for a while when he hit a wall. That's what had happened with the case he'd been working on in West Memphis. He'd allowed it to consume his every thought, every move. He prayed that when he returned home, he would be able to focus on more than his grief to bring the killer to justice.

He planned to return to West Memphis with a fresh set of eyes after he helped Ellis with whatever situation he had going on. He still did, but now it would be after solving Ellis's murder. His investigation in West Memphis was too important to mess up. Too personal.

Ellis drowned the same day Jace arrived in Pocahontas. Ellis's decision to go out on his boat left Jace clueless about the nature of what Ellis wanted him to investigate. If only he knew what Ellis uncovered, solving his murder would be a lot simpler. Jace's mind kept going to Old Davidsonville. Then, the school. As the former history teacher, what if Ellis uncovered something before retiring? Or the Pocahontas Police Department? Obie Wilson, Ellis's best buddy, won the last Sheriff's election by a landslide, so that couldn't be it. Or maybe it could. It was too early to discount any of these scenarios.

He stared at the picture of Ellis's girlfriend, Lorene Pankey, on the murder board he'd made. Could she have killed him for money? Probably not, but she was the main suspect for now.

He needed to find out who Ellis left his assets to. As a well-known wealthy man with extensive rental properties across town, money could have been the motive.

So many unanswered questions. Could it be tied to the supposed treasure or a random murder? Or maybe a simple fishing accident cost Ellis his life? But that didn't add up. At least it didn't to Jace. He rubbed his temples and took a swig of his lukewarm coffee.

The distinct sound of a barking dog caused Jace to sit straight up on the sofa. He holstered his Glock 19 and slipped out the back door. No one on their street had a dog.

Two doors down, a sweet-looking older model Bronco sat in the driveway. It must belong to Miss Ruby's daughter, Tammy. He'd only seen her once from a distance since they'd graduated high school. She'd missed Ellis's funeral. At least he hadn't seen her there. He filed that fact away for later. He needed to focus on the here and now. Tammy must be here to check on her mom. But why the barking?

Even though he figured trouble lay on the other side of the door, he made his way up the steps. Snarls joined the barks. Instead of knocking, he tried the knob and eased the door open when he found it unlocked. He eyed the mess and padded toward the back of the house.

The scene he walked in on could've easily been one from the movies. A large pit bull lunged at a man in a black mask. Tammy stood beside the bed with a gun pointed at the floor, her hands trembling. The masked man fired a shot, and the dog's body jerked and dropped to the floor. Tammy screamed like she'd been the one who took the bullet. The dog shot upright and raced the man, teeth bared. The man cried out, raised his weapon, and this time he pointed it straight at Tammy's head. She dropped to the ground. The bullet whizzed above her head and shattered the window behind her.

Jace's heart gunned into overdrive, and within a split second, he pulled the trigger. Blood stained the man's shirt as he collapsed on the floor. The dog stopped and glanced at Jace, almost in appreciation. Tammy didn't spare Jace or the injured man a second look. She crawled beside the dog and whispered words of comfort.

Jace checked the man's wrist for a pulse. He breathed a sigh of relief as he dialed 911. To the man's left, a half-open duffle bag lay with what looked to be a jewelry box sticking out. Crimes like this happened in Pocahontas about as often as in Mayberry. Where was Andy Griffith when you needed him?

Tammy turned, and he took a step back when he got a good look at her. Many years had passed since he'd seen a woman with such feminine yet stern features. Her eyes popped like the sun on a rainy day. Golden brown and full of life.

And they currently speared Jace with the same fiery, hot gaze as the last time he saw her.

chapter five

Tammy laid her hand on Castle's hip and sobbed. He raised his head and looked at her like she needed to stop. The bullet had nicked his side but didn't appear to be life-threatening. Even so, he needed to see a vet as soon as possible.

She glanced from the corner of her eye at the man speaking with a 911 Operator. Uncle Ellis's tenant, Jace Eubanks. His caramel skin stood out against the white t-shirt he wore, making Tammy's skin seem pale and drab in comparison. He paced the floor as he spoke, his tall frame still as lean and toned as it had been in high school.

Mama had sent Tammy a few pictures of him over the past couple of weeks. She'd wanted them to reconnect. Tammy, not so much. She didn't want or need anyone in her life. Especially a lying, cheating pig like Jace Eubanks.

Tammy found it too much trouble to invest in a relationship. So why even start again? The last one was exactly that. The last one. She had Castle to keep her company. And so far, he'd been way better than any man she'd gotten involved with.

Jace hung up the phone and glanced at Tammy. "Do you want to put some pressure on that man's wound, or are you too busy worrying about a dog?"

Her head spun around so fast it could've lifted off her shoulders. "Excuse me? You're the one who fired the shot. Not me." Her eyes narrowed into slits. "Why don't you do it and keep your nose out of my business."

He ripped his t-shirt off and stomped over to the man on the floor. Tammy's eyes doubled in size as Jace wadded the shirt into a ball and placed it over the bullet hole. He slipped the mask off the burglar's face and asked a question without looking at Tammy. "Do you know him?"

Tammy swallowed and adjusted her view away from Jace's bare chest. The would-be burglar reminded her of the countless people she'd dealt with over the years who'd lost themselves to addiction. Sores covered his sunk-in face, giving him the appearance of a sixty-year-old. She pressed her lips together and shook her head. "He looks strung out. Is he breathing?"

Jace kept one hand on the t-shirt covering the bullet hole and put his ear close to the burglar's mouth. "Yeah, but it sounds labored."

"I have to find Mama." Tammy talked more to Castle than anyone else. She looked inside the closet and found nothing but enough clothes and shoes to open a boutique. Once she'd looked under every rack, she marched out of the room. Within minutes, she came back in and sat beside Castle. She sighed.

"You didn't find Miss Ruby?"

"Nope." She glanced through the bedroom window. The moon cast a glow on the backyard. It reminded Tammy of a horror movie just before the killer let loose. "I can't imagine where she'd be so late at night."

Castle raised his head and let out a low growl. Tammy rubbed behind his ear and rested her forehead on his. "It's okay, baby boy. Help will be here soon."

Sirens sounded in the distance, and red lights flashed through the open curtains. Jace continued to put pressure on the man's wound, steadily mumbling something under his breath.

What could Mama have been thinking when she talked to her about Jace being back in town? There's no way the two of them could ever rekindle old feelings. No matter how attractive, she still found him. Deep brown eyes you could dive into had always been her weakness, but his were off-limits.

Within minutes, the place swarmed with medical personnel and police officers. Tammy's head pounded from all the questions she couldn't answer. She needed to get Castle taken care of and find Mama. Two EMTs loaded the unconscious criminal into an ambulance and sped away with a cop car on their tail.

"Ma'am?" A woman in a navy blue EMT polo and khaki pants pulled a few long black flyaway hairs behind her ear and leaned beside Tammy. "May I see about your dog?"

"Yes, we'd appreciate it. Wouldn't we, Castle?" Tammy's face flashed with a smile for the first time that night. She moved over to give the woman, whom she recognized as Nicole Eubanks, some room when she caught Jace gawking at her. She scowled and turned back to Castle.

The woman spoke to Castle in a low tone as she pulled out her supplies. So far, he seemed to be okay with her. She bandaged Castle and turned to Tammy. "I'm Nicole Benson, by the way. Not sure if you remember me."

"I do remember you, Nicole." Tammy smiled at Nicole. "Thank you for helping Castle. I know it's not your job."

"Not a problem. I've got him bandaged, but we need to get him to the vet for stitches. The bullet went through his side and luckily missed everything it needed to."

A wave of relief washed over Tammy. "I appreciate you. Where's the vet?"

Nicole's lips twitched at the corners. "You're in luck. The vet is my husband, and his clinic is beside our house the next street over. I can take Castle there now if that's all right."

The tension in Tammy's shoulders lessened. "You have no idea how much that would help me. I still need to find Mama," she said.

"I think Miss Ruby is on a date," Nicole said.

A date? Mama didn't date.

Jace crossed the room and stopped directly beside Tammy. "Do you have somewhere else to stay tonight?"

He hadn't changed a bit. Always Mr. Protector. Even when he couldn't stand the sight of someone. Still trying to process that Nicole thought Mama was on a date, Tammy answered without meeting his gaze. "I planned on staying here or at Uncle Ellis's after tracking Mama down."

Mama picked that moment to sashay through the front door, the local sheriff close to her heels. "Good grief, Tammy Gail, what in the world have you done?"

chapter six

The following day, Tammy poked her head inside the room where Castle slept at the vet's office. "Hi, baby boy."

He cracked open his eyes and rose like someone stuck his backside with a needle. She dropped to the floor and hugged him to her chest. The tension in her shoulders faded away with the hug.

"He's doing great," Harry Benson, the vet, said. His smile exposed a full mouth of straight, white teeth.

After receiving care instructions, Tammy and Castle headed to Mama's. She'd set up a big fluffy bed at the end of the sofa for him. He scanned the room before curling up and going straight to sleep.

She entered the kitchen, where Mama stood at the stainless-steel stove, waiting for a pot of tea to boil. Her silky baby blue pajamas pooled at her ankles, and even after last night's events, she still looked as if she'd just stepped off the pages of Southern Belle magazine.

"I still can't believe you went on a date with Sheriff Obie Wilson last night." Tammy paused with the dustpan in her hand.

Mama patted the sweeping blonde curls that fell to her shoulders and jiggled her eyebrows. "Well, believe it. I've decided it's beyond time for me to have a life, Tammy Gail."

A shudder traveled down Tammy's spine as she stared, unseeing, at the line of white cabinets. "Either way, I'm glad you weren't here when that thug broke in."

Mama grabbed a wooden spoon from a flowery ceramic jug and squeezed a lemon into a mason jar full of iced sweet tea. "Me, too. That was the Lord watching out for me. And maybe that means He approves of my relationship with Obie."

"I wouldn't go that far," Tammy said under her breath as she emptied the dustpan into the garbage.

The spoon Mama used to stir the tea clunked against the side of the mason jar. "What was that, Tammy Gail?"

"Nothing." Tammy bent down to scratch her ankle. She had been back in Arkansas for less than twenty-four hours and already had a mosquito bite. "Was that your first date with the sheriff?"

A giggle left Mama, and she mumbled something Tammy didn't hear. Really? A giggle? In all her forty-five years, Tammy had never heard Mama do that. Now, she does it at sixty-three. Over the sheriff. Oh, boy.

"Tammy Gail? Did you hear me?"

"Sorry, I didn't." She poured a cup of coffee, mixed in cream and sugar, and plopped down on a black leather bar stool at the island. "What did you say?"

"I said we've been on five or, I guess, six dates now." Pink stained Mama's cheeks. "We discussed moving our relationship to the next level last night."

The barstool screeched across the floor as Tammy shot up. "What do you mean by that?"

"It means we're going steady." The pink stain deepened on Mama's cheeks. "What did you think I meant?"

She swallowed the lump in her throat. "I don't know. Marriage crossed my mind for a second."

Mama laughed sweetly. "Of course, we're not getting married. We enjoy one another's company. That's all."

Tammy released the breath caught in her chest. "Okay then. Do you want to go to the station? Detective Bromley said he has a few more questions for me."

"I sure do. I have questions for him. How am I supposed to feel safe after that man came into my home and tried to steal my stuff?" She lowered her voice and leaned her waist across the kitchen island. "With a gun?"

Tammy's face relaxed as she reached for Mama's hand. "I'll be here a while, Mama. If that's okay with you."

"It's more than okay with me. I can't wait to spend time with my sweet girl." Her face brightened, and she squeezed Tammy's hand. "Please say you'll stay here instead of at Ellis's place."

"I will, Mama." Tammy took a sip of coffee and eased back onto the barstool. "I still can't wrap my head around Uncle Ellis leaving me his house."

"All his houses and everything else." Mama looked at Tammy as if trying to figure out her thoughts.

The delicate features of Mama's face never ceased to amaze her. Mama had an angelic, sweet face, and Tammy had high cheekbones and a more sculpted look like her Daddy.

Mama continued, "You know he had at least ten rentals. You need to meet with the attorney to finalize everything while you're here."

"I don't want to leave Castle alone." Tammy rubbed the scar the bullet had left on her chest and sighed. Now, she had to deal with rental property on top of everything else.

"Obie said he'd keep an eye on him," Mama said as she handed Castle a meaty treat. "We won't be gone that long."

When they arrived at the station, they learned that an eighteen-year-old drug addict, Sonny Perkins, had been the burglar. He had a bag of Mama's jewelry and some cash she'd kept on her bedside table. Luckily for him, the gunshot had been clean, so he'd be out of the hospital and in the county jail soon.

A couple of hours later, Tammy clicked the blinker to turn onto Bettis Street as she drove from the police station. Wind from the open window lifted Tammy's hair and did the same for her mood. The air smelled nice and clean, like fresh-cut grass.

Mama crossed her arms and tapped her foot. Tammy had no doubt she fumed over the detective telling Mama the "incident," as he called it, was a one-time thing. The man who'd broken in recently lost the job he'd had for only two weeks. They blamed the burglary on desperation and his drug addiction. That hadn't given Mama the reassurance Tammy knew she needed.

She might be aggravated, but at least her hair stayed firmly in place. Tammy wanted to say that to Mama. Instead, she kept the conversation light and avoided anything that would worsen Mama's mood. "Did you want to grab lunch on the way home?"

"Can we stop by the pharmacy first? I need to tell Heather about Vivian White's money situation."

A grin ruffled her lips. "Okay, Mama. Who is Vivian White?"

"She's new to town." Mama's smile slipped into a frown. "Unfortunately, Sonny Perkins is her nephew."

Tammy nearly choked on her spit. "Nephew?"

"Yes, but she can't control his actions." A smidge of anger laced her tone. "She's had a hard time since they moved from Los Angeles. The ladies from church want to help her."

She passed the courthouse, mashing the brake to the floor, when a group of kids walked in front of the car. "What would make them move to Pocahontas from LA?"

"Vivian's husband recently passed away, and she was all the family Sonny had left. She said he had been in trouble and even wanted to join a gang."

"Why Pocahontas?" Tammy asked as she eased into an empty parking spot.

Mama pooched her lips out. "I don't know, Tammy Gail. I guess she liked the name of the town. She said she just wanted to get him away from Los Angeles."

"So, she moved him here where he could rob you? Where are his parents?"

"From what I understand, they died a few years back." Mama's eyes bore into Tammy's. "Now, don't you try to stop me from helping her."

"Wouldn't dream of it."

As the owner of one of the oldest pharmacies in Arkansas, Mama made it her business to ensure all the elderly folks had medication, even if it meant losing money on her end. Tammy's heart flipped. If only one day she could have half the tender heart Mama had, she'd be all right.

Every familiar sight, from the imposing old courthouse to the intriguing museum and the bustling historic square, tugged at Tammy's heartstrings and filled her with a longing to return to the carefree days of her childhood. The comforting feeling of home washed over her, and she couldn't help but smile.

After securing an empty parking spot right in front of the pharmacy, she decided to seize the opportunity to indulge in a nostalgic treat. Making her way to the old-fashioned soda fountain, she reveled in the memories of doing the same as a child. The thought of enjoying a delicious ice cream in that familiar setting brought a sense of warmth and contentment.

Tammy skipped past the red stools that lined the bar and washed her hands. Mama had always wanted Tammy to attend pharmaceutical school and take over the family business. She spun around, debating what she wanted before grabbing a cone from a glass jar. For a moment, she wished she had followed in Mama's footsteps instead of Daddy's. She probably wouldn't have a bullet scar to deal with. She took a bite of vanilla ice cream and sighed.

After they left the pharmacy, a glance in the rearview mirror put a frown on Tammy's face. The same maroon Ford Taurus with dark-tinted windows that Tammy had noticed when they left the house this morning trailed behind them. She made a sudden turn down a side street and parked in front of a random house, her eyes glued to the rearview mirror. Sure enough, the Taurus turned down the same street. Tammy's heart accelerated as her hand rested on her gun.

"What are we doing?" Mama's voice cut through Tammy's nerves.

What if the car stopped? Would she be able to protect them? Had someone from Atlanta followed her here? She'd arrested many hardened criminals over the years who would want payback. Her heart pounded, and she held her breath, her eyes glued to the car.

The car zipped right past them and turned left on the next street. Tammy let out a breath and closed her eyes. Perhaps she needed to seek medical help for her paranoia.

chapter seven

I DRIVE PAST DETECTIVE Sharp and turn down the next street like I'm out for a Sunday drive. I even threw my hand up in a wave. Not that she can see it through the tinted windows. But it is neighborly to wave when we pass people.

Word around town is Ellis Martin left her everything he owned. He'd just handed it to her on a silver platter. She'd always been lucky, even as a child. Her father, the real Detective Sharp, had doted on his little girl, Tammy. He'd been a good man up until the day he died. I'd respected him since the day he stood up to my sister when we were in grade school. I'd give his daughter a little leeway because of him.

After all, she could change life as I know it with a little direction. Everything I've searched for is within reach as long as she plays her part without getting sidetracked. Yes, this could end well for me as long as I stay focused.

Could all the years of pretending to be someone I'm not finally be coming to an end? Everything I've done has brought me to this point. My destiny awaits. What would Mother think of me now? Would I finally be good enough for her? If she could see how far I've come, would she look at me with tender love instead of my twin sister? Would it be my sister getting locked in the closet at night when Father was away and me on the outside taunting her?

No. I would have helped her escape. How could I have allowed my twin to suffer such pain, fear, and humiliation? Unlike my twin, I have always been a good person.

I need to stop by Sharp Pharmacy for my high blood pressure medication, but I won't be able to do so today. There are still four pills in my current bottle, so it can wait until tomorrow. I must focus on my next steps to finally have the life I deserve. Should I choose a companion to spend the rest of my life with? I loved someone a long time ago, but they were selfish.

Maybe I should warn Detective Sharp to keep her nose out of things that don't concern her. No, not just yet. That can come after the instructions. I'll write her a detailed letter like Mother taught me. Detective Sharp needs to be told what to do, and then all I'll have to do is watch and wait. I've had many years to practice being patient.

Doesn't the Bible say patience is a virtue? I can still hear Mother's voice in my head, telling me it does say that. Once, as an innocent child, I tried to sneak a biscuit before supper was ready. She hit my arm with the spatula over and over until it bled. I can still feel the sharp edge cut into my skin.

After she hit me, she squatted to the floor and wiped the tears from my face. "How many times have I told you patience is a virtue?"

I nodded as I watched blood drip onto the floor. I knew I had better clean it up without Mother asking me. If I didn't, she'd make sure to shed even more of my blood before the night was out.

After I cleaned the floor, I wrapped the same towel around my arm. That was the last time I ever ate one of her biscuits. They were no longer safe after what she did to me. She forced me to retaliate by adding rat poison to the batter every time she made them after that night. She had to pay for how she treated me. Father always said actions have consequences, even for her. I may have been only ten, but I knew better than to eat rat poison.

At that point in my life, I didn't want her to die–I just wanted her to feel some of my pain. When she took ill and was in bed for over a week, I stopped adding the poison.

My sister and I had to handle all the extra chores around the house. Sister took on more than her fair share when my hand got cut. She would've been so mad had she known I did it to myself. Occasionally, she was helpful to me as a child.

I have every intention of giving Detective Sharp the same courtesy. Her life will remain in her hands as long as she is a valuable asset. Little does she know, if she causes trouble in Pocahontas, her days are numbered. No matter who her father was.

chapter eight

AFTER MEETING WITH THE attorney about Uncle Ellis's finances, Tammy kicked off her shoes and threw her purse on her bed. She grabbed her phone and dialed Thomas's number.

He picked up after two rings. "Hi there, T-Sharp."

"Hey. I need a favor." She shimmied out of her leggings and pulled on the skinny jeans at the foot of her bed.

"What's up?"

"I need a check on Sonny Perkins. Originally from California, moved to Arkansas less than a year ago."

"Yep. He has a string of misdemeanors out of Los Angeles. Nothing major. Seems to me this punk is a wannabe on the fast track to prison."

Tammy grinned. "So, you have been checking up on him already?"

"As soon as you texted me last night."

"I have a weird feeling about this dude."

"Let me know if you need anything. Sybil and I can be on the next flight to Arkansas."

After ending the call, she wrote everything she could about Uncle Ellis's life in a notebook. He'd spent over thirty-five years teaching History at Pocahontas High School. Outside of that, he loved the outdoors. Hunting and fish-

ing had been two of his passions. Tammy always assumed he led a quiet, peaceful life.

She added Sonny's name to the corner of the page with
a big question mark beside it.

She pressed the middle of her chest and breathed in.
Even though the bullet hole had faded to a nasty-looking
scar, her chest ached. Worrying about Mama on top of
her new rental business hadn't helped her anxiety.

She thought spending some time inside resting would
help calm her nerves. Nope. If she spent another three
days cooped up in this house, she might go crazy. So,
when Nicole invited her over for dinner, she jumped at
the chance to get out of the house. She knocked on
the solid white front door of the vibrant blue home and
stepped back.

The house next door cast a long shadow as the sun descended in the sky, painting the evening clouds in shades
of orange and purple that glimmered above the roof. A
warm breeze brushed against her arms, reminding her
of the sweltering heat that often enveloped Arkansas.

Harry Benson opened the door with a smile. His tan
joggers and white polo shirt made Tammy think of Miami.
They flowed well with his perfectly styled, dirty blonde
hair, which probably wouldn't move even if a windstorm
blew into town. He stepped to the side. "Good evening,
Tammy. Please, do come in."

"Hello." Tammy closed her eyes as a whiff of garlic and
basil washed over her. "Something smells amazing."

The front room had a caramel sofa and two quirky
burnt orange chairs arranged around a stone fireplace
that covered an entire wall. On the other side of the
room, a wooden table and chairs with seating for six to fit

comfortably filled the space in front of a picture window. Several photos and relics from Nicole's Native American ancestors decorated the area. Tammy wondered if Jace displayed his heritage like his sister or if his home was sterile. Like his personality seemed to be.

Nicole marched through an open doorway with a pot in her hands. Her teal jumpsuit made Tammy feel under-dressed in her Calvin Klein skinny jeans and black tank top. Nicole set the pot on the table and turned to Tammy. "It's lasagna. I got the recipe from my mother-in-law, and it tastes as good as it smells."

Jace strode from the same direction as Nicole with a basket of breadsticks. He froze and rested his gaze on Tammy. His throat rippled with a swallow before he glanced at Nicole. "I didn't know you were having company for dinner."

After saying a quick prayer for patience, Tammy plastered a smile on. "I can leave if I make you uncomfortable."

He held onto the breadsticks like they were his lifeline. "I didn't say that. Your being here is just a surprise."

Nicole bit her bottom lip. "Sorry, you two. I forgot to say we would all be here."

This was a setup if Tammy had ever seen one. It would serve Nicole right if she left. But two things kept her from it. First, Nicole and Harry both helped Castle. Second, she couldn't wait to taste the lasagna. So, it was settled. She'd stay and pretend like Jace wasn't there.

With a solid plan in place, Tammy shrugged and waved a hand. "It's fine. I'm good if he is." Liar. If she was good, then why was her heart trying to beat its way out of her ribcage?

A half-cocked smile slid across his face. "If it's not a problem for you, then it's not a problem for me," Jace said as he held Tammy's gaze hostage.

"Then we're all set. Because I never said it was a problem for me." A cheeky smile nearly caused her face to break. She'd rather eat a bug than allow Jace to get under her skin like he had in high school. He would never know how her stomach flopped when she heard his voice. Nope. "You're the one who made a big deal out of it."

The sparkle in his eyes reminded her of the Jace she knew and loved so long ago. It spelled nothing but mischief. And she wanted no part of it. None. Right?

Harry sat at the head of the table, and Nicole sat to his left. They both looked at Jace like they were ready to throttle him.

Jace dropped the basket between the lasagna and a salad and sat to Harry's right. "Let's just eat before it gets cold," he said.

Tammy ignored his comment and situated herself beside Nicole. After they each made their plates, Harry led them in a blessing. The first bite of lasagna, and Tammy had no doubt she'd made the right decision. The sweet, garlicky sauce rolled around her tongue and tasted like pure bliss. It seemed like she'd survived on takeout and frozen dinners for the past year. Maybe longer. The last homicide case she'd worked on had almost consumed her. And yet, she'd failed to realize Chip Reeker needed professional help.

Enough with that line of thought. "This is delicious. Mama's having her crew over to play dominoes, and I needed to give her some space. Thank you both for inviting me."

"Anytime. I'm just glad you're back in town." Nicole looked at Jace, and Tammy could've sworn she kicked him under the table. "How long are you staying in Pocahontas?"

Tammy took a swig of her Strawberry Lemonade and puckered. "I plan to be here for at least a few months."

After she wiped her mouth, Nicole grinned at Tammy. "That's great news. I hope we can renew our friendship while you're here."

"I would love that."

Harry laid his fork down and pushed his plate away. "How's Castle today? I assume he has greatly improved since last I saw him."

Tammy used her breadstick to wipe up the rest of her sauce. "Other than being mad at me for leaving him behind, he's good."

That earned a part chuckle, part cough from Jace.

Nicole scooted her chair back and licked her lips. "We have a pecan pie for dessert. Jace, come help me make the plates."

Tammy's hand flew to her stomach. She didn't think she could eat another bite until Nicole put a piece of the pie in front of her.

"It's fresh from the oven," Nicole said.

After dinner, both Jace and Tammy stayed to help clean up the dishes. Somehow, they'd managed to go through the entire meal without saying a word to one another. Tammy hadn't acted like such a child in years. She would have to be more mature around him. That or avoid him altogether.

As he reached up to pull the ponytail holder out, his black locks spilled onto his broad shoulders in a silky cascade. She couldn't help but recall the countless occasions when she had been the one tugging the ponytail holder from his hair so she could braid it. Or at least that was the excuse she'd used. All she'd wanted was to run her fingers through it. She had loved the feel of his hair in her hands.

He turned, and their eyes connected. Had he noticed the look on her face as she thought of their past?

Her cheeks heated.

Tammy almost asked him if he remembered the time she told him he looked like the Native American hunters who used to live in this very area. Instead, she swallowed and glanced at the front door. "Thanks again for having me over. I'm going to head over to Mama's."

"Hold up, I'll walk you home," Jace said as he squirted soap into his hands.

She shook her head. Walking home with Jace would only cause more memories she didn't want. "I'm a Homicide Detective in Atlanta. I think I can walk two blocks in Pocahontas, Arkansas, without getting into trouble."

As Tammy descended the sidewalk, the stars and moon hid behind a dark sky. Without the one streetlight working, it would be pitch black out. She made a mental note to contact City Hall about replacing the bulbs.

Headlights from a car creeping by nearly blinded her. She shielded her eyes with the back of her hand as the vehicle continued to drive by at the pace of a wounded turtle. As soon as her eyes got used to the changing light, she turned toward the road.

The same Ford Taurus from before stopped several feet away from Tammy. The driver's side door creaked open a few inches. No inside light came on, so Tammy couldn't see the driver. As the person exited the car, the street light flickered a few times, putting off enough light for Tammy to lay eyes on someone wearing a ski mask and holding an envelope.

She groaned. Not again. This had to be someone from her past. No one from Pocahontas would do this to her. She reached for her gun. Only to find it gone. Instead of taking it to dinner, she'd opted to leave it behind. It looked like she'd have to do things the hard way. She made a straight line toward the masked man.

Before she reached him, he got in the car and sped away, leaving Tammy choking on gas fumes. She locked her eyes on the muddy license plate and could only make out an A.

"Are you okay?" Jace yelled as he jogged up the sidewalk two houses up the street.

A host of emotions ran through Tammy as she worked to control her labored breathing. "I'm fine. Like I said, I can take care of myself."

He stopped beside her, his face full of questions. "Who was that?"

She shrugged, wheeled around, and left Jace standing on the street, calling her name. So much for being more mature.

chapter nine

ANOTHER NIGHT, HE ENTERTAINED thoughts of the past, of how he had wronged Tammy. He could still picture the pain on her face when he told her all those years ago that they'd never be together. He closed his eyes and willed his mind to think of anything else.

Even so, a picture of Tammy consumed his thoughts. He scowled. Even after she'd managed to dodge him the past week or so, he couldn't get her off his mind. The one time they ran into each other at the grocery store, she'd brushed off his concerns from the night a car had pulled up to her.

He couldn't shake the feeling that something terrible was going to happen. Why else would someone hide his identity behind a mask? The driver of the Ford Taurus spelled trouble with a capital T. He scanned the parking lot of the apartment complex where he sat, waiting for the driver of the Ford Taurus to show up. No one stirred yet—not many people are up and about at four in the morning. The muddy license plate hid the tag number, but Jace had a good feeling that this was the same car that pulled up to Tammy. Now, he needed to be pa-tient. Someone would come out at some point. His stiff knuckles bit into the cold steering wheel, and he regretted running the air conditioner on high. He switched the temperature to cool and rested his eyes.

A car door slammed. His blood hummed excitedly when the Ford Taurus's tail lights lit up red as it backed out of the parking spot. He would've seen who got in if he had kept his eyes open. Oh well. He gave the driver time to pull onto the road before he started his car and followed behind at a safe distance.

Tammy said she didn't need his help. It's more like she didn't want it. What else could he expect? Should she welcome him back with open arms? Tell him she'd love to be friends. If Tammy had the same temper as she had in high school, he figured he better just be thankful she hadn't shot him.

Seeing Tammy had brought all those old memories right to the surface. Speaking of old memories, if he planned to open the recently acquired newspaper, he'd better get busy cleaning the place up. After living in West Memphis for the last twenty-five years, Jace never would've dreamed he'd be reopening the newspaper where he spent his high school summers working. Mr. Gleason Murphy had given Jace a job delivering papers to area businesses and doing odd jobs around the office. Before long, the job had pricked a love in his bones for investigative writing.

Jace owed his career to Mr. Murphy. Right before he retired, he put the newspaper up for sale. It had been closed for almost a year but had everything needed to reopen. Maybe Jace had acted impulsively when he offered to buy the place, but he couldn't change that now. He had every intention of getting the place running and hiring an editor and enough staff so he could return to West Memphis.

After ten minutes of driving, he pulled into an old barn's gravel and dirt parking lot with a red sign with white letters spelling out AUCTION. He stopped beside the Ford Taurus and met a man's gaze who looked to be in his early forties. The man's eyes widened when Jace hopped out of his black Mustang and approached him. He had the same build as the masked man from the other night. Jace's heart kicked up a notch.

"I don't know what you're trying to pull, mister," the man said as he pulled a small pistol out of the back of his jeans.

Jace whirled around in a circle and kicked the pistol out of the man's hand. He unsheathed the knife he kept strapped to his ankle and laid it across the man's throat. "Pulling a gun on me was probably not the best idea."

The muggy air surrounded them, and a fine sheen of sweat glistened on the man's upper lip. "I'm sorry, man. I ain't got much money here, but I'll give ye what I got."

Jace's tone suggested danger. "Why are you following Tammy Sharp around?"

The man's frantic gaze met Jace's stony eyes. A look of complete confusion crossed his face. "Who?"

"Detective Tammy Sharp." He applied pressure with the knife. "Why did you try to accost her the other night?"

"I swear I don't know what you're talking about."

The ch'chunk sound of what Jace had no doubt was a pump action shotgun pricked his ears from behind. "I suggest you step away from my employee, or you'll find your head rolling on the ground."

Jace mentally kicked himself. "Your employee has been stalking my friend. I'm just here looking for answers."

The man's Adam's apple jerked up and down. "Boss, I ain't never stalked no lady named Tammy Sharp. I swear I ain't."

"Tammy Sharp?"

Jace kept the knife tight against the man's jugular as he swiveled around. He met the eyes of his former high school math teacher. Both their mouths fell open. "Mr. Remington?"

"Well, I declare." Mr. Remington lowered the shotgun. "It's been a long time, Jace. How about you take that knife away so we can settle your misunderstanding with Brian there."

Jace sheathed the knife but kept his eye on Brian. He told Mr. Remington what had happened and finished his story with, "So you see why I followed him here."

"Yes, I do, but there's no way Brian is the stalker. Brian, you want to tell Jace where you've been?"

Brian lowered his head. "I been in jail for getting into a fight over at the pool house."

Jace's breath caught in his throat. "Jail? When did you get out?"

"I got out yesterday," Brian said.

"Where has the car been?" Jace asked Brian but looked at Mr. Remington.

"Right here." Mr. Remington pointed behind the barn at a metal fence with barbwire around the top. "It's been locked up. You're welcome to take a gander at the video from my cameras."

After Jace offered Brian an apology, he accepted the offer to view the cameras. Mr. Remington gave Jace free rein in the security office, and afterward, he insisted he show Jace around. The car hadn't moved since Brian had been in jail. Jace pursed his lips. He should have known things wouldn't be so easy.

An hour later, he parked in front of the Pocahontas Star Herald. As soon as he strode inside, the aroma of old newspapers enveloped him. He stood at the entrance, absorbing everything around him. A spacious area with a counter led to the office, and beyond the desk, he fixed his gaze on the trees outside the window. What a stunning view! The historic building had stood the test of time. With some effort and updated furniture, it would be as good as new.

A slight smile touched his lips, and an image of teenage Jace sneaking a kiss from Tammy by the old copy machine entered his mind. He ran his hand across his mouth before lowering himself into the old school sunflower-yellow office chair.

Those memories had no place in his life now. After the way he'd ended things, he'd be better off forgetting he even had a past with Tammy. He had no hope she'd ever forgive him. And for some reason, he acted like a spurned schoolboy whenever she came around. He couldn't stop himself. She brought out a side he forgot he even had.

His foot slid on a piece of paper when he scooted the chair under the desk. He leaned down and laid eyes on an envelope. Odd. He didn't remember that being there the last time he was here. After using his foot to scoot the envelope closer, he scooped it up.

He furrowed his brow as he read the note. Someone had cut out letters from a magazine and glued them to the paper, but that wasn't what caught his attention.

What the message said validated everything he'd been thinking since Ellis's drowning.

ELLIS MARTIN WAS KILLED. DO NOT GO TO THE POLICE. THEY MAY BE IN ON IT. PLEASE LOOK INTO WHAT HAPPENED. OLD DAVIDSONVILLE. THANK YOU.

Someone took the time to use magazine clippings. They could've just come to him. Unless they had a reason not to. Even though the message said not to contact the police, Jace's first instinct was to get them involved. But he needed more solid evidence first.

He detected a slight floral scent coming from the envelope, which gave Jace the idea that a woman had left it. Interesting.

In Jace's experience, fear was one of the top reasons people kept quiet in times like this. That or money. So, which was it? And what did they mean by Old Davidsonville?

Ellis had been fishing off the Black River. Could he have seen something go down at Old Davidsonville while he fished? No, that couldn't be it. How would the person who wrote this note know that? It had to be the legend of the lost gold and jewels.

Jace tapped an ink pen on his chin. He couldn't rule out the possibility of the note writer being in the wrong place at the wrong time. They could've witnessed Ellis's murder. Maybe they kept quiet until they could safely leave. He grabbed his keys off the desk. He wouldn't find answers sitting here wondering about the writer.

Ten minutes later, he slipped through the back door to Ellis's place. It's a good thing Ellis had left Jace a spare key in his rental. A low moonlight stream gave the kitchen a mysterious glow as Jace clicked the door shut.

Even though Ellis had been gone almost two months, a whiff of Old Spice cologne still hung in the air. Jace shook his head. He wished he'd gotten more time with Ellis. After Jace lost his father at twelve, Ellis stepped up. Jace had thought maybe he and Mom would hit it off, but she married someone else and moved to Oklahoma after Nicole graduated from high school.

Jace's hand hovered over the light switch above the sink. But before he could flip it on, a piercing crack hammered into his skull.

Maybe he should've called the police after all.

chapter ten

Unless Tammy counted how many times Mama and Sheriff Obie had been out, two weeks passed without anything odd. They'd only skipped one night. One!

Aside from being forced to watch Mama and Sheriff Obie, taking a break from her high-stress job had been a blessing. Since coming home, Tammy had spent her days resting and writing about Uncle Ellis's life. She didn't want to rush into anything that could hinder her from discovering what happened. Bringing his killer to justice burned her very soul. She'd take her time and do things right. At least, that was the plan.

In her current situation, Tammy watched Sheriff Obie twiddle his thumbs as he waited for Mama to get ready for yet another date. His white button-up shirt and pressed Wrangler jeans gave him the look of a sheriff from the eighties. All he needed was a cigarette hanging from his mouth, and the picture would be perfect. He took a break from twiddling to run his hand through spiky salt-and-pepper hair cut so short it screamed former military.

Tammy cringed as condensation from his glass of tea pooled onto Mama's antique Victorian coffee table. She grabbed a napkin, cleaned it up, and moved the glass of tea to a nearby coaster.

Sheriff Obie laughed nervously, took a sip of tea, and carefully placed it back on the coaster. He and Mama didn't match. His larger frame seemed to tower over Mama's petite one, and they had no business being together. She grudgingly admitted he was an attractive older man, but it didn't matter how he looked.

She leaned both elbows on her knees. "Sheriff Obie, what can you tell me about what happened to Uncle Ellis?"

He wiped his full gray mustache with a thick hand. "You're probably too young, but have you ever watched the old western with John Wayne called The Man Who Shot Liberty Valance?"

"I can't say that I have," Tammy answered as her brow tightened.

"Well, that one came out in, I believe, 1962 or maybe 1963. Anyhow, the main character returned to town to attend his friend's funeral. I feel like that man must've felt." He picked up the glass of tea and held it. "Saddened by losing a man I respected and cared for."

Tammy sat up straighter and pressed her lips together. "I understand you also experienced a great loss. I miss him so much, and I want to know why he died. Don't you?"

Another line of condensation formed on the outside of the glass. Sheriff Obie swirled the ice and wiped the moisture from the outside. He seemed to ponder how he to answer the question.

"I wish I could tell you I knew why he was out there fishing, but he and I didn't speak the day he died."

Mama flitted into the room. Her hot pink capris, white sandals, and white glittery top gave her the look of a much younger woman. Wow. "Tammy Gail, would you like to join us for dinner?"

"Not tonight, Mama." Tammy's mind raced for a good excuse and came up short. "I just don't feel like it."

Relief crossed Sheriff Obie's face, and Tammy almost burst into laughter. She cleared her throat and tried to talk herself into going to spite the sheriff. She would do it if she were interested in watching them coo over one another all night.

"If you keep holed up in this house, you'll dry up and blow away," Mama said.

"Don't worry. I'll go out tomorrow." She'd traded Thomas and Sybil pestering her to find a good man back in Atlanta for Mama staying on her in Pocahontas. Maybe they were in a secret group determined to see Tammy settled.

Mama kissed Tammy's cheek. "I'll bring you a doggie bag."

After Tammy locked up, she ran a hot bath and read twenty chapters of Pride and Prejudice as she soaked for almost an hour. Mixed feelings for Mr. Darcy caused more than one gasp as she turned the pages of Mama's book.

Chapter thirty-four got Tammy's blood boiling. That man had a lot of nerve the way he asked Elizabeth to marry him! For a moment, she allowed an image of Jace on one knee declaring his ardent love and affection to float around her mind. As she walked away, he would run after her, and she'd tell him he was the last man on earth she'd ever be prevailed upon to marry.

Her stomach gurgled, interrupting her daydream and reminding her she'd been hungry since lunch. She shook her head at her silliness. What would make a grown woman think things like that? Certainly not a man like Jace Eubanks.

A little later, comfortable in her black sweats and gray Atlanta Homicide Unit t-shirt, she popped a chicken pot pie out of the oven. She almost had a tiny sliver of regret for staying behind when she glanced at her plate. And that doggie bag Mama promised would probably be more like lunch tomorrow. Even though it pushed nine o'clock, there had to be something open to grab a decent bite. She moved the plate away and pulled herself out of the chair.

Castle's backend wagged, and he danced a jig when Tammy grabbed her purse. "Come on, Castle. Let's go find something to eat."

She donned her shoulder strap and slipped her Glock 19 inside. After everything that had happened since she'd been home, she figured better safe than sorry.

Once outside, Tammy headed toward her Bronco, but Castle bolted toward Uncle Ellis's. Now what? Tammy ignored her empty stomach as she raced after Castle. He planted himself in front of the back door and watched Tammy take two steps at a time. She put her finger to her mouth and raised her brows at Castle. He clamped his mouth shut and cocked his head while Tammy slipped her gun out of the holster.

She tried the doorknob. The door creaked open, and Castle shot inside. He stopped beside a man who lay in front of the sink. Tammy clicked the light on and kept her gun trained on the man. He groaned and tried to sit up.

Jace. She should've known. There was no good reason for Jace to be here. Could he be involved in Uncle Ellis's death? She squinted her eyes as the thought swirled around, landing in the pit of her stomach.

Castle gently licked Jace's face as a surge of heat consumed Tammy's senses. "What are you doing in Uncle Ellis's house? Did you break in? Why are you on the floor?"

He rubbed the back of his head and winced. "I didn't have to break in. Ellis gave me a key."

She holstered her gun as she glanced around the spotless kitchen. "Well, the place now belongs to me, so you can leave the key on the counter on your way out." She paused. "You didn't say why you are on the floor. What happened?"

"Ellis left his house to you? If I recall, you didn't even show up at the funeral, so why would he leave his house to you?"

"Don't worry about it. I'll ask one more time. What happened?" She stopped and glared at him.

He took his hand away from his head and grimaced. "Someone knocked me in the head!"

Knots coiled in her stomach. There was no reason to feel bad. Jace was fine. Besides, he'd been the one to trespass, so anything that happened was his own fault. Still, she went back to the kitchen and grabbed an ice pack. "You were hit inside this house?"

He took the ice pack and nodded.

"We need to file a police report."

"No. Please hold off on that."

"Someone broke the law." She narrowed her eyes. This had to be tied to the man in the Ford. "Why were you here in the first place?"

He placed the ice pack on the back of his head, raising his shoulder. "Working a hunch."

"Hunch?" She pinned him with her gaze. "Tell me what you're talking about."

"Look, I'd rather not say anything just yet. I promise I will tell you soon. Take my word for it. We can't call the police yet."

"Well, I'd like you to leave." She opened the back door and motioned for him to go. "Oh, and Jace, don't come back without my permission."

He moved past Tammy like a robotic soldier. "Fine by me." After he walked through the door, he paused. "Do you want me to move out of the rental? Ellis told me I could stay there a few months, but I'll be happy to leave."

"I'll honor whatever Uncle Ellis told you."

He gave a curt nod before he continued down the back steps.

She waited until he crossed to the other lawn before she slammed the back door so hard it echoed across the kitchen. She slid onto the floor, unable to silence the cry she'd held at bay for so long. Castle sat down beside her and cocked his head. The sob racked her body as she held onto Castle.

After her tears dried up, she stood and looked around. Now she could get to work investigating who'd been in here. When she figured that out, she'd know who drove the Ford Taurus and murdered Uncle Ellis.

chapter eleven

The conversation between Detective Sharp and Jace Eubanks was highly amusing. It appeared Detective Sharp had hard feelings toward Jace Eubanks. That should make things interesting.

Jace Eubanks showing up at Ellis Martin's had almost prevented me from placing a listening device inside the home. He's lucky he got away with only a cracked head. That man had an uncanny ability to appear at the worst possible times.

First, he'd ruined my chance to give Detective Sharp a letter the other night, and now this. I may not get another opportunity to catch her alone, so I'm forced to mail the instructions I've so meticulously outlined. I smile at a man walking on a cane as I hold the door to the post office open for him. I dropped the letter addressed to Miss Tammy Sharp in the mail. How else will she know what's expected? I am fair, so she won't be held accountable until told what to do.

If Mother could see how I'm showing Detective Sharp grace, she'd be proud. I modeled myself after the way she treated my sister. After all, she showed her grace time and again. My punishment came before grace ever did. Mother always said I had to be an example for my sister since I was a few minutes older. Was I ever shown grace?

Who was my example? The scar running down the length of my leg burned. I got it when Mother shoved me into the stove. I tripped and somehow hit the axe. Sister said I pulled her hair, so I was punished without a chance even to say I was sorry.

No matter. This wasn't about me.

Detective Sharp would be given a chance to do right. A simple test would gauge her worth. It was only fair to allow her to prove herself. I owed the real Detective Sharp that much. I know he would appreciate the way I'm handling things with his daughter. He'd probably even thank me.

In the meantime, Jace Eubanks better keep his distance, or he'd meet the same fate Ellis Martin had.

chapter twelve

UNCLE ELLIS'S HOUSE HAD never been this clean. It's like someone had hired Molly Maid to come in, remove all the clutter, and disinfect the place. But why? And how was Jace involved? His cagey behavior told Tammy he knew more than he was letting on.

Tammy massaged her forehead as she took another turn around the office. She'd spent over an hour scouring every room. Other than the sparkling clean space, nothing stood out.

Her stomach gurgled, and a wave of dizziness threatened to overcome her. When had she last eaten? Castle had enjoyed his dinner before they left, but Tammy hadn't eaten anything since a soggy bowl of Cheerios for lunch. And by now, all the restaurants would be closed.

She drifted near the front door before glancing at Castle. "Looks like I'll be forced to warm that pot pie up unless Mama is home with leftovers." Her tongue seemed to protest as it stuck to the roof of her mouth. "That or another bowl of cereal."

As they made their way across the dark yards, a rake of shivers crawled up Tammy's spine. She shoved around on the ball of her foot and scanned the area. Nothing seemed out of place.

Hundreds of bugs buzzed around the lone street-light between Mama's and Uncle Ellis's. A flash of head-lights hit Tammy in the face. Her heart lodged in her ribs as she ran toward Mama's house with Castle on her heels. As Tammy's feet touched the steps, a white Chevrolet Silverado pulled into the driveway.

Sheriff Obie got out and raced around the truck. "Evening, Tammy."

Mama thanked Sheriff Obie for opening her door before her gaze moved to Tammy. "Tammy Gail, what in the world are you running from?"

"Nothing. I'm just starving to death." Tammy let out a breath, thankful the darkness covered her burning face.

"I figured you'd be hungry." Mama handed Tammy a container and followed her up the steps. "Where have you been?"

"Uncle Ellis's."

Mama leaned close to Tammy and lowered her voice. "You should've left the porch light on. I know it's kinda scary coming across the yards in the pitch dark."

A laugh sprang from Tammy despite herself. Her tone matched Mama's when she spoke. "I'll know for next time."

Sheriff Obie stuck his hands in the belt loops of his jeans. "Good night, Ruby. I enjoyed dinner."

Gentle laughter sprinkled the air. "I loved it. Thank you for taking me, Obie." Mama looked expectantly at Tammy.

Now what? Did they want Tammy to go inside? Sure-ly, they didn't expect her to leave them out here alone. Did older people kiss? No, that wasn't possible.

Mama fidgeted with the strap on her bright pink Coach purse. Sheriff Obie scratched his head and swallowed.

Talk about awkwardness.

Tammy didn't care. She didn't plan on budging. They wouldn't be swapping spit on her watch. Nope. And they better believe she had enough patience to wait them out. Once, she'd holed up in a little foreign Yugo shoebox car for six hours, waiting for her suspect to make a move. This happened to be nothing compared to that. It didn't even matter that a mosquito and its three sisters had taken to attacking her bare ankle. Who cares that her entire leg would more than likely be swollen the next day? She was winning this round.

By the time Sheriff Obie gave up, the mosquitos' cousins had joined them and were going at her arms. He pressed his lips together and nodded. "You ladies have a good night. I hope to see you tomorrow, Ruby."

"I'll be counting the hours." Mama flitted down the steps and kissed his cheek. "Good night, Obie."

She was lucky Tammy didn't trip her.

A big grin flashed across his face, and Tammy figured she could've counted his teeth if she'd taken the time.

His eyes crinkled as he stole a glance at Tammy. "Night, Tammy."

"Good night, sheriff."

Tammy opened the door, and Castle bounced inside, going straight to his food bowl. Some days, she thought he ate more than an elephant.

As soon as the door closed behind them, Mama started in. Her sweet country twang came out a tad bit higher than usual. "Tammy Gail Sharp, what has gotten into you?"

"Nothinnnnn." A sweet smile that could rival Mama's on her good days crossed Tammy's lips, and she used her best country twang. "Why?"

Mama slipped her shoes off and padded by Tammy, clicking her tongue. Guess that was answer enough.

"Oh, Mama?" Tammy fell in behind her. "Did you have Uncle Ellis's place professionally cleaned?"

Worry lined Mama's forehead as her lips tugged downward. "No, honey, I haven't been able to go through his things yet. I'm sorry."

Tammy put her arms out to comfort Mama. Or maybe Tammy needed a bit of comfort. "It's okay."

After they hugged a while, Mama leaned back and eyed Tammy. "Do you want me to clean it out so you can stay there?"

"No, that's not it." Tammy chewed on the side of her lip. Should she tell Mama what she suspected?

"Tell me what's on your mind," Mama said.

Why did Mama have to go and use her stern voice? The one that made Tammy feel like she had to spill every secret she ever had, or she'd be in deep trouble.

Seconds ticked by as Tammy tried to find the best way to tell Mama. There would be no easy way. She grasped Mama on her forearms and stared into her eyes. "Mama, I have a gut feeling Uncle Ellis was murdered."

A spark of anger ignited in Mama's eyes, and her mouth slid into a firm line. "I know he was murdered, Tammy. Why do you think I started dating Obie?"

chapter thirteen

TAMMY'S BROW FURROWED, AND her head jerked sideways. "Mama! I knew you and that sheriff didn't match–"

Mama interrupted her. "I said that's why I started dating him...but he's kinda growing on me."

"I still think you can do better, but I guess we can talk about that later." A scowl slid across Tammy's face. "So, what do you know about Uncle Ellis's drowning?"

"Go ahead and eat your dinner while I change. Then we can talk."

"Okay," Tammy said as she opened Mama's leftovers. The delicious smell of green peppers and onions hit her. She layered a fajita shell with steak and slathered sour cream on top, added the vegetables, and sunk her teeth in.

She almost groaned when the perfect amount of spice exploded on her tongue. She inhaled the first and was two bites into the second one when Mama strode by wearing a set of pink fuzzy pajamas. "Good, huh?"

After the last bite, Tammy licked her fingers and nodded. "My favorite."

"I know it is." Mama lowered herself into the recliner and waited until Tammy swallowed the last bite before she spoke again. "What makes you think Ellis was killed?"

Tammy guzzled a swig of water and stuck a leg underneath her body on the sofa. "Initially, it was just my gut telling me he didn't drown by accident. Now, things just don't add up."

"What things?"

"Gut feeling. But I'm being followed by someone driving a Ford Taurus." Tammy fiddled with the strap on her gun holster. "I need you to be careful and call me if you see anything suspicious."

"I sure will," Mama said, her lips flattened. "I wonder who's driving that car."

"I plan to find out. What makes you think his drowning was no accident?"

"For one thing, Ellis was too smart to fall over the side of his boat like that."

Turmoil swirled inside Tammy. She patted the sofa, and Castle jumped onto the spot beside her. He laid his head on her lap and sighed. She rubbed his side as she stared into the distance. The boy that shot her had taken more than her self-respect. He'd taken her ability to be there for her family during a tragedy.

"Mama, I'm sorry you were at the hospital with me instead of here when Uncle Ellis drowned."

Mama jerked herself out of the recliner and sat on the other side of Castle. He wrenched his leg out from underneath her and nuzzled Tammy's hand. "Honey, that was not your fault."

She would not cry. It didn't matter if her throat burned worse than the last time she sucked on a piece of Fireball candy. "Yes, it was. If I hadn't gotten shot, you would've been here."

"I couldn't have helped Ellis. His fate was sealed by whatever he had going on in his life." She leaned across Castle and gripped Tammy's hand. He twisted his head and looked at Mama. "You're my daughter, my priority, and you needed me there. Don't ever be sorry for needing me."

With her throat on fire and chest in knots, Tammy could no longer fight back the tears. "I missed saying goodbye to Uncle Ellis because of my weakness. I should've just pulled the trigger. Daddy would be so disappointed in me."

She examined a plaque she'd been honored to receive for solving the murder of a couple and saving their daughter from a kidnapper. Mama had been so proud at the dinner when Tammy was given the plaque that Tammy let Mama take it home. She had proudly displayed it on her fireplace mantle for the past few years. What happened to that detective?

Castle nuzzled his head on Tammy's side, doing his best to provide comfort. That's why she loved him. Pitbulls mostly got a bad rap, but this sweetheart had so much love to give. Tammy rubbed his side with her free hand as her chest heaved.

"No, he would be proud of you. I'm proud of you. Do you hear me?"

"I hear you, Mama."

"And you were the light of Ellis's eye. That's one way I know he didn't accidentally drown. He wouldn't have been out on Black River trying to catch a fish while you were in the hospital."

Tammy wiped her tears away. She needed to focus. "I thought the same thing."

Mama braced her forearm on the back of the sofa. She looked out the window, and a thin smile graced her beautiful yet haunted face. "No, the last thing he told me was to tell you he loved you and would be back at the hospital the next day. He even had another flight booked."

Her blood chilled as she let what Mama said sink in. "Did Uncle Ellis say anything else?"

"Just that he had a meeting with Jace that day before heading out." Mama sipped her iced tea and ran her hand down Castle's side. He beamed with the attention. "He was excited about whatever he had going on and said he needed Jace here to help him."

"Help him with what?" Tammy's body tightened. That must be why Jace lived in the rental house next door to Uncle Ellis.

Her forehead scrunched, and she shrugged. Not a regular shrug but a shrug of aggravation. A shrug of almost knowing what happened to her brother but needing more information. Tammy understood the feeling. "I'm not sure, and neither was Jace. Ellis drowned the night before they were supposed to meet."

"So how does you dating the sheriff factor into finding out what happened to Uncle Ellis?"

"I'm hoping Obie knows something he'll share with me."

Tammy raised a brow. "I know you like him more than you're letting on. I've been here over a month, and the two of y'all have been on almost that many dates."

Mama closed her eyes for a second. When she opened them, her gaze bore into Tammy's. "Sometimes, we do what we have to for our family. Although I will admit, I find Obie charming and very attractive."

A big yawn came from Mama, and she tried to cover her mouth. Tammy followed suit with a yawn of her own. They both stood up. Castle jumped off the sofa and headed to the room he shared with Tammy.

"Why don't we go to bed and talk about this in the morning? We can make a list and see about getting to the bottom of who murdered Uncle Ellis."

A spray of light flashed inside the living room, and Tammy headed toward the front door, but Mama made it there first. "It's just Obie. Let's go to bed."

Tammy creased her brow. "Why would he drive by at almost eleven o'clock at night?"

Mama set her empty glass of water in the sink and waved her hand. "I asked him to after that awful man broke in here."

Tammy peeked out the window beside the front door. "Okay then. Good night, Mama, I love you."

Mama kissed Tammy's forehead. "Night, my sweet girl. I love you."

Tammy checked the windows and doors to make sure they were locked before heading to her room.

Close to three hours later, Tammy woke to Castle growling. She patted the bed and rolled over. "Hush up."

He nudged her shoulder, jumped off the bed, and went to the window. After looking out a second, he barked a shrill-sounding bark that caused Tammy's head to pound.

Her eyes shot open. The hairs on her arm raised. It was a good thing she kept her gun on the bedside table. She slipped her silky pajama bottoms on and grabbed it.

Before Tammy could reach the door, Castle let out another round of barks. If he didn't stop, the entire neighborhood would be awake. The barks turned into a whine and then a menacing growl. He hopped to the bedroom door and clawed underneath as if he desperately wanted out of this room. His nails screeched across the old-school wood floor, and Tammy dreaded seeing the damage. Mama would strangle them both.

She opened the door and gasped. A puff of white smoke circled the back of the house. Her stomach pitched as her police training kicked in. She tried to open Mama's door, but it wouldn't budge.

Instead of allowing the anxiety that threatened, Tammy balled up her fist and pounded on the door. "Mama!"

The door opened with a bang. Mama stood there tugging her earlobe. "What time is it?" Her eyes grew wide the moment the smoke hit her. "Where's the fire?"

Castle continued barking as he ran toward the front of the house. He stopped midway there and stared at them until they started in behind him. He planted himself at the front door and waited for them to get there.

Tammy turned the doorknob, but the door didn't open. Sweat prickled her scalp as she jerked on the door. It didn't budge.

Mama moved Tammy's hand and pulled on the doorknob. Nothing happened. She jerked on it almost hysterically. "Why won't the door open?" Her body moved as she put her weight into opening the door.

"Wait here." Tammy made her way to the back of the house. Her heart dropped. That way wouldn't work, either. The door wouldn't budge, and flames licked at the cute patio set Mama had been so proud of.

A dark figure stood there, staring in Tammy's direction as the rest of the porch rose in flames.

chapter fourteen

NO MATTER WHAT POSITION he lay in, Jace couldn't get comfortable enough to go to sleep. He rolled over on his left side, sticking his leg out of the cover. He punched his pillow a few times and groaned.

His mind kept drifting back to the day his wife died. He'd traveled to Memphis to pick Leo up from the airport. Una said she had things to do around the house, but Jace knew she wanted to give him some father-daughter time with Leo. She'd been working as an intern in Washington, DC, for almost a month.

Leo's boyfriend at the time, Slate Sanders, had to work, so Jace had been happy to pick her up. The flight had been delayed, so Una had been home alone for about three hours. Long enough for someone to take her away from them.

The scene Jace walked in on had chilled him to the bone. He could still smell the heavy stench of iron that permeated the air and feel the fear that settled into his bones as he ran through the house. Una's body lay crumpled on the kitchen floor, her lifeblood pooled around her.

Leo tried to bring her suitcase inside. He held her back as they waited for the police. The look on Leo's face would forever haunt him. He didn't think he'd ever be able to get a whole night's rest again. Not that he deserved to sleep after how Una died. He should've been there to protect her.

He pulled on a pair of pajama pants. Now what? Growing up, he'd always thought he'd enjoy living alone. But life after losing Una had not been all he thought it would be. Even after three years, he missed her company. He missed how she'd laugh after chewing him out in their native Cherokee language.

He'd married her against his better judgment, but he'd never say he regretted it. He'd made a promise to his cousin that couldn't be broken. Once they said I do, his life belonged to her. He would've gladly died in her place so she could've been here for their daughter, but that's not how things worked.

He opened the refrigerator and leaned his head against the freezer. Bare shelves seemed to mock him. He pulled out a bottle of water and took a swig. A glance at the clock on the stove revealed that it was after two a.m.

Castle barked in the distance. He stepped onto the back porch to stargaze, but that notion left him immediately. A man stood at the back of Miss Ruby's house, watching the porch rise in flames.

Jace swung his body off the back porch and made a beeline toward Miss Ruby's. The man must have noticed Jace. He took off down the street and disappeared before Jace got there.

Castle's barks got louder and louder. Jace prayed that was a good thing.

He ran around the side of the house and turned on the water faucet. Water spurted out of the hose. Jace sprayed the burning porch as quickly as his legs would move. An overhanging piece fell off the roof and landed on Jace's arm. His arm hair seemed to melt into his bones as the fire enveloped the skin where it hit. Despite the intense burn, he shrugged it off, determined to saturate the area with as much water as possible.

As soon as the porch crumbled, he kicked the back door in. He eyed a thick nylon rope hanging from the charred doorknob. What in the world? Whoever started the fire had tried to trap Tammy and Miss Ruby. Glass shattered from inside the house. Jace's heart nearly vacated his body as he charged inside. "Miss Ruby? Tammy?"

Castle barreled through the laundry area. Tammy called his name from the front of the house. Jace covered his mouth with his shirt and followed Castle. Tammy had her arm wedged through the glass on the front door. She pulled her hand back and shoved the door with her shoulder. After it burst open, Tammy held her arm out to Miss Ruby. Jace got on the other side of her and helped them outside.

They collapsed in a fit of coughs. Jace met Tammy's gaze. "Are you both all right?"

A storm brewed. But not in the sky. This particular storm came from the most beautiful woman he'd ever seen.

"Why were you in our backyard in the middle of the night?" she asked.

He'd much rather the storm come from the sky. He opened his mouth and promptly closed it. She didn't need his smart response on top of everything else.

She helped Miss Ruby off the ground, and her hand flew to her hip. Her once-white silk pajama set had turned gray. "Well?"

"I couldn't sleep, so I stepped onto my back porch. That's when I saw a man standing in your yard watching the fire burn."

Miss Ruby found her voice. "Did you recognize him?"

His arm chose that moment to remind him of the burn. He glanced at it and shook his head. He'd break his teeth off before he allowed Tammy to see his pain. "He wore a mask."

"Oh my, you're burned, Jace." Miss Ruby pointed at Ellis's house. "Come on, let's get your arm seen about and call the police."

Almost like she conjured him up, blue lights flashed as a car pulled into the front yard, and within seconds, Sheriff Obie stepped out. "Ruby!"

She met him halfway and fell into his arms. "I must be the unluckiest woman in Pocahontas. First a robbery and now this."

"Luck had nothing to do with it. Someone has targeted my family," Tammy said as she leveled a dark gaze on Jace. "You better start talking, and I mean now."

Castle stood directly beside Tammy, giving Jace a look that made him forget the searing pain in his forearm. He'd never had to fight a pit bull, but he guessed there was a first time for everything. Not that he wanted to. Tammy would surely hate him if he hurt her dog.

Sirens blared, and an ambulance pulled in, followed by another police car. Tammy scrambled over to Jace, her eyes narrowed to mere slits. "This conversation is not over. You know something you're not sharing."

His nostrils flared as Nicole bounded out of the ambulance. After determining that Miss Ruby and Tammy weren't hurt, she gently grabbed his wrist and shined a flashlight on his arm. "You need medical attention. The burn looks to be at least second-degree."

Tammy's gaze fell to his arm, and she didn't flinch. His skin had already started to bubble over with tiny blisters. He'd broken his arm a few years back, which was nothing compared to this.

She blocked the path to the ambulance. "There are two scenarios in my mind. Either you're in on it, or you're trying to help. You better pray it's the latter." She flipped around and headed toward Miss Ruby and Sheriff Obie.

He had a sinking feeling Tammy played the "bad cop" like a pro during interrogations, and for some reason, his name landed at the top of her list of suspects.

So why did he have a zip of excitement coursing through his blood?

chapter fifteen

My chest feels like fire burns inside me. I want to crack my windshield, but I will not allow myself to lose control. Detective Sharp thought she knew what had happened to Ellis. She had no idea he had caused his death. He stirred up the hornet's nest when he started investigating things he should've left in the past.

Why can't she leave things alone? It's not like I enjoy taking lives, but survival comes at a cost. Detective Sharp will be safe if she focuses on finding the gold instead of wasting time on Ellis Martin. I need that gold. Without it, I'll never get out of Pocahontas. I'll never get to move to Switzerland. I'll be stuck here until I die if it's not found. That can't happen. I deserve more than what this place has to offer.

What could be keeping her from following instructions? The letter had been clear. Did she think herself superior? Or was she stupider than she let on? After her colossal failure tonight, there could be no other explanation. Hadn't her daddy taught her anything before he died? He had been an intelligent man. That's why I chose him to be my best friend. I still mourned his loss. If only he had believed my sister died of natural causes, things could be so different right now. Why he zeroed in on me as his top suspect was another mystery. I was his best friend. He should never have betrayed me. I had high hopes for his daughter. Even so, I hadn't decided if she would live or not.

I continue coasting down the gravel road until I see the old, abandoned homestead. The no-trespassing signs ensured most people steered clear out this way, making the dilapidated barn out back the best place to relieve some steam.

Dried-out corn stands tall and brown as if begging to be reaped. People these days call it harvesting. But I've always liked the sound of reaping much more.

A rabbit hopped around the side of the barn. I fired a round in its direction. It was close but a miss. The rabbit scurried into the cornfield, living despite almost getting hit.

Almost.

Over the years, I've grown to despise that word.

Almost.

Almost in love.

Almost a family.

Almost rich.

Almost dead.

If not for that nosy Jace Eubanks, the Sharp women would be dead by now. Detective Sharp had missed the opportunity to prove her ability. Her worth. She had the chance to save herself and Ruby from the fire, but instead, she had to be saved by Jace Eubanks. Again.

Sonny may have started the fire, but I gained knowledge from it. Still, he would pay for that mistake.

Maybe I would be better off finding the gold without her help. Heat licks at my skin, and my vision flashes red. I press my palm to my heart, willing the beats to slow down. My anger must not get the best of me. I must have clear thoughts in the days ahead.

I need an outlet – someone deserving punishment. It was time for a trip to a nightclub. I had plenty of time to get to Missouri.

My mind drifts to my sister as I set my cruise control to seventy. After her husband died, she'd become a loose woman. She'd been an embarrassment to me. One time, I confronted her, and she told me she was looking for love.

Love! Mother loved her all her life. She'd babied my sister while she used me as a whipping post. She hated me. If anyone needed to look for love, it was me. Not my sister. But I'd never do that. I was not that type of person.

By the time I reached my destination, I'd calmed down. My sister was dead. She had no bearing on my here and now.

Mind-breaking country music blasted into my brain as I stepped inside. The first person to catch my attention inside the smoky bar was a man with dark hair and a small frame. He seemed depressed as I took the seat next to him. I ordered a drink. Before I spoke, a dark-skinned woman wrapped her arms around his neck. He pushed her away before walking out of the bar.

She turned to me and smiled. "Hi, I'm Kendra Burton. What's your name?"

"Nickie."

"Hi, Nickie. What are you drinking?"

I shrugged. I'd be drinking water, but no one would know that. "What are you drinking?"

"Whatever I can get people to buy me." She barked a laugh that quickly turned to a sob. A fake one. I could tell by her eyes it was a big joke.

"Are you okay?" I eyed the woman.

"Not really. My son got took away from me."

I nodded toward an empty booth. "Wanna sit and tell me about it?"

After we settled into the booth, Kendra Burton guzzled her drink and shrugged. "My neighbor called social services because I spanked him."

"Spanked? Can't a person spank their child?"

"I left bruises. He is a bad kid. I promise he is."

My heart pounds as anger coursed through my veins. I managed to smile anyway. "I bet. Aren't they all?"

I pretended to care about this woman for a few more minutes before excusing myself to converse with a man playing pool. I couldn't be seen spending much time with Kendra Burton.

Two games of pool later, I excused myself and left the bar.

My mind is centered around Kendra Burton as I park behind an old country store down the road from the bar. Didn't she deserve swift justice after treating her child the way she did? Any parent who hurts their own should not be allowed to live.

I can't stop the grin as I decide to follow Kendra Burton home. I had plenty of rope in my trunk and could easily pin her death on Sonny. Yes, that would be fitting.

As my mind drifts to Jace Eubanks and the Sharp women, I savor that they have no idea they're like the dried-out corn from the field. On the verge of being cut down.

And when the time was right, they would be reaped. Just like Kendra Burton.

chapter sixteen

Lorene's Love Locks stood in a cute little hot pink boutique-style building on the outskirts of town. Tammy pulled into the parking lot beside a forest-green Pontiac Grand Am.

She chuckled as she made her way inside the salon. If Thomas saw her walking into a hot pink beauty shop dressed like she was, he'd laugh at her for hours. He loved giving her a hard time about how she always wore dark clothes to work. Not that she didn't have a feminine side, but she kept that side neatly tucked away from her work life. She couldn't imagine taking down a hardened criminal wearing a pastel suit. Not where she worked, anyway.

Today, she wore one of Mama's mango orange button-up shirts and a pair of loose boyfriend jeans with some simple white Skechers. She'd even taken five minutes to dab on a bit of makeup. Mama had seemed pleased as a pickle when Tammy left the house. Castle, not so much. He'd tried to go with her and pouted when she said he had to stay with Mama.

A woman Tammy didn't recognize handed Lorene Pankey a check. Lorene scanned it and let out a humph. "Hey, Brenda? Make sure you come to see me before your hair gets so bad next time. I'm not in the detangling business."

Tammy recognized the woman as Brenda Honeysuckle, the high school librarian. "You keep getting smart, and I'll go to The Clip Joint next time."

Lorene's mouth dropped open. "You go right ahead. You know me and the owner are friends, right? Who do you think does my hair?"

"You're lucky we went to school together." She nodded at Lorene before half-smiling at Tammy on her way out. She stuck her head inside the door. "Have a good one."

Lorene's tall frame spun around as the door snapped shut. "Tammy? I was beginning to think you forgot I exist."

"Of course, I didn't forget about you," Tammy said as she shook her head. "How are you doing, Lorene?"

Lorene's eyes misted over, and she hugged Tammy tightly. The way Lorene held Tammy, you wouldn't know they'd only seen each other a few times since she'd started dating Uncle Ellis.

After Lorene lowered herself into a hot pink upholstered accent chair, she ran her hand across close-cropped brassy hair. "I cut my hair off after losing my Ellis. I miss him so much I can hardly stand it."

Tammy claimed the seat next to Lorene and glanced at the barber's chair. The last time she'd been in this shop, Uncle Ellis sat there while Lorene trimmed his hair. Tammy swallowed the bulge in her throat and patted Lorene's hand. "I know you do. I miss him too."

Lorene's chin tipped toward the fluffy white area rug, and her mouth turned downward. "I just hate you didn't get to be here for the memorial service. It was beautiful."

A muscle ticked in Tammy's jaw, and her throat tightened with a hard swallow. "Me, too. Kinda had a gunshot wound to deal with, or I would've been here."

Lorene leaned forward, the whites of her eyes visible. "I didn't mean to imply you could've been there," she said.

Tammy forced her spine to relax. "You didn't. I'm sorry, I can get a little defensive when I feel guilty over things."

Lorene lifted herself out of the chair and went to the tiny refrigerator. She returned with two bottles of water and handed one to Tammy. "Don't you worry yourself none. I know you've had a hard few months." Her eyes widened. "What in the world happened with the fire?"

"I don't know all the details. The fire inspector is supposed to let us know what he found this week."

"I heard they think it was a serial arsonist."

"You heard that already?" Tammy ran her hand across the back of her hair. "I'm not so sure about that."

"Didn't somebody bar the doors closed?" She leaned one elbow on her knee. "Is that true? That's just unheard of."

"No, they weren't barred closed." Tammy stood. "That's not what I came to talk about."

"Oh?" Lorene scratched the side of her neck, leaving red patches behind. "What can I do for you, hon?"

"I have some questions for you. But first, can I borrow your restroom real quick?"

"Sure. It's right through the hall on the left."

Once Tammy returned, Lorene tilted her head. "Now, what brings you by?" Her eyes raked over Tammy's hair. "Needing a cut and style?"

Tammy shrugged. It *had* been six months, so a cut and style wouldn't hurt her, but she needed to stay focused. "I wanted to ask you some questions about Uncle Ellis."

"Tell you what, you sit and ask the questions while I trim your hair. I can't let you leave here with dead ends like that." She swirled the barber's chair around and patted the seat. "It could damage my reputation as the best stylist in Pocahontas, you know."

"I don't know –"

"You should've seen Brenda's hair when she got here. It looked like a family of dragonflies had built a nest in her hair." A proud grin crossed her face. "Did you notice how good it looked before she left?"

"Her hair did look pretty." No sense in arguing. Maybe if Lorene focused more on Tammy's hair, she'd let her guard down. "All right, but I only want the dead ends cut."

Lorene's face lifted into an even more pleased smile as she picked up a hairbrush. "That's fine with me. I'll trim first, then wash and style."

Tammy met Lorene's gaze in the mirror. "Are you aware of anything dangerous Uncle Ellis was working on?"

The hairbrush Lorene held in her hand hit the floor. She picked it up and pulled it through Tammy's hair. "What do you mean?"

Tammy winced when Lorene tugged a tangle out of her hair. If Lorene didn't calm down, Tammy would leave with worse than dead ends. She'd be bald.

"Was he involved with criminals or working on anything dangerous?"

A brittle-edged laugh left Lorene as she snipped the ends of Tammy's hair. "Why, of course not. Why would you ask such a question?"

Tammy clamped her gaze onto Lorene's. "Do you think his death was an accident?"

"That's what the police said, right? I wasn't out there investigating it myself." She adjusted her view away from the mirror. "Let's get you washed real quick."

A few minutes later, Lorene had the blow dryer on high, trying to burn a hole in Tammy's head. As soon as she laid the dryer down, Tammy creased her brow. "Was Uncle Ellis having problems with anyone?"

"Not that I know of." The chair circled, so Tammy faced Lorene.

"So you don't know if anyone had threatened him over anything? Or if he had any new friends that made you feel uneasy?"

Lorene tapped her foot as she ran a straightener through a section of Tammy's hair. "Why all these questions?"

Heat from the straightener threatened to singe Tammy's scalp. She moved her head to the left before Lorene pulled it through another piece of hair. "I just need to figure out what happened."

"Ellis drowned, honey. Leave it be." She swiveled the chair around and smiled at Tammy in the mirror. "Whatcha think?"

Tammy's head felt lighter after Lorene took off at least two inches. "It looks pretty, Lorene. Thank you." Her voice changed to all business. "If you know anything, please tell me. With Sonny Perkins breaking in and now the fire, things have gotten dangerous."

Lorene met Tammy's gaze in the mirror. "You have no idea how dangerous things can get here in Pocahontas."

Tammy bounded out of the chair. "What is that supposed to mean?"

"It means stop asking questions. Believe me when I say Ellis wouldn't want you getting mixed up in anything that could get you killed."

The words Lorene spoke caused knots to coil in Tammy's belly. "Like what?"

"That's all I can say, Tammy. I mean it." Her lips drew into a hard line, and she pinned her arms across her chest.

The bell on the door dinged. A woman and a young girl stepped inside. Lorene's mouth quivered into a smile as she greeted the pair.

That put an end to Tammy's questions.

As Tammy drove away, she had no doubt Lorene knew more than she said. She made a mental note to have a more formal meeting with her very soon.

chapter seventeen

It only took Tammy two days to locate Sonny Perkins. She slowed down as she passed one of the known houses where druggies hung out near Walnut Ridge.

When the pavement turned to gravel, she flipped around and headed back toward the house. She tapped the brake and pulled into the driveway. Strips of dirty tan siding leaned against the side of the house. Overgrown bushes made a fortress around the front porch.

For a moment, Tammy reconsidered her plan to talk to Sonny alone. After scanning the area for a Ford Taurus, she pushed aside the feelings of doom and stepped onto the porch. Heavy metal music rattled the windows and blared from inside.

The front door swung open. Sonny stood on the other side. His lips slid into a smirk. "Well, well, well. Detective Sharp." He stepped aside. His oversized jeans seemed to be ready to hit his knees. "Please do come inside and make yourself at home." His sarcastic tone didn't escape Tammy. Without another glance, he strode over to the stereo system and turned the music down. "What do you want?"

Tammy sat on the edge of a stained light blue chair and met Sonny's stare. He couldn't have been the man in the Taurus. Not with his tall, skinny frame. "I want information."

"I been here about six months." He skulked to the window and pulled one of the black curtains back. After peering out for a few seconds, he tossed himself onto the couch. "You'd be better off asking somebody else."

"Why did you and your Aunt Vivian move here?"

"That woman ain't my aunt. Well, she was married to my uncle, but anyway, she brought me here right before I turned eighteen. What's it to you?"

"I want to know why you broke into my mama's home."

A scrawny man without any teeth walked into the room. "Hey man, turn that music back up."

Sonny nodded in Tammy's direction. "We have a visitor. Give us a few minutes."

The man shot a nasty look at Tammy before disappearing the way he came.

Her gaze left Sonny, and she took inventory of the room. The living area opened into a kitchen with an island big enough for two. A bent spoon, cotton, cut cigarette butts, and orange needle caps littered the dirty bistro-style dining table. It could've been a cute place without the remnants of drug use, heaps of clothes, and random shoes scattered about. "Have you ever heard the name Ellis Martin?"

"Yeah, no."

"Then why did you break into my mother's home?"

"Look, I'm going to court over that, you know." He pinned his arms over his chest as his brows melted together. "You can't be here harassing me."

"Did you start the fire?"

"What fire?" His look told Tammy he thought she was stupid to even ask.

Anger spread like flame through her bones. Being in this house titillated every nerve to the point she could pinpoint them individually in her body. "You know what fire."

"I for real don't have to tell you nothing, lady." He snickered. "You're just a normal person like me. You ain't no cop."

Another man came from the back of the house. His eyes darted at Tammy before he opened the refrigerator. He popped the top on a drink and stood at the island. One of the barstools teetered when he knocked into it. A tall drinking glass hit the tile and shattered.

Time seemed to move in slow motion as Tammy's heart drummed into her ribs. Chip Reeker's face swam in her vision. Her chest seized, and she imagined another bullet hitting her in the same spot as before.

"What's wrong with you?" Sonny screamed in Tammy's face. His breath smelled like he'd shared his last meal with a few vultures.

The question, mixed with the stench, snapped Tammy back to reality. Using the palm of her hand, she slapped his chin, shoving him away from her. "Nothing is wrong with me, you punk. I want answers."

He barked a laugh, teetering on unsteady feet as he fell onto the sofa. "Well, you won't be getting them here. I suggest you go on back to Atlanta, where you belong, before something bad happens. It would be a shame if another fire got started."

Her face hardened as she allowed fierce anger to whip through her body. She surged upright. Her arm snaked out, and she wrapped her hand in Sonny's shirt. She dragged him off the couch. "If you ever threaten me again, I'll cut your tongue out."

His eyes narrowed as he grasped her hands. His tone came out labored. "I thought you was a cop. You can't do nothing to me."

She applied pressure until his face reddened. "Didn't you say I was a normal person, just like you?"

He tugged at her hands and nodded.

"I'll be back to talk to you soon. You may want to think about telling me the truth." She kicked his kneecap as hard as she could. He crashed into the stereo system. She punched his nose and leaned close to his ear. "That was for shooting my dog."

The other man hurried toward Sonny as Tammy marched out of the house.

chapter eighteen

FALL IN ARKANSAS HAD to be one of the best times of the year. The Fall Festival had a packed crowd of people hitting up the various booths and enjoying a taste of some of the homemade goods the locals had to offer.

The vibrant orange and yellow leaves made Tammy want to run out and buy a bunch of pumpkin pie-flavored desserts. For now, she would settle for the Pumpkin Pie Espresso from Copperhead Coffee House and a warm slice of pumpkin bread from a local vendor. She breathed in the warm, rich aroma while savoring the first sip. Yeah, there was no settling going on with this cup of coffee. It had to be one of the best she'd ever tasted. Tammy had no doubt she would've gone broke if they'd been open when she'd lived in Pocahontas.

A couple of girls that couldn't have been more than ten or so skipped by munching on candy apples and giggling. A sprig of longing entered Tammy's bones. When she decided to become a Homicide Detective, she also promised herself she wouldn't have children. After losing Daddy at ten, she'd never want her child to grow up without a parent like she had. The time to change her mind had passed long ago.

"Tammy, we want you to go on a hayride with us," Mama said as she dragged Jace by his hand over to where Tammy sat on a bench.

Tammy pitched the wrapper in a nearby trash can as her mind worked out a way to get out of this new situation.

Jace clutched at the collar of his black and white striped crew-neck sweater, half grimaced as his lips quirked. "I don't think Tammy is interested in going on a hayride with me, Miss Ruby."

Instead of saying something, Tammy stood there like the woman who'd walked into Tammy's bathroom stall at the convenience store the week before. The woman seemed to want to turn away but stared at Tammy for a moment instead.

Yes, while Tammy was on the pot.

At this very moment, Tammy could relate to the woman. She couldn't take her eyes off Jace. It had taken Tammy clearing her throat for the woman to snap back to her senses and close the stall, mumbling about how sorry she was. For Tammy, it took Mama laying her hand on her arm to snap her out of her daze.

Tammy remained silent a moment longer as her eyes traveled from Jace's snug dark wash jeans to his pristine white sneakers. He must've grown out of the graphic hard rock t-shirts and holey jeans he used to sport around town. Too bad. Nobody else in the entire school had ever been able to rock a pair of Levis like Jace.

He cleared his throat. He seemed as uncomfortable as he had the day he told her he'd married another woman. Tammy's fingers tightened around the cup of coffee. She had to let that go. Jace lost his wife a few years back, so was there even a point to Tammy holding on to the anger?

"Now, why would you think that, Jace? I love hayrides." She swallowed the last swig of coffee, threw it in the trash can, and headed toward the people waiting in line. "Come on, you two."

Jace's brow raised as she passed him by, but he fell in behind Tammy. "The new back porch looks good," he said.

"Obie did a fabulous job, and I just love it." Mama fanned herself after they got in line behind the crowd.

A tall woman with the oddest Crayola orange hair color came around the tractor-trailer full of hay. She stopped in front of Mama and tugged a tuft of hair out of her eyes with slim fingers. "Miss Ruby, I didn't get a chance to thank you for making sure I got my medicine this month."

Mama waved her hand. "Now, Vivian, you know I told you we help one another in our community. It's what we do."

Miss Vivian looked at the ground. "I didn't expect you to help me none after my nephew broke into your home." She put her hand on her neck and choked up as she spoke. "I hope you can forgive me."

"You didn't do anything to be forgiven for." Mama patted Miss Vivian on her back. "Let's forget about it, okay?"

She smiled, revealing pearly whites that surprised Tammy. "I thank you. I'm going to mosey over to a bench so I can catch my breath."

After Mama introduced Tammy and Jace to Miss Vivian, they said their goodbyes, but Tammy kept an eye on the woman while she waited for their turn to board the tractor-trailer. A man who looked like a less stocky version of Chuck Norris with a close-cut white beard sat on the far end of the bench. He and Miss Vivian seemed to be making small talk.

A wrinkle cut across Tammy's forehead. "Mama? Who is that with Miss Vivian? He looks familiar."

She followed Tammy's line of sight. "Oh, that's Lewis Carter."

"Are they kin?"

"Not that I know of. Why?"

"I was just wondering." Tammy cast one last glance at the pair on the bench as she followed Jace and Mama up the steps and claimed a seat on the hay.

Once they got settled, Jace leaned closer to Tammy. "Lewis Carter owns the bait shop on the outskirts of town."

She held her breath when a whiff of citrus, lavender, spice, and a magical forest permeated her senses. It should be against the law for a man to smell that good.

"I remember him now. We used to stop by his shop for worms…" Tammy swallowed the lump in her throat.

Uncle Ellis should be here. She thought about her next steps in the investigation to avoid getting more emotional. She needed to speak to Lewis Carter. Since he owned the bait shop, maybe he saw something he hadn't told the police. If they even interviewed him. Focusing on bringing the killer to justice was about the only thing that kept her sane.

After the ride, Mama excused herself to walk around with Sheriff Obie. Jace's eyes darted to Tammy, and he grinned.

She fought the urge to roll her eyes. Before the night ended, she'd talk to Mama about her sneaky ways. "I'm going to head to the house."

He slipped his keys out of his pocket. "I think I'll head out, too."

A gunshot rang through the air when they got to the parking area. Tammy dropped behind her Bronco. Her chest rose with her pounding heart as she slipped her gun from its holster.

chapter nineteen

JACE LOWERED HIMSELF TO the ground beside Tammy. He breathed in the smell of peaches and cream from her hair. "It's okay, Tammy. A car backfired."

She kept the gun pointed up like she planned to drop a bird. "A car backfired?"

"Yes." He pointed at a truck that looked to be on its last leg. Gas fumes poured from the pipe. "See that old Ford?"

She followed his gaze and nodded. "Yeah." Her eyes narrowed to slits before she holstered her gun.

He raised a hand to offer comfort but let it drop to his lap. She'd probably knock it away or, worse, attempt to loosen some of his teeth. "What's going on? Are you okay?"

She pressed her back against the Bronco's tire. "I'm fine."

He swiveled his head to stare at her face. "Did you think that was a gunshot?"

A young couple strolled by hand in hand. The girl giggled as they disappeared behind another row of cars.

Tammy stared at the couple and pressed her fingers against her temples. "Why are you here, Jace?"

"I heard there were a lot of baked goods, and I'm a sucker for chocolate muffins." He jiggled his eyebrows, but Tammy's stony face told him she wasn't in the mood for jokes.

Her mouth tightened, and she glowered at him. "No, I mean, why are you in Pocahontas? Why are you suddenly back?"

Not caring for the direction the conversation took, he shrugged. "I have my reasons."

Her head tilted upward to get a better look at his face. "Do those reasons include taking Uncle Ellis fishing?"

A rush of blood clogged his head, and he struggled to keep his voice at a level lower than a shout. "What are you asking? Do you think I had something to do with what happened to Ellis?"

Her unblinking gaze didn't budge from his. "It is odd he drowned right after you moved back to town."

"How so?" His eyes clamped onto hers.

She jabbed a finger in his direction. "You come back, and he drowns. You're living in one of his rental houses, which happens to be next to his."

He opened his mouth to defend himself, but she held the same finger she'd pointed at him straight up. "I found you in Ellis's house, where you had no business being. You just so happened to be awake the night of the fire. I mean, the list could go on."

The rush of blood that clogged Jace's head turned into a waterfall. Could Tammy honestly think this poorly of him? "I take it I'm at the top of your suspect list?"

She shrugged and cocked her head.

She did think that poorly of him. "What about you?"

Her spine visibly stiffened. "What about me?"

The seconds ticked by as he attempted to think about what he said before saying something he'd regret. "I overheard Miss Ruby talking about you inheriting more than Ellis's house. He left you everything."

She heaved off the ground and took a step away from Jace. "So?"

He rose and closed the space between them. They stood mere inches apart. "You didn't show up at the funeral. Why not? Guilt keep you away?"

Her hand flew up, and she cracked him across the cheek. The quiver of her bottom lip as she stared him down without saying a word caused shame to course through his veins.

Maybe he needed to work on not saying something he'd regret. Because that last question could've been reworded. He lowered his gaze, regretting his lack of self-control. "I deserved that."

"Yes, you did."

"I'm sorry." He worked his jaw back and forth, still stinging from the slap. "We can stand here all night throwing accusations around or work together to find out who killed Ellis."

"I got shot." She ran her fingers across her chest.

Concern riddled his bones. "Shot?"

"That's why I wasn't at Uncle Ellis's funeral." A quiet sob left her lips. "I asked Mama not to say anything about it. I'm shocked she listened."

"I had no idea," he said, hanging his head. "The subject of you has definitely been off limits."

"I let a young punk get the better of me," she said as she tapped her chest. "He got me right here."

"Oh, wow, I'm so sorry. I know that had to be hard." He squeezed his eyes shut. "I'm glad you're okay."

"Hard's an understatement. So, what do you think? I killed Uncle Ellis for a few rental houses I don't even want?"

"I did think money could play a part in his death." The shame he'd felt earlier intensified. "That's a heavy motivator for some."

She opened her Bronco door and paused. Before she climbed inside, she affixed her gaze to his. "Unlike others I know, nothing could ever be a strong enough motivator for me to hurt the ones I love. That's not how I'm built."

Ouch. That was a dig if he ever heard one. "I'm here because Ellis asked me to come. He said he'd found something big and needed my help investigating it."

That seemed to get her attention. "What did he find?"

"That's the thing, he died before we had a chance to talk." He pulled a piece of paper out of his pocket. 'Someone left this on my desk at the newspaper office the other day."

After scanning the note, she met his gaze. "Old David-sonville? What do you think that means?" A look crossed her face like she'd only registered what he said. "What do you mean by *your* desk at the newspaper office?"

"I recently bought the place off Gleason Murphy."

"Hmm. I'm going to grab Castle and head over to Uncle Ellis's place for another look. Would you like to join me?"

For some reason, Jace couldn't help but think she wanted him close so she could keep an eye on him. But that didn't matter, not if he could ask for her forgiveness. "I do. Don't you think we should clear the air?"

"No, I don't. You broke up with me by marrying some-one else. There's no air to clear." She closed the door and drove away, leaving Jace staring at the back of her Bronco.

Working with Tammy might be the stupidest idea ever. That or he was a glutton for punishment.

chapter twenty

TAMMY STEPPED INSIDE UNCLE Ellis's with Castle on her heels. She plopped down on the couch and buried her head into the plush cushions. After sniffing around for a few minutes, Castle lay beside her. She figured he wanted her to know he'd found nothing amiss.

He nuzzled her hand until she scratched behind his ear. "Why did I ask Jace to come over here?"

"I don't know, why did you?" Jace folded his arms across his chest and leaned against the doorframe.

That's what she got for leaving the door open. The traitor Castle hopped off the couch and galloped over to Jace.

She squeezed her eyes closed and smacked her lips. "Don't ask me. I was hoping Castle would know the answer."

He took a couple of steps inside the living room. "Listen, I'm sorry I hurt you, but I felt I had no choice at the time."

"We really don't have to rehash something that happened when we were teenagers." She wiped her sweaty palms on her jeans and stood. "Let's just focus on the task at hand. Figuring out what happened to Uncle Ellis. That's what's important right now. Wouldn't you agree?"

"I do. Just wanted to make sure you understand..." His voice trailed off as Tammy escaped into the office.

He followed her inside and stuck his hands in the front pockets of his jeans. "What's on your mind?"

Her eyes landed on a framed copy of her college diploma on the wall. A small, sad smile played on her lips as she ran her finger over the wood frame. She'd never noticed this before today. "Do you remember visiting Uncle Ellis with me in high school?"

"Yeah, he always baked snickerdoodle cookies that were so good. Why?"

"Was his house ever this clean?"

One shoulder lifted as he scanned the office. "I don't really remember. What are you thinking?"

"Uncle Ellis was always sloppy. You know, he'd leave books and papers lying around. I've even known him to leave a bunch of dishes in the sink."

He cocked his head. "You think the killer cleaned Ellis's house?"

Now that he said it like that, maybe she sounded ridiculous. "I don't know, but I think it's somehow connected. The clean house and the burglar."

"You mean the kid who broke into Miss Ruby's the night you arrived?" He slid over to the window and pulled the curtain back. "You think he's connected to what happened to Ellis?"

She shook her head. "I do." She filled Jace in on her visit to Sonny.

"You should've taken me with you." He rested his shoulder against the window frame. "But I do have a thought about the clean house. Do you think Lorene Pankey could've cleaned it since they were an item?"

Tammy sat behind the desk and flipped through the desk calendar. "That's possible. I questioned her the other day. She knows more than she let on."

He stared at the framed diploma for a few seconds before landing a smile on Tammy. "Sounds like it's time to question her again."

"Mama said she's out of town the next week or so visiting family in Missouri." She pushed away from the desk. "Let's put that on the agenda for when she returns."

After an hour of searching Ellis's place, they had no more clues than when they started. Tammy opened the refrigerator and stared at its contents. A twinge swirled around her belly. Oh, how she missed Uncle Ellis.

She twisted the lid off a two-liter root beer, which didn't fizzle even a bit. She hated flat drinks. The lid fell from her hand and landed between the refrigerator and cabinet. With a groan, she dropped to her knees and shined the light from her phone. The lid lay behind a tiny pill.

"Hey, Jace, will you hand me a skinny spoon?"

He rummaged through several drawers before he handed her a teaspoon. Tammy used the spoon to drag the pill to her. She flipped it over in her palm. Uncle Ellis had a phobia of taking medications. So why would a Valium be there?

A chill crept up her spine as she thought about the pills she had been carrying around since she'd been released from the hospital. She put the pill in a small bowl and grabbed her purse. She removed her pill bottle and emptied the contents on the counter. Her heart liked to have dropped to the floor as she counted nineteen pills. There should be twenty since she'd not touched any since Dr. Patel prescribed them to help with her anxiety attacks.

"I don't understand how I'm missing a pill. There's no way my pill should've been on the floor in this house."

Jace seemed to be comparing the pills. "Has anyone had access to your purse since you've been back here?"

After a bit of mental retracing her steps, she only had one name. "Lorene Pankey."

chapter twenty-one

I RUB MY HAND down the puppy's soft fur and listen to the fake Detective Sharp's conversation with Jace Eubanks. That man and his ridiculous ideas. He could talk her into almost anything. Detective Sharp seemed to be about as bright as Lorene Pankey. A box of rocks could shame them in an IQ test.

If they thought they would be interviewing Sonny, they had another thing coming. He was currently visiting some of his drug buddies outside of Walnut Ridge. After helping him make bail, I supplied him with enough meth to last a while. At least until I need his assistance again. Which may be never after he bungled the break-in at Ruby's. All I'd asked was for him to find anything that could lead to the gold. Instead, he decided to steal her things. Stupid man. Then there was the matter of the fire. I push the thought away. Now was not the time for anger. Not with this sweet baby in my arms.

Several knocks on my front door, followed by a few pings to my doorbell, snapped me out of my thoughts. Someone had stopped by unannounced. A few neck pops, and I feel the tension ease away. I kiss my puppy on the head before walking out of the room. I love dogs more than words can express. They're more loyal than any human I've ever met.

I owed Detective Sharp thanks for prompting me to get a puppy. After seeing Castle, I knew I was ready for my own. Maybe I will adopt Castle if something happens to her. Yes, that would be perfect. It would be a way to show her my appreciation.

I feel my heart skip as I lock eyes with the visitor. I can't believe how happy I am to see none other than Ruby Sharp standing at the front door, holding a basket. She'd always been a fine Christian woman.

My smile is genuine as I step aside to let her in.

chapter twenty-two

As much as Tammy hated calling Sheriff Obie, she swallowed her pride and dialed his phone number. After he answered, Tammy cleared her throat. "This is Tammy Sharp. Have you seen Mama?"

"Howdy, Tammy. Ruby told me earlier she planned to spend the day visiting folks in the community."

"She's not answering her phone. Do you know who she's visiting?"

"Nah, but she normally leaves her phone in the car when she visits, so she's not distracted."

"All right, thank you."

Tammy paced the floor. Castle paced beside her. She looked through the bookshelf until she found the church directory. After she spoke to the preacher and called half the members, she was no closer to finding out where Mama was. One lady said she'd been there two hours ago, but that was the only lead.

Tammy's legs took off toward the front door when a car pulled into the driveway. As she stepped on the porch, she staggered at the sight of Mama. "Where have you been?"

"Excuse me?" Mama's forehead tightened so hard her brows nearly melted together.

"I've been looking everywhere for you." Tammy pulled her into a hug.

Mama's back relaxed as she wrapped her arms around Tammy. "I'm sorry, honey. I didn't think about you being worried."

"Since coming home, your house has been broken into, and someone tried to burn us up in it. I thought…"

Mama hugged Tammy tighter before she led her inside. "I'm fine and even made sure I was back in time to go to the bank with you."

Relief passed over Tammy, and she almost laughed. She never would've acted like that before she got shot.

An hour later, Tammy settled into a chair beside Mama at the First Trust Bank. She needed access to Uncle Ellis's bank statements. Hopefully, she'd find charges there that would give some clues about what he researched that could've gotten him killed.

The branch manager, Douglas McCoy, insisted he be the one to help them due to the nature of their visit and the large amount of money Uncle Ellis had in the bank. Tammy cocked her head. It was hard to believe Douglas used to have a crush on her. One time, he'd practically begged her to leave Jace and give him a chance. Jace had to step in and tell him to stop bothering Tammy before he got more involved. From that moment on, Douglas refused to speak to either of them. Even when he graduated top of their class, he acted like Tammy and Jace didn't exist when they congratulated him.

He looked Mama up and down before briefly glancing at Tammy. "Give me a few minutes, and I'll transfer Mr. Martin's accounts to your name. Since you're the beneficiary, I only need the death certificate."

Guess he still wasn't much for small talk. Tammy handed him the certificate. "That's fine."

Mama crossed her legs, and her light yellow wide-legged dress pants swished when she moved. "Douglas, how is your sweet daddy?"

A slight frown tugged at his lips. "The last time I saw him, he was all right. He stays to himself like a hermit most days."

Mama's left eyebrow twitched a little, and Tammy wanted to moan. Whenever Mama got that look, it meant she had a mission. "That won't do. He's going to waste away if he's not more active. You should bring him over for dinner tonight."

He didn't respond to Mama as he typed away on his keyboard a few minutes before he put his reading glasses on the desk. "Miss Sharp, the new account is active and ready for you to log on."

She clicked the bank app on her phone and nodded. "You can call me Tammy. I mean, we did go to high school together."

He gave a curt nod before his eyes darted to Mama, smiling so big his dimples could've made the five o'clock news. "I've been hoping to get an invitation for dinner at your place." He paused and looked pointedly at Mama. "What time should we be there?"

Mama tugged a piece of hair from behind her ear as a tinge of pink colored her cheeks. "Seven on the dot."

Seriously?

"We'll be there." He continued ogling Mama even though he spoke to Tammy. "What are your plans now that you're filthy rich, Miss Sharp?"

Mama put her arm around Tammy's shoulder and pulled her upper body across the chair. "Now that Ellis has set her up for life, she can quit that dangerous job and move back home."

She didn't remember Douglas McCoy being so nosy. Or flirty with older women. Maybe with her but with Mama?

Instead of answering, Tammy stood and offered a handshake. Douglas followed suit. "Now, you come back and see us when you're ready for a financial plan. We'll take good care of you."

"Sure. Let's go, Mama." Tammy emphasized the last word in case Douglas forgot Mama's age.

"Before you go, I have somewhat of a personal question." Douglas walked around his desk and stopped in front of Tammy. "Would you consider selling Ellis's home to me?"

Tammy looked up at Douglas. Wow, he must be six feet tall. "No, I'm not interested in selling."

Even though a smile crossed his lips, the light left his eyes. "I hate to hear that. Maybe something will happen that'll change your mind."

Tammy's spidey senses screamed that Douglas McCoy had a mean side he hid well. Still, she held her ground. "I doubt it."

He started toward the door and held it open for them to exit. "Looking forward to seeing you both this evening."

After they drove off, Tammy chuckled. "Can you believe that man was flirting with you?"

Mama crossed her arms and let out a huff. "Yes, Tammy, I can. You may not believe this, but men flirt with me all the time."

"I didn't mean that like it sounded." Tammy clicked the blinker to pass a van. "I just mean, you're way older than Douglas."

After a fake gasp, Mama shook her finger at Tammy. "You better quit while you're ahead, missy."

"All right, but don't go getting no ideas. Douglas McCoy is not a nice man."

Mama's voice climbed an octave. "Tammy Gail! You quit being mean. Douglas has always been nice to me."

How was it Mama always thought the best of people? Tammy must've gotten her cynical, untrusting attitude from Daddy. Luckily, Mama wouldn't be dating Douglas McCoy, so she'd let the subject drop. "I forgot to tell you I need to swing by Nicole's to grab Castle before we go home."

A beep sounded from Mama's purse. She pulled her phone out and scanned the screen with a grin. "Not a problem. We have plenty of time before Obie and the McCoys stop by for dinner."

"Sheriff Obie's coming over tonight, too?"

"Yes, I have a pot roast in the crockpot, and I hoped you'd make some Mud Cookies."

"Sure. Is there enough roast for a couple more people?"

"There's enough for several more people. I'm going to throw together a squash casserole, salad, and some mac and cheese."

A vision of Mama's homemade oven-baked mac and cheese had Tammy licking her lips. She pulled into the driveway and smiled. Castle had a football in his mouth, doing his best to keep Nicole and Harry from getting it.

His backend wagged so hard as he ran back and forth across the yard.

Castle spit the ball out when Tammy stepped out of the Bronco. He skidded across the yard until he sat in front of her. Tammy leaned down and let him know how much she missed him today.

Nicole patted Castle's head. "Castle has been so calm and nice playing with the other dogs today."

"That's Mama's good boy," Tammy said as she smiled at Castle. She glanced at Nicole. "Hey, are you and Harry available for dinner this evening? Mama made a roast, and I'm making Mud Cookies."

"That sounds good." Nicole's smile faded. "Would it be okay if we brought Jace? His stove went out, so I invited him over here."

Internally, Tammy screamed no a thousand times over. She should've kept her big mouth shut. When said big mouth opened, she found herself giving an answer she disagreed with. "That's fine."

She'd forgotten how living in a small town meant rubbing elbows with people you may not want to. There was a difference between having Jace help figure out what happened to Uncle Ellis and eating dinner with him. Mama had told her how Jace had played a part in solving a few cases over the years. So, he could be valuable. She could put aside her feelings for Uncle Ellis. But spending personal time with that man had no appeal to her. None. If it did, that would make her pathetic. And that's one thing she was not. Right?

chapter twenty-three

Tammy drank in the aroma of what had to be pumpkin pie spice as she sunk her teeth in a chunk of pot roast. She lifted her nose and got another whiff of ground nutmeg, cinnamon, ginger, allspice, and cloves. Her stomach gurgled as she chewed another bite. The spicy sweetness couldn't be mistaken. "Mama, did you season this roast with pumpkin pie spice?"

Mama leaned one elbow on the table and grinned. "I knew you'd recognize the taste. Do you like it?"

Tammy nodded as more proclamations about how delicious the roast came from around the table. Sheriff Obie, who happened to be sitting at the head of the table with Mama to his right, clenched Mama's hand before he shoveled another bite of roast in.

"You could put this roast up against the best of the best and come out a winner." Sheriff Obie's eyes brightened. "Have any of you watched that cartoon Ratatouille?"

Nicole grinned. "That is one of my favorites."

"I watched almost the entire movie at my doctor's office here a while back." His mouth slid into a straight line. "The blamed nurse called me back when we only had fifteen minutes left. That movie was so good that I rented it that very night to see the ending."

"I believe it." Harry, who sat directly to Sheriff Obie's left, nodded. "Nicole has forced me to watch it six times since we've been married."

Sheriff Obie laughed. "Well, anyhow, for those who ain't watched it, it's about a rat who can cook better than the finest chefs in Paris. This little rat saves a restaurant from closing down." He cut his gaze to Mama's. "My Ruby don't need no rat to save a restaurant. She could do it all on her own."

"I would have to agree with you, Sheriff." Harry elbowed Nicole a few times. "Nicole, asking Miss Ruby to share some of her recipes would be beneficial."

Nicole rubbed Harry's neck, not bothering to hide the fact she rubbed harder than she should have. "We may be coming over every night after this." Nicole's mischievous look caused Tammy to grin.

Harry winced as the rubs intensified. He grasped her hand and kissed her palm. "I was only teasing. You have nothing to worry about in the cooking department."

Tammy's grin stayed on her face, but inside, she cringed. Was that jealousy she felt? Surely not. No man had been able to catch her attention long enough to build anything lasting. Did she even want a relationship? A year ago, she would've given a resounding no. But now? Well, she couldn't be sure. Being home brought back memories she'd buried many years before.

Fred McCoy filled his fork with mac and cheese and nearly groaned as he chewed. "Sheriff Obie's right. This is mighty good." His eyes twinkled as he leaned across the table to look at Harry. "This here would tempt me to join you and your lovely wife at Miss Ruby's table every night."

Douglas elbowed his dad. "I take it my cooking isn't as good as Miss Ruby's?" He clutched his chest. "I'm highly offended, Dad."

Laughter filled the room, and they settled into a comfortable silence as they ate, drank water, and sipped their sweet tea.

Tammy openly watched Jace as his eyes darted around the table. He looked everywhere except at her. If she didn't know better, she'd think his nerves had him on edge.

Could he be the reason her emotions jumped all over the place? She pushed those thoughts aside. There was no sense in getting worked up because nothing would ever come of it. She'd return to Atlanta in a few months, and he could go wherever he pleased.

"You should've called me about the stove, Jace."

He met her gaze. Finally, she had his attention. Not that she wanted it, but it wasn't nice for him to ignore her completely. He scratched under the collar of his teal button-up and shrugged. "It's no big deal." Even though he wore a button-up instead of a t-shirt, his arm muscles strained against the fabric. The shirt would surely bust if he made a sudden move with his arm.

That line of thinking made Tammy think about the old-school Hulk and how his shirts would rip apart when he started changing. Then she imagined Jace turning green as his shirt fell off in shreds. A wide smile spread across her face, and she held back her laughter by biting the side of her cheek.

Mama shot a glance at Tammy from the corner of her eye. "Tammy Gail, would you like to share what's so funny?"

Tammy pressed her lips together. "Nope. I was just about to tell Jace I'd have someone over to fix the stove this week."

Jace grinned and raised a brow. She'd never been so thankful in her life that people couldn't read minds. She'd read a book one time about a vampire named Edward who knew what everyone thought. Well, everyone but his love interest. She'd be in trouble if people could read her thoughts.

By the time she snapped back to reality, Mama had changed the topic to the rental properties Uncle Ellis left Tammy. "I think she needs to quit her job and stay here."

Nicole's head bobbed as she set her ice water on the table. "Me, too," she said, her lashes flying high. "We would have so much fun if you moved back home."

Douglas chewed a piece of ice as his gaze penetrated Tammy. "I'd be open to taking all the rental properties off your hands, Miss Sharp."

Tammy considered taking him up on the offer, but she couldn't do that to Uncle Ellis. "I don't want to sell, but thank you for the offer, Mr. McCoy." He wanted to keep things professional. That's what she'd do, too.

Mama shook her head and pinned Tammy with her gaze. "What if the person who tried to burn us up comes back? Don't you want to be here to help since they never caught him?"

"Of course I do, Mama." Tammy squirmed in her seat. "But remember, we installed a security system with the best cameras. And don't forget, the police continue to drive by." She nodded toward Sheriff Obie. "Right, Sheriff?"

Mama continued as if Tammy never spoke. "They don't even have any suspects. You could hire Gleason Murphy to manage the property so you wouldn't be tied to it. That's what Ellis planned to do." Mama's mouth quivered, and she swallowed hard. Sheriff Obie rubbed her hand, and Mama smiled a smile that could've won her the title of Miss America.

Tammy narrowed her eyes. Mama said she just wanted to find out who killed Uncle Ellis, but she liked Sheriff Obie a lot. This could be trouble if he's hiding something, so she made a mental note to keep a closer eye on him for Mama's sake.

"I thought Gleason Murphy owned the newspaper."

Mama stuck her fork into her side salad. When she brought it out, Italian dressing dropped from a piece of lettuce. "Oh, he sold the paper a couple of weeks ago."

Both Tammy's brows shot up. "Really? Who bought it?"

Jace cleared his throat and laid one arm on the table. "Remember, I told you I bought it the other day."

"Oh, that's right. I'm not sure how I forgot that."

A car door slammed from the front of the house, allowing Tammy to process what he had just said. So, Jace bought the paper. Why? Whatever the reason, that meant Tammy could never move back home. How had she forgotten him telling her something important?

"We were leaving the fall festival, and it was noisy," Jace said as he bit into a mud cookie.

Yeah, she'd just had a meltdown because she thought she heard a gunshot. That's how she'd forgotten. Her anxiety got the best of her sometimes. She listened with half an ear as someone said something about Gleason leaving town on a mission trip.

The doorbell pinged, and Mama excused herself. Castle stirred from his nap and accompanied Mama to the door.

Within a minute, she returned with a dozen red roses in a beautiful purple vase.

That Sheriff Obie was a sneaky one.

"Who would be sending you roses?" Mama set them on the counter and turned to Tammy, hand on her hip. "Do you have a man I don't know about, Tammy Gail?"

Tammy almost fell out of her chair. "Who are they from?" Castle sat beside Tammy and laid his head against her leg.

Mama pulled the card out. "It says I look forward to rehashing the past with you."

Heat burned Tammy's throat as she skewered Jace with a glare. "Do you know anything about this?"

His eyes widened as a look of hurt crossed his face. "Why would you ask me that?"

"Remember the other night I told you I wasn't interested in rehashing the past?"

Douglas snickered. Tammy shot a look riddled with anger at him. He squirmed in his seat and took a sip of his sweet tea.

"I didn't send the flowers." Jace's mouth set in a grim line as he pushed away from the table. "Miss Ruby, thank you for the delicious dinner, but I do believe I've outstayed my welcome. Have a good evening, everyone."

Mama waited until Jace walked out the front door before she turned to Tammy. "You keep acting like that, you'll never get a man."

Tammy scowled. It's not like she wanted one anyway.

chapter twenty-four

UNEXPECTED ANXIETY CURLED IN Jace's stomach. After the disastrous dinner, he couldn't help but think he'd made a mistake taking over the newspaper. His life had been spent investigating things, not running a business. Maybe he should call Mr. Murphy to see if it's too late to back out. No, that wouldn't work. He'd already signed the papers, so wasting regrets on a done deal would do more harm than good. And it's not like he had a timeline to reopen the place. He would take his time to make sure it was as near perfect as possible.

Not that time was on his side when it came to his daughter. If Leo had her way, he'd be back in West Memphis before the night was out. She didn't understand how desperately he needed time to rethink everything about Una's murder. After three years with nothing but a bunch of dead ends, he needed fresh eyes.

Thankfully, his old friend Arnold Davidson had been assigned to the case after the lead detective over the investigation retired. Arnold promised Jace he would make solving Una's murder a priority. But he'd also asked Jace to give him a few months to look at Una's case without Jace's input or interference. Jace had agreed. Leo, not so much. He understood her frustration in wanting the killer brought to justice. Knowing the person who murdered

Una was still walking the streets made Jace's blood turn cold. But he'd step back so the detective could do his job, at least for now.

He moved from room to room, mentally updating the space. His gaze landed on a bookshelf. What looked like an ancient copy of Great Expectations caught his attention. Odd. It didn't weigh more than a candy bar.

He carried it to the desk and opened it. What lay inside got his investigative juices flowing. The book had been hollowed out and filled with newspaper clippings stored in individual bags. He thumbed through the bags, his eyes glued to the various headlines.

The first one read:

DENNIS HOWARD CLAIMS HE FOUND GOLD!

The second one read:

DENNIS HOWARD GOES MISSING

The third one stayed along the same lines:

WAS DENNIS HOWARD MURDERED?

The fourth article gave the answers:

DENNIS HOWARD'S BODY FOUND ON BLACK RIVER!

After he read the headlines, Jace backtracked and read the articles. Dennis Howard went missing well over forty years earlier. He stayed gone for a year before his body washed up on the shore of the Black River. Even though he claimed to find gold, his death had been ruled an accidental drowning.

Jace picked up a piece of paper and found yet another article dated the current year.

The headline read:

ELLIS MARTIN DROWNS ON BLACK RIVER

The hairs on the back of Jace's neck stood up. What in the world? Who had put these here? Gleason Murphy? No, that couldn't be. Gleason Murphy had always treated Jace like a son. He didn't have the demeanor to kill.

A little voice in the back of Jace's head whispered that most people could kill if they had what they thought to be a good enough reason.

Still determined not to put this on his old mentor, Jace's mind raced toward other possibilities. Who else could it have been? No one else came to mind. This had been Mr. Murphy's office, so why would someone else put this book here? Could he be the one behind Ellis's death? What if he killed Dennis Howard and Ellis found out? Why else would these articles be hidden here?

Nothing made sense. Why would Gleason Murphy leave something of this magnitude behind? Surely, he would've taken this with him if he'd killed Ellis and the other man.

Right?

A tiny slip of paper fell on the desk when Jace stacked the articles. It looked like a piece of a letter signed by someone named Constance. Maybe the word love came before her name. He couldn't tell, but that word made the most sense.

He took his phone out and snapped pictures of the box and its contents as his mind wandered to possible explanations. A bang came from the front door and interrupted Jace's thoughts. He gathered everything and deposited it in the desk drawer.

Sheriff Obie leaned into the opening of the door. "I was hoping to find you here. We need to talk."

Jace stepped aside. "Come on in. We can talk in the office."

After he looked over the bookcase, Sheriff Obie claimed one of the only two wood chairs across from the desk. "I don't figure you've watched a movie called Hondo?"

Jace shook his head.

"It's an old western. An army scout named Hondo, played by John Wayne, protects a woman and her child during a war."

"Sounds interesting, but what does that have to do with me?"

"I'm just going to cut to the chase. You and Tammy need to stop looking into Ellis's death."

The office chair creaked as Jace leaned back. "What makes you think we're investigating Ellis's death?"

He snorted. "Tammy's a Homicide Detective. You're an Investigative Journalist."

Jace picked up a stress ball and rolled it around in his hands. "That doesn't mean we're -"

Sheriff Obie raised his hand as he cut Jace off. "Tammy wouldn't be caught dead in the same room as you without a good reason."

Well, that stung. "Yes, she would."

He clicked his tongue while his head bobbled back and forth. "Didn't you run off and marry another gal while y'all was engaged?"

That question socked Jace in the stomach. His jaw clenched as he lifted himself out of the chair. "I'm not discussing this with you."

As Sheriff Obie stood, his eyes flashed. "Suit yourself. I'm just trying to help."

"If we need your help, I'll make sure to ask," Jace said as he coiled his fingers into tight balls.

"Just remember, you ain't no Hondo, and you sure ain't no John Wayne." With one last glance at the bookcase, he ambled out the door.

The front door shut with a bang. Jace placed both hands flat on the desk and stared at the chair Sheriff Obie had vacated.

Looks like he may have just found their killer.

chapter twenty-five

CASTLE NUDGED TAMMY ON the shoulder. She pulled the cover up to her neck and rolled over. He huffed air out of his nose and pressed against her side. She cracked an eye open and gave him the dirtiest one-eyed look she could muster.

After a glance at the clock, she groaned. "Can you hold it?"

Another nudge. Why did he have to go outside at four o'clock in the morning?

A few short pings sounded against her window. She grabbed her gun as another, louder ping hit. She eased the curtain back an inch and grinned before she could stop herself. Jace stood there with a flashlight and a bag of sweet tarts. The screen lay on the ground.

They were around fifteen years old the first time they'd gotten into a fight. Tammy had gone home mad and locked herself in her bedroom. That night, Jace pecked on her window. When Tammy opened it, he'd apologized and handed her a bag of sweet tarts. She'd accepted his apology, and all was right with the world. At least for a while.

She deposited the weapon on the table and raised the window. Since she had on her flannel pajamas, she made a quick decision. She met Castle's gaze. "Give me a minute, and I'll let you out to potty."

After she disarmed the alarm, she slipped on her house shoes and flopped one leg through the open window. As she shimmied her way outside, she remembered that this was much easier as a teenager.

Jace held her hand as she landed on her feet. Heat blasted her neck and head as memories of the first time she'd done this assaulted her. Thirty years ago, Jace had held her hand the same way. Except that time, when she had landed on the ground, she'd pressed her lips to his.

Their first kiss.

She could almost feel the excitement and love fifteen-year-old Tammy had experienced. A tingle spread through forty-five-year-old Tammy's veins as she imagined herself reenacting that kiss.

For one captivating moment, Jace's lips lingered mere inches from Tammy's. A sweet yet tart lemon scent surrounded her. Even though shivers spiraled down her spine, she stepped back until she hit the wall. At fifteen, she'd vowed only to kiss Jace. He had forced her to break the promise she'd made to herself when he married Una.

He swallowed and took a few visibly deep breaths. "I'm sorry for making things difficult for you." He pressed the sweet tarts into her hand. His fingertips left a trail of goosebumps where he touched.

For some reason, the only thought in her mind centered around the kiss they could've just had. Had he wanted to kiss her? Wait. What's wrong with her? Those thoughts were banned. She licked her lips as she tore the box open. "Thank you."

"I promise you I didn't send those roses."

Water flooded her mouth as she crunched on a light pink sweet tart. "After thinking it through, I already came to that conclusion."

He shifted from one foot to the other and sighed. "When Mato got shot, I was so distraught. His blood covered my hands and clothes from where I'd tried to help him." A sob racked Jace's shoulders, and he lowered his head.

Tammy laid her hand on his shoulder. "Hey, you don't have to get into this. I know Mato got shot in a senseless drive-by, and I was so sorry. I wish I'd been here for you instead of out of the country."

He raised his head and locked eyes with Tammy. "I do have to get into this. Mato getting shot changed both of our lives, Tammy, and I'm so sorry."

She squared her shoulders but kept silent. He needed to say something, and Tammy didn't have the heart to stop him.

"Mato lay there screaming for Una and his unborn child."

Tammy gasped but didn't say anything. Unborn child?

"He begged me to take care of her and his baby." His hands shook as he rubbed moisture from his eyes. The words rushed from Jace. "I made a blood brother promise to marry Una and raise the baby as my own. We went to the justice of the peace that day. I married her with Mato's blood still on my hands. Please forgive me. I should've done things differently."

For a moment, Tammy allowed herself to think of what Jace went through from his point of view. The despair he must've felt as he witnessed his best friend pass from this life.

As her heart ached for the young Jace, Tammy stepped forward and ran her hands through his hair, stopping on his shoulders. The depth of Jace's silky gaze swaddled her like a velvety afghan in front of a fire on a cold night. Before she thought better, she raised on her tippy toes and pressed her lips to his.

chapter twenty-six

JACE'S STOMACH PITCHED AS Tammy's lips touched his. How many times had he dreamed of kissing Tammy over the past couple of weeks? Too many to count. The comforting kiss Tammy offered hadn't been what he had in mind, but he'd take it. His hands trembled as he caressed her shoulders, careful to keep his touch light.

Tammy broke away and stepped back, coming to a stop when she hit the wall. She clutched the sweet tarts to her chest with one hand and ran her hands through her hair with the other. "I'm sorry."

He swallowed several times before he found his voice. "I'm not."

Her eyes widened. "Thanks for the sweet tarts. Good night, Jace." With that, she darted around the front of the house.

Jace picked up the screen and clutched it to his chest. The desire to follow Tammy almost overtook him as his heart banged out of control.

Tammy marched around the house before he made up his mind whether to put the screen on or go after her. She shrugged. "The door's locked."

He made a step out of his hands. "I'll give you a boost."

Tammy bit the side of her lip as she glanced from Jace to his hands.

He chuckled. "I promise it's just a step."

She narrowed her eyes. "No funny business this time."

He nodded. "Promise."

The last time Tammy snuck out through her window, they'd been around seventeen. They'd leaned against her wall for over an hour, watching the stars and eating candy. When she'd started yawning, Jace made a step like the one he made tonight. But instead of letting her step inside, he'd only wanted to steal kisses. Miss Ruby had cleared her throat before chewing them both out. She'd told Jace no more funny business.

After that, Miss Ruby said they could watch the stars from the back porch, with her keeping an eye on them. Jace's chest tightened as he thought about the life he and Tammy should've lived. Yes, he'd grown to love Una, but that love had never been a love like he had for Tammy.

Tammy stepped into his hand, and he boosted her inside. As he installed the screen, she leaned into the window. "Thanks again. Good night."

"Good night, Tammy. Lock the window behind me." He stood there until the lock clicked into place.

As he meandered through the yards, the sky glowed with red, purple, and orange highlights in the distance. He stopped and stared, trying to decide whether to tell Tammy to look.

He swiveled around as a door closed behind him. Tammy came through the yard toward Jace, Castle on her heels, until he shot off into the backyard.

"Castle needs to potty."

Tammy paused, seeming to drink in the view. She took his breath away. The curves of her face screamed for his touch, and every strand of hair invited him to run his hands through it.

That thought sent Jace's blood into a tizzy. His desire to see Tammy the past few years hadn't been about begging her to forgive him. At least not entirely. He'd wanted to see her because he still loved her.

His breath went jagged as the feelings he'd buried for so many years hit him in the gut. Even though Tammy only meant to comfort Jace with that kiss, it ignited a fire like he'd never known.

Now, he couldn't deny he would do whatever it took to win her back.

chapter twenty-seven

Hot water streamed onto Tammy's head as she rinsed the conditioner from her long locks. The events from earlier that morning still baffled her. What in the world caused her to kiss Jace?

Heat ran up her neck as she thought about how he touched her shoulders. No, no, no. Tammy would not allow herself to get hurt by Jace again. He'd married Una behind her back, and she had no idea if she could ever fully forgive him for that.

How could she trust a man who up and married someone else like Jace had? A small voice in the back of her mind whispered a reminder of why he'd done it. She pushed the voice further back until she no longer heard it as she grabbed a towel. The days of Jace Eubanks owning a piece of her heart were over.

At least, she hoped they were.

She dried off and donned a pair of faded black boyfriend jeans and a cream turtleneck sweater. A wild hair stuck out on her brow. Yuck. She tucked her feet into fluffy purple house shoes and grabbed her black Coach purse to look for tweezers. After she waded through a glass fingernail file, three quarters, a dime, four pennies, and three pieces of peppermint, she laid her hands on the tweezers. She gasped. A small pill was wedged in with the tweezers. Her missing Valium. Wow. She remembered taking a pill out one time when she felt out of control. It must've been in there the entire time.

Thankful for solving one mystery, she went to the kitchen and poured a cup of coffee before she settled into the breakfast nook. Now, she had to figure out the owner of the one she found by Uncle Ellis's refrigerator.

A book about the history of Old Davidsonville sat on the counter. Interested, she sipped her coffee as she perused the pages. What kind of trouble did Uncle Ellis stumble into? Could he have really uncovered something about the historical settlement? That sounded like something he would've loved to research.

Mama strolled into the kitchen just as Tammy downed the last of her coffee. She focused her eyes on the book and avoided Mama's gaze. "Morning, Mama."

A glint touched Mama's eyes when she kissed Tammy on the forehead. "Morning." She pecked her fingers on the counter and looked at Tammy. "Why do you look so guilty?"

Tammy sat the book on the table, stood, and headed to the coffee pot. "I don't look guilty," she said with a smirk. "What would I have to feel guilty about?"

Sunshine cascaded through the window, shining on Tammy's face like a beacon. She clinked the shades down before she sipped her fresh coffee.

Meanwhile, Mama's eyes roamed over Tammy like an inspector looking for a problem. "So that you know, Castle woke me up early this morning."

"Sorry about that. I'll start keeping my bedroom door closed." Tammy flipped through the book's pages. It was time for a subject change. "I want to go out on Black River and stop by the bait shop this afternoon. Do you know where Uncle Ellis keeps his boat?"

Mama lowered her eyes as she poured a glass of tea. "Yeah, it's stored on Gleason's lot at the storage complex. The Ford Ranger you inherited is there with the boat and trailer."

"Goodness, I haven't even thought about that." Uncle Ellis had left Tammy everything she needed to start life over in Pocahontas. But did she want that? Atlanta had been home for the past twenty years. Could small-town living be the change Tammy needed after all this time?

The iron skillet landed on the stove with a thud. Tammy glanced up as Mama grabbed a pack of bacon from the refrigerator. "I have a taste for a BLT this morning. Do you want one?"

A BLT did sound pretty tasty. "Sure. I'll slice a tomato."

"No need. I have the lettuce and tomato ready to go. You sit down and enjoy your coffee." Bacon sizzled as Mama laid a few pieces in the skillet. "I understand you had a long night."

Tammy's eyes grew wide as she stared inside the very interesting cup of coffee. "I'm not sure what you mean by that."

Silence greeted Tammy. Good. Maybe she'd drop the subject. Tammy got out the bread and saucers as Mama finished the bacon.

Sandwiches done, Tammy reclaimed her spot with a fresh cup of coffee. Mama slid across from Tammy and clicked her tongue. "I thought the days of sneaking out your window to meet Jace were long gone."

Not only did Mama not drop the subject, she picked it up and ran with it like a superstar quarterback with a football. Tammy opened her mouth and then clamped it shut. Oh boy, she hoped Mama didn't witness that kiss. She'd definitely move back to Atlanta if she had. That's something she'd never let Tammy live down.

"He's the one that stopped by. No big deal."

After blessing the food, Mama took a bite from her sandwich and thoroughly chewed it before answering, "Mmm-hmm." She took a swig of tea, and her eyes clouded. "That terrible Sonny Perkins is still out and about. You need to be careful."

Castle joined them in the kitchen. He greeted them with special Castle kisses and headed to his food bowl. She should've known he'd wake Mama up. He better be glad she loved him, or he'd stay behind with Mama when she returned to Atlanta.

"I'll be careful. He probably won't come back here anyway." Tammy bit into her sandwich and grinned. Mama made the best bacon. Hers always had a crispiness to it that Tammy could never get. "What are you doing today, Mama?"

"I planned on stopping by the pharmacy, but now I guess I'm going to Black River with you."

A knock at the door interrupted Tammy's thoughts. Mama entered the living room and returned with Officer Rayburn and Sheriff Obie.

After they exchanged greetings, got cups of coffee, and made small talk, Sheriff Obie cleared his throat. "Ruby, we need to talk to you and Tammy about the night of the fire."

Officer Rayburn sat his coffee on the table. "Have either of you remembered anything new from that night? Maybe something or someone strange?"

"Nothing. We didn't even know about the fire until Castle woke us up." Tammy cut her gaze from Officer Rayburn to Sheriff Obie. "Why?"

"A woman from Missouri named Kendra Burton died in a house fire a few nights ago."

"That's horrible." Mama's voice cracked when she spoke. "What happened?"

"Like the fire here, both the front and back doors had ropes tied to them." Sheriff Obie tapped his fingers on the table. "But the ropes didn't match."

"At first, we suspected her ex-husband." Officer Rayburn picked up his coffee cup and held it mid-air.

Mama gasped and put her hand across her chest. "This is awful. I mean, just the worst news we could've gotten."

Tammy's mind worked overtime. Had the fire been random? No, she didn't think so, but for now, she'd keep those thoughts to herself. "Could her ex be the killer?"

"No, he has a solid alibi." Officer Rayburn pressed his lips together. "He was out of town for work."

"Like I said before, I think it was Sonny Perkins," Tammy said.

"We're looking into that possibility."

After Officer Rayburn and Sheriff Obie left, Mama and Tammy sat silently for a few minutes. A text buzzed on Tammy's phone. She scanned the message and bit her lip.

Mama craned her neck as she leaned across the table. "Who's that?"

Tammy shrugged. If only she could lie to Mama, she'd tell her it was anyone but who it was. Better rip off the proverbial bandaid. "Jace wants me to stop by the newspaper office this morning."

"Really?" Her face brightened as a brow raised.

Tammy's fingers ran down the side of the warm coffee cup as she avoided Mama's gaze. "It's not like that. We're trying to figure out what happened to Uncle Ellis, and that's it."

"After the fire, I think it may be too dangerous for you to be digging into things. Don't you think it would be best to leave the investigation to the police?"

"They're not investigating, so I will." Tammy bit into the sandwich and almost forgot what she was saying. Soft bread, sweet tomato, crispy bacon, and crunchy lettuce had to be the perfect combination for a sandwich. "It's what I do, Mama."

"I don't want you getting hurt, and you know Ellis would forbid it if he were here," Mama said. "You can spend time with Jace doing something else."

"Jace married another woman, Mama. While we were together." She pushed the coffee cup away. "I will never be able to forgive or even trust him. What I'm doing is for Uncle Ellis."

Mama stayed quiet for a few minutes but kept her gaze on Tammy. She could stare all she wanted. As long as that was all she did, Tammy would be fine.

After Mama cleared the table, she reclaimed her seat. Something close to disapproval gleamed in her eyes. "Remember in the Bible, how Joseph's brothers thought about killing him but ended up selling him instead?"

Tammy should've known the silence wouldn't last. "Yes, but that has nothing to do with Jace and me."

Mama's southern voice sounded so sweet it could've rivaled Dolly Parton's. "Joseph was hurt, and I mean deeply hurt. Right?"

Tammy got up and poured another cup of coffee. She'd only thought she could cut back on coffee after taking a break from the police force. "Right."

"Did he help his family during the great famine?" She pinned Tammy with her gaze. "Including the same brothers who sold him?"

A long breath escaped Tammy, and she squirmed in her seat. "Yes, Mama. I remember you teaching this in Bible class."

"Then you need to start living it. Look at how quickly poor Kendra Burton's life ended. It could happen to any of us. Tammy Gail, you're closer to fifty than forty, but you act like you've got all the time in the world to find love."

"I found love, but love hurt, so I'm no longer looking." Tammy stood and grabbed the book. "I'm going to finish getting ready."

chapter twenty-eight

The Pocahontas Star Herald held a special place in Tammy's heart. Memories bombarded her as she got out of her Bronco. The train caboose she'd spent many hours of her youth playing on looked the same as it always had.

A small smile drifted across her lips as she took a moment to take it all in. The sudden loud blast of a car horn, followed by car tires skidding across the pavement, came from the road. Tammy swiveled around in time to see a Camry barely miss getting hit by a Jeep. As she turned back toward the building, a flash of green caught her eye. Her brow furrowed, and she jogged in that direction with Castle on her heels.

Sonny Perkins peeked at her from behind the caboose. They locked eyes before he high-stepped it toward the park. Fire lit under Tammy's feet as she raced to catch up with him. As soon as she got close enough to reach him, she lunged.

Castle's fur seemed to stand on end as he waited for Tammy to give him an order. She had trained him only to intervene if she was down or if she gave him the go-ahead.

A high-pitched scream came from Sonny as they hit the rocky ground. He landed a blow to the side of Tammy's head.

She shook it off, spun around, and slammed her foot into his knee. He let out a yelp and collapsed to the ground, holding the place she kicked. His leg snaked out, and he knocked her legs out from underneath her. A rock dug into her palm when she landed. Sonny wasted no time knocking his foot into her side. The same rock cut her cheek when her face crushed into the dirt. Her blood surged. She flipped over and found her feet.

He threw a punch, barely missing her wounded cheek. "Did you really think I'd let you get away with punking me out the other day? I was wasted, you know. That's why you got the better of me."

"I'll find out what you're up to. Even if I have to beat it out of you."

Sonny slipped a switchblade from his back pocket and jabbed it toward her stomach. "You think you're big and bad? I've beat better than you with a broken arm."

Castle growled and made a move toward Sonny. "Castle. Stay." Tammy wanted the pleasure of beating Sonny Perkins on her own.

Tammy kicked the knife out of his hand. Her face throbbed. A surge of anger coursed through her veins. She moved behind him and circled her arm around his throat. At that moment, she fully intended to squeeze the life out of him. "I thought you said you had nothing to do with the fire."

"I didn't!" Sonny said as he clawed her arms. "Let me go."

Liar. She shoved him away from her. "Then why are you spying on me?"

A furious look marred his features as he landed on the ground. "I wasn't. I was already here when I saw you."

"You're lying." A vein in Tammy's forehead throbbed as she took a step toward Sonny. "You know more than you're letting on."

Gravel crunched behind Tammy as Jace strode in their direction. "What's going on?" Tension oozed from Jace's voice, and his back visibly bristled.

Sonny Perkins stammered when he spoke. "I don't know why she attacked me. I legit was just out here looking around."

Tammy took a step in Sonny's direction with both hands balled into fists at her sides.

"It's true!" Sonny's voice cracked.

Jace grabbed Sonny by the nape of his neck and pulled him into a standing position. "I better not ever catch you near this woman again." Danger dripped from Jace's tone. His grip tightened. "Do you understand?"

His face turned visibly red as Jace put more pressure on his throat. "Yeah, I understand!"

Jace brought Sonny into the same breathing space. "I don't even want you in the same store as Tammy, or you will answer to me."

Sonny nodded several times before Jace let him go.

Tammy watched Sonny scuttle away with mixed emotions. This side of Jace did something to her she didn't like. She didn't need a man to protect her. But at the same time, it felt nice. Nice enough that her heart seemed determined to beat out of her chest.

"Are you hurt?"

"I'm fine."

Jace's eyes roamed over Tammy. When he seemed satisfied she had no serious injuries, he nodded. "Come inside, we need to see about the cut on your cheek. And

I'll get you a cold drink to put on your head. It's already bruising."

As she adjusted her shirt, she inhaled through her nose and exhaled through her mouth a few times. "I'm right behind you."

The place reeked of stale ink and old newspapers. Tammy loved it. The aroma that greeted her reminded her of her younger years. Of days following Mr. Murphy around, asking a million questions about how to write the best articles, days of holding Jace's hand, days of sneaking kisses. She remembered how she'd thought about becoming a reporter for a short time.

Then Jace left her, and everything changed. She figured out that she'd only wanted to be a reporter because of him. Finding killers brought Tammy a joy she couldn't describe. That had been her calling.

The man on her mind took out a first aid kit from the desk and bandaged her face. A trail of fire lingered behind everywhere his hand brushed. The bruises and cuts paled in comparison to the feelings Jace stirred as his breath caressed her cheeks. He drew in a long breath before handing her a cold drink. He sat behind the desk, seeming deep in thought.

Her gaze lowered. The color of choice for his daily t-shirt was a deep purple. It looked nice against his tan skin. Tammy inwardly groaned. Stop it. Just because a man has nice arms doesn't mean looking at them is okay.

Castle bounded over to Jace, his nails clicked on the wooden floor as he danced a jig. That boy and his showing off! He'd do anything to get his head scratched.

Jace patted Castle on the side a few times, which earned Jace a special Castle kiss on his arm. The burn Jace had gotten from the fire at Mama's had faded to a light pink with a few hard-looking spots. A sliver of guilt passed over Tammy as Castle settled beside the desk.

The cool aluminum felt good against the place where Sonny hit her. She held it in place, walked over to a bookcase, and looked over her shoulder. "How's the arm? It looks better."

"It's healing nicely." He picked up a pencil and twirled it in his hand. "Do you believe Sonny being here was a coincidence?"

"It is possible. He's a drug addict, and I think he could've been hiding out here." She shrugged. "It's not like Pocahontas is a huge town with lots of places to go."

"You have a point."

"Even so, I think he's hiding something. If he didn't set the fire, he knows who did."

"I agree," Jace said, his Adam's apple bobbing. "Will you sit down for a minute? I need to talk to you."

Tammy's spine stiffened. "As long as the topic has nothing to do with our past."

He shook his head and plopped the pencil down. "No, this is about Ellis's murder."

Her heart rate kicked up a notch. At least this time, she had something to blame it on.

chapter twenty-nine

After claiming the chair across from the desk, Tammy focused on Jace. "What have you uncovered?"

He laid an old book on the desk. Tammy bit her bottom lip. What could a copy of Great Expectations have to do with Uncle Ellis's murder? Once he opened the book, it made sense. Jace laid out a few old newspaper clippings.

After she read through them, she cocked her head. "What does Dennis Howard's drowning from forty years ago have to do with Uncle Ellis?"

"I would say nothing if not for this." He laid a more recent clipping on the desk, and a pang struck Tammy in the middle.

She angled her body so she could reread the articles. Her eyes narrowed once she finished reading. "Where did you get these?"

Jace hoisted himself to his feet and moved to the bookcase. "I found it right there."

She followed. "Wow. Either the killer left it there, or someone close to Dennis Howard has been investigating his death."

"And they've somehow tied his death to Ellis's."

Her gaze bounced from him to the bookcase. "Maybe they were murdered by the same person."

Jace grabbed two massive books leaning against the wall and placed them on the desk. "We need to find every article we can about gold," he said.

She flipped the book on top open to a newspaper dated 1975. "I agree." Castle let out a huff. Tammy ruffled his ears with a smile. "Let me grab Castle a treat and some water."

Castle stood at attention as soon as he heard the word treat. Jace chuckled as he emptied a stack of papers onto the desk. "Sounds good."

Two hours later, they both plopped down in the office. They'd found several articles about Old Davidsonville but not any about lost gold.

Jace glanced at his watch. "You hungry? It's past lunchtime."

Castle laid his head on Tammy's lap, and her stomach answered Jace's question. "I could eat."

"Wanna grab a taco?"

She allowed a grin to spring across her lips. "It's not often I'd turn down a taco." She stood and grabbed her purse. "Can we stop by Gleason's storage building before we eat?"

"Sure." He clicked the lock into place before heading down the steps. "What's at the storage?"

She fell into step beside Jace. "I want to see if I can get Uncle Ellis's truck and boat started so I can go out on Black River this afternoon."

Jace led her to a shiny black Mustang. He grinned as he opened the passenger door for her and Castle. On the way to the storage building, Jace pecked his thumb on the steering wheel. "At some point soon, I want to show you a board I've put together on Ellis's murder."

She ran her hand down Castle's side. "I'd love to see it. I've been jotting things down in a notebook but planned on getting a board together."

"You can share mine if you want." He stuttered and scratched the back of his neck. "I mean, we'll make more headway working off the same one, I think."

"Yes, we will." She stared out the window for a minute before she met his gaze head-on. "This is about Uncle Ellis and bringing his killer to justice. And that is all."

Did he wince? It didn't matter. He needed to understand that she only accepted his help to find Uncle Ellis's killer. They weren't friends.

He visibly swallowed as he turned into the storage complex. "I believe we need to look at Sheriff Wilson."

A frown tugged at her lips. "Why?"

Before he answered, a gasp came from his lips as he stopped in the parking lot. Tammy followed his line of sight. A surge of anger bit into her bones.

All the tires had been slashed on Uncle Ellis's truck and the boat trailer. STUPID DETECTIVE had been spray-painted across the white truck with bright red paint. The way the letters dripped, Tammy couldn't help but be reminded of blood.

chapter thirty

In Jace's experience, dealing with the police in a small town had pros and cons. Those in the big city stayed mainly in a hurry, going from call to call, leaving no time to get personal. Small-town Arkansas, not so much. In between questions about Tammy's past, present, and future, she finally got a police report made.

Officer Rayburn's lips stretched into a smile that took over his entire face. "Tammy, I'm just so glad to have you back in town." A few splotches of pink covered that same face. "Not that I'm glad about the vandalism, mind you."

Officer Rayburn had been a staple in Pocahontas for as long as Jace could remember. He'd been a rookie cop when they were in high school.

Tammy touched Officer Rayburn's wrist as she returned his smile. "Oh, I know that."

His smile got even more prominent, if that was possible. After they said their goodbyes, Tammy ran a hand through her hair and glanced at Jace. "I want to speak to the new history teacher this week. It looks like this afternoon is open. Do you want to join me?"

Shivers covered Jace's skin. He'd like to blame the cool breeze, but that would be a lie. He never would've believed he and Tammy would interact like this again. Even though she only had him around to help solve Ellis's murder, he couldn't stop the feelings he'd been having. Not that he wanted to. "Sure. How about we grab that taco first?"

The sky turned gray and menacing from out of nowhere. Thunder boomed, followed by a streak of purple lightning that circled the sky, turning it into a beautiful scene.

One minute, he stood gawking at the vivid sky. The next minute, a sheet of heavy rain slapped him in the face and drenched his clothes. As he allowed the rain to pepper his body, Jace pitied the person who never had rain to hit their face as a smell of earthy musk surrounded them.

Moments like this reminded him of Una. Her laugh had been contagious the last time she'd danced in the rain. A pang of guilt pierced his heart as Una's face swam around in his mind. They'd spent over twenty years together before he lost her—twenty good years—great, even.

He could never bring himself to regret their time together. She'd been a good wife and mother to Leo, and he loved her. He could almost hear her sweet laughter as she teased him about not wanting to get his hair wet in the rain.

Tammy grabbed his hand and nudged him toward the front lot where he'd parked his car. As soon as his legs started moving, Tammy dropped his hand like he had a wad of poison ivy in his palm.

He sighed. It was odd how Una came to him a few months before she passed to discuss him finding love again if she died. Convinced he'd be the one to die first, he'd shrugged the comments off. She'd been persistent and gained his promise. He had also made her promise to do the same if he passed before she did.

What would she think about that love being with Tammy? Since they'd spoken about her over the years, he knew the answer to that question. Una felt guilty for taking Jace away from Tammy. One time, early in their marriage, she offered to divorce him so he could marry Tammy. He'd declined. Marriage was for life. When and if he ever remarried, it would be the same.

Castle stared at Jace from the back seat as he opened the passenger door for Tammy. He closed her door and ran around to the driver's side.

By the time he got in the car, Tammy had squeezed between the seats and had Castle's water bowl in her hand. Jace twisted around to see what she was doing. She refilled the bowl and placed it on the floorboard. When she tried to get back to the front seat, she turned, and their faces nearly touched. They both froze. Her eyes doubled in size.

The fragrance of cotton candy washed over Jace, and his gaze dropped to her mouth. Her body inched closer to Jace as he moved toward her. Another millimeter and their lips would meet. He latched his gaze onto hers, almost daring her to make a move.

The tip of her tongue ran between her lips as she edged back into her seat. She looked straight ahead, seeming to want to act like nothing almost happened. The way her shoulders heaved in rhythm with her chest told Jace another story.

Castle capped his eyes on Jace. If Jace didn't know better, he'd think the dog looked disappointed in him. Jace knew the feeling. After a second of sizing Jace up, Castle curled into a ball and closed his eyes.

The rain hadn't slowed, so Jace turned his lights on and eased onto the road. "Do you want to talk about what just happened?"

"Nope."

"Still want that taco?"

"Nope."

"Want to go home and change and maybe try to see the history teacher?"

She looked at Jace, her mouth flattened into a frown. "Just take me to my car."

He shrugged. "Whatever you say."

The extra few minutes it took to get to the newspaper were filled with hammering rain and silence. Tammy wouldn't even look at him.

As soon as he pulled beside her Bronco, she hopped out. Castle followed without her having to ask.

She kept her eyes averted as she slammed the door, got into her Bronco, and sped away.

chapter thirty-one

Maybe Tammy needed to make an appointment to be reevaluated by her therapist. Obviously, her sanity was in question. Why else would she have a strong desire to kiss Jace Eubanks? Again.

The vent blew heat that could rival even the best bonfire. That had to be why Tammy's face and neck felt hot. That and maybe the fact that the sun had peeked from behind the clouds. The rain had moved on to another part of Arkansas.

She shouldn't even consider giving that man a second glance. Why did he have to be so attractive? Some of the men from her graduating class had aged like they lived in dog years. But Jace? He'd aged like Tammy's 1973 Bronco.

Beautifully.

The truck in front of her turned right at the stoplight. She screamed in frustration as she stepped on the gas when the light turned green. Her tires spun on the slick street. If Castle hadn't started whining, she would've been happy to keep going until Officer Rayburn cited her for reckless driving. Instead of getting a ticket, her foot eased off the pedal, and she rubbed the only visible part of Castle, his head. His favorite Scooby Doo blanket covered him from shoulders down.

The spoiled brat.

"You probably think I've lost my marbles." Castle leaned into her touch, seeming to disagree with her assessment. At least, that's what she told herself.

"I know, I know. That man does something to me that I don't like." She clicked the heat down a notch and eased into Miss Vivian's driveway. Maybe she would know what Sonny had been up to.

The outside reminded Tammy of an updated shed, but it had a homey feel. Maybe the blinking Christmas lights clinging to the two bushes on either side of the door and the gingerbread man wreath did the trick. Odd since Christmas was still a couple of months away, but to each his own.

With no luck getting an answer at Miss Vivian's, Tammy decided to call it a day and go home. A white BMW and an older model maroon Tahoe sat in the driveway behind Mama's car. Two men stood outside with her.

Tammy sped up. Her brow furrowed when she got close enough to see who the visitors were. Douglas Mc-Coy stood in front of Fred McCoy. Both had clenched fists.

When Tammy parked, Fred crossed in front of the Tahoe, opening Tammy's door. Even though a smile crept across his face, he looked angry.

After Tammy got out, she traded a look with Mama, whose eyes had taken the shape of the Bronco's hubcap. What in the world?

Douglas lifted his chin toward Tammy. "Miss Sharp." Disappointment seemed to weigh his face down.

Tammy planted a hand on her hip after she shut the door to keep Castle from getting out. He fed off emotions, and right now, they seemed high. "What's happening?"

Mama took a few steps to the Bronco and let Castle out. She waved one hand and stroked Castle's head with the other. "Oh, it's just a small misunderstanding."

Fred barked a laugh as he opened the door to the maroon Tahoe. "It's all good, Miss Sharp. My son and I were both here to ask your beautiful mama on a date."

Forevermore. How had her and Mama's roles reversed? She remembered how Mama had to fight off the boys after Tammy had blossomed into a young lady.

That is until she and Jace bonded at the newspaper office.

She inwardly groaned. Why did her thoughts have to drift back to that man?

Douglas stared Fred down before he got into his BMW and backed out of the driveway without so much as a see y'all later.

Fred let out another chuckle before he strolled over to Mama and kissed her hand. "Apologies for the way my son and I acted."

Mama's lips twitched, and she shook her head. "It's not a problem, Fred. Maybe I could've handled things better."

"You were perfect." He got in the Tahoe and rolled the window down. "Good day, ladies."

Odd. Tammy sensed Fred and Douglas were into it over something else. Their tension had to stem from something more than a date.

Tammy watched him back out with her mouth wide open. After a second, she closed her mouth, scratched her head, and met Mama's gaze. "I'm gonna have to lock you up."

Mama raised a brow as she disappeared through the front door. "Oh, hush. I can't help it that men find me irresistible. Are you going to tell me what happened to your face?"

"Just a misunderstanding." As the door snapped shut behind Tammy, she breathed in the aroma of chili powder, onions, and garlic. She stepped into the hallway and raised her voice. "I didn't know you were making chili. It smells amazing."

Mama stood at the island, tapping her fingers. "So, what happened?"

Tammy sighed. "I may have lost my temper when I ran into Sonny Perkins earlier."

Fear emanated from Mama. She put one open hand to her throat. "How?"

"You know it doesn't take much for me to lose my temper."

"No, I meant, how did you run into him?"

"He was outside the newspaper, and I thought he was following me. We got in a tussle before Jace came out and threatened him."

A smile beamed across Mama's face. "Jace threatened Sonny? Good for him."

"Yeah, let's not make a big deal out of it. Okay?"

"Okay. I need to get ready anyway."

"For what?"

"Remember, we're having a gospel meeting this week. I'm making chili for potluck tonight. We need to get ready to go."

The only place Tammy intended to go was bed. She stepped into her bedroom and peeled her damp clothes off. After rustling through her drawers, she slipped on a fuzzy pajama set and padded to the kitchen. All she needed was a cup of coffee as big as her head. That and some Advil.

A few minutes later, Mama strolled out of her bedroom wearing a cream sweater covered with embroidered pumpkins, a pair of burnt orange slacks that fell to her ankles, and a pair of brown Skechers. "Make sure you cover that bruise before we leave."

Tammy nursed the cup of coffee on the way to her bedroom. She stuck her head out the door. "I'm going to pass. I have things to do."

From the sound of the creaking floor, Mama hurdled down the hall like a rhinoceros chasing a hyena away. She jerked Tammy's bedroom door open. "You will not pass. Now, get in that shower and make yourself presentable."

Tammy's brow rose as she stared Mama down. After a few seconds, Mama bestowed one of her sweet smiles on Tammy. When she spoke, her tone matched the smile. "I'll be waiting in the kitchen. With the chili."

"Fine. I'll get ready." Tammy paused. "But first, I want to ask you a question. Do you remember Dennis Howard?"

Her brows knit as she landed expressive eyes on Tammy. "Of course. Why?"

"Just wondering. Do you know if any of his family is alive?"

"His dear mama lives at the nursing home in Walnut Ridge."

Tammy's face lit as her heart kicked into gear. "I need to go see her."

"I'll be happy to take you later in the week." Mama swatted Tammy's rear. "Go on and get ready. Be sure to cover that bruise."

A half smile graced Tammy's lips as the hot water hit her face. What had her life come to? She'd gone from taking murderers down in Atlanta to reliving her teenage years in Arkansas.

And so far, she didn't mind the change.

chapter thirty-two

During Tammy's time in Atlanta, she'd opted to skip most social gatherings. Her job kept her busy, so showing up for worship and leaving before too many people could speak to her became easy. During the rare times people had the opportunity to talk to Tammy, they asked her to stay for fellowship, but she'd always used work as an excuse. Now that she thought about it, it had been years since she'd been to a potluck before a gospel meeting.

Her current situation included a potluck and a room full of people. Some gawked, but most had spoken to her and hugged her neck. Rectangle tables lined the room, making two long tables with two more on the end, forming a u shape.

Mama and Sheriff Obie had already made their plates. They sat at the end of one table, entertaining a group of older folks. One of the ladies Tammy recognized as the Vivian woman Mama had helped with her medicine.

When Vivian looked up, she bestowed a half smile on Tammy. What a timid, sweet woman. Tammy smiled back and headed in her direction. "Hi, Miss Vivian."

"Hi, Tammy." Miss Vivian ran her hands down the orange sweater that matched her hair. "It's nice to see you here."

"You, too." Tammy met Miss Vivian's gaze. "Have you seen your nephew since he was released from the hospital?"

Miss Vivian pressed her lips together and shook her head. "He stopped by for a few minutes and showered a few nights ago, and I ain't seen him since."

Tammy handed her a business card. "Will you ask him to call me when you see him?"

Vivian stuck the business card in her purse and nodded. "I'll ask him."

Tammy thanked her and headed to the end of the line. She passed the dessert table, almost stopping there first after eyeballing a pumpkin cheesecake. Instead of grabbing the entire dish, she dragged herself to the other line.

The table looked like a Southern café had exploded. Tammy passed by meatloaf, pot roast, spaghetti, potatoes, greens, goulash, and various soups. But she had her eye on the chicken and dumplings. Once she piled a bowl full, she sat in an empty seat beside Nicole and Harry.

Lorene Pankey claimed the chair to Tammy's left. She leaned her elbows on the table close to Tammy and lowered her voice like they shared a secret. "You should stop by the shop in the morning so I can show you how to curl your hair."

That statement had Tammy blinking. She ran her hand down the side of her head and shrugged. Miss Pankey must take her job seriously. "I normally just flat iron it or let it air dry."

"You must've let it air dry today." Lorene scrunched up her nose. "It looks awful frizzy."

Tammy gaped at Lorene. "Do you normally try to entice customers by insulting them?"

Lorene tilted her head to the left and patted her finger on her chin. "Look, I'm just trying to help you out." Her eyes seemed to take stock of Tammy. "You have a beautiful face and a nice figure. I think it may be your hair keeping the men away."

Next to Tammy, Nicole choked on her ice water. Harry patted her back and glanced wide-eyed at Tammy and Lorene.

"Nothing is keeping the men away, Lorene." Tammy swallowed the smart remark that burned the tip of her tongue. "Thank you for your concern, but I don't want or need a man right now."

Lorene raised a brow before her eyes lingered on something above Tammy's shoulder. The woman across from Nicole let out a soft squeal as her gaze followed Lorene's.

Even though something told her not to do it, Tammy turned to see what had their attention. Of course, Jace strutted inside. He met Tammy's gaze before letting the door slide shut behind him. Confidence emanated from Jace as he threw his shoulders back. The pink and white plaid button-up shirt tucked into tan slacks caused Tammy's insides to tingle.

Lorene raised her brow and elbowed Tammy. "Don't you wish you'd spent a tad bit more time on your appearance now?"

The woman across from Nicole took a folding fan out of her purse and fanned herself. Lorene rolled her eyes. "Dear Sadie, don't get your hopes up. I'm sorry to be the one to tell you this, but you are not good-looking enough to grab that man's attention."

Sadie and Tammy both drew in a breath. Sadie propelled herself out of the seat, levied a glare on Lorene, and stomped toward the other side of the room.

Tammy blew the breath she'd been holding out and leaned close to Lorene. "You should be nicer," she said.

Lorene's mouth dropped open. "That was nice. I was trying to keep the poor woman from wasting her time."

When Jace rested his eyes on Tammy, she started to run after Sadie to see if she had a spare fan she could borrow. Instead, she spun around and stared at her bowl of chicken and dumplings. Heat radiated from her face and neck, and she prayed no one would notice.

Tammy grabbed her bottle of grape soda and rubbed it on her neck. That should cool her down before anyone noticed. Satisfied her neck had returned to its normal color, she took a swig of the soda. As soon as she put it on the table, she met Nicole's curious gaze. "Having a hot flash, I guess."

"I see that." Nicole snickered.

Lorene pulled the chair next to hers out and switched seats. She must've wanted the people driving down the street to hear when she spoke. "Yoohoo, Jace." She patted the now empty seat beside Tammy. "We have a seat for you right here."

He nodded at Lorene and got in line behind a man Tammy didn't recognize. The man's blonde curls reminded Tammy of how Mama wore her hair when Tammy was a little kid. Super tight and full of gel. Now, there was someone for Lorene to hit up for a beauty salon visit. Surely, he had to know he'd look much younger with a different hairstyle. That style screamed the eighties, but Tammy guessed it could be making a comeback.

A tapping on her forearm caused Tammy to snap out of her fog. Lorene jiggled her eyebrows. "See how easy that was? Once you learn how to style your hair, I give it a week before you snag that handsome man."

An ache settled right at the bridge of Tammy's nose. She needed to get out of there before she lost it on Lorene. Someone chose that moment to push out from under the table. The metal chair legs hit the floor, causing a screech to explode into Tammy's eardrums.

The ache in Tammy's head intensified. Before she moved, her watch buzzed with an incoming text message. She glanced at the watch screen and blinked several times before looking at it again.

Why are you ignoring my instructions?

Tammy clenched her jaw as she fumbled in her purse for her phone. She kept the phone low so no one could see her screen as she responded.

What instructions? Who is this?

Find the map showing where Ellis buried the gold.

Who is this?

No answer.

> *I don't know about any gold.*

Still no answer.

> *Did you kill my uncle?*

Dots appeared, letting Tammy know the sender had finally decided to answer.

> *Ellis Martin committed suicide.*

> *Suicide?*

> *Find the gold, and I'll tell you what happened.*

Tammy called the number. No answer. She sent several texts with no answer.

Suicide? Tammy didn't think so. And what was this about gold? Solving Uncle Ellis's murder was going to take a lot of detective work.

Tammy hoped she had it in her.

chapter thirty-three

THE BORROWED LINCOLN CONTINENTAL flew down the dirt road at breakneck speed. Why did Detective Sharp continue asking so many questions? She was focusing on the wrong thing!

How had she survived as a detective so long in Atlanta? It seemed she had to be shown everything. She had no sense of direction. Who killed Uncle Ellis? Why is his house clean? Blah, blah, blah. She was always whining. Never stepping up to find the gold. If only she were half the detective her daddy had been, she'd already have the gold. Or she would've figured out about me, so maybe her lack of smarts was a good thing.

For a short time, I'd thought she was an intelligent woman with enough sense to find the gold. But I couldn't have been more wrong. I hate being wrong. A savage scream boils from my chest, flowing into the car. She's lucky I can't allow my feelings to hinder the ultimate reward, or she would be dead.

After Ruby told me Tammy got them out of the house the night of the fire, I had a glimmer of hope. Ruby had been so proud when she told me Tammy got the front door open before Jace Eubanks barged in.

I want to tear something apart as I think about the fire that should've never happened. Sonny had no business going behind my back. He said he wanted Tammy to pay for getting him arrested. He forgets his place. He could've cost me everything. EVERYTHING!

His court date was next week. What would he say? Was he planning to tell them I was behind it all? Sonny Perkins can't be trusted.

A curve loomed ahead. I push the gas pedal to the floor. For a moment, a thought of hitting the massive Oak Tree and ending things passes through my mind.

But that would make things too easy on Detective Sharp. And that would never work. She should've kept her nose in Atlanta and out of Arkansas. I push the brake at the last minute, slowing down just enough to make the curve. Excitement courses through my veins when the car fishtails.

A figure stands beside the old barn a few miles down the road. My helper, who, as it turns out, is not so helpful. I turn into the bumpy driveway and exit the car.

Sonny Perkins took a drag off a cigarette before dropping it to the ground. He smashed it with his heel and ran a shaky hand across his shaved head. "What took you so long? I been waiting for over an hour."

"I had things to do in town." I take a step toward Sonny, the butt of a Smith and Wesson 9-millimeter handgun pressing into my side.

Sonny's eyes darted to my hands, and a flash of panic crossed his face. His voice trembled when he spoke. "Hey. Why are you wearing gloves?"

"You've become a liability. I never gave you permission to set Ruby Sharp's house on fire."

My heart rockets to a wicked beat with the thought of what comes next.

chapter thirty-four

THE BEST PLACE TO start researching gold had to be the Randolph County Heritage Museum. Tammy tapped her chin as she walked through the building for the third time. Nothing about lost gold had jumped out at her. She'd even asked the volunteer working that day, and she wasn't familiar with anything in the museum about lost gold.

When her phone buzzed, she dug it out of her purse.

Tammy Gail, this is your mama, Ruby.

Tammy burst into laughter when she read the message. Another message popped up.

Look beside my bed. I found a part of an article you may find interesting.

Thank you!

A little later, Tammy stood in Mama's bedroom, feeling the need to grit her teeth. Even though the article seemed like a good lead, it was incomplete. She closed her eyes, scolding herself for being so negative. Her heart skipped a beat as she reread the story. This could very well pertain to the lost gold the killer was looking for. A jeweler named Henry Corey was killed in 1867 by three men who planned to steal a compass from his jewelry business. The story ended midsentence with one of the men admitting they'd planned to loot the place.

This story needed to be followed up on. She called for Castle and headed to Uncle Ellis's, hoping to find something else about this jeweler who had lived in the area many years earlier.

As Tammy and Castle stepped into the house, her phone buzzed. Thomas's name flashed across the screen. "Hey there, T-Riggs."

"What's up, T-Sharp?"

Tammy filled him in on everything she and Jace had uncovered.

"Why don't I see what I can dig up on Black River drownings and the jeweler?"

"That would be great. While you're at it, see what you can find about anything weird happening at Old Davidsonville. Focus on stories linked to lost gold."

He barked a laugh. "I see going home hasn't made you any less bossy. You better be glad you're great at your job..."

"Well, I was before I met Chip Reeker."

Rustling and then a FaceTime request. Tammy accepted.

Sybil pushed Thomas out of her way. "You still are. The best."

"Excuse me?" Thomas put his hand on his hip.

A grin tugged at Sybil's lips as she cocked her head toward Thomas. "Besides my wonderful husband, of course."

A few minutes later, they ended the call. She spun around Uncle Ellis's living room and bit her bottom lip. "What would you think about moving here, Castle?"

Too often, while living in Atlanta, Tammy longed for a simpler life. She often pondered moving back to Arkansas to live closer to Mama and Uncle Ellis. If only she'd done it sooner, maybe Uncle Ellis would still be alive.

Castle raised his head from the bed he'd made on the sofa and gave her a look that warmed her heart. She plopped down beside him and scooted his upper body onto her lap.

Was that something Tammy should seriously consider now that Uncle Ellis had passed, leaving Mama without any other family? Tammy had enjoyed spending time with Mama. When not searching for clues about gold, they studied the Bible, watched movies, cuddled on the couch, cooked, and talked. Tammy hadn't realized how much she missed those moments until now. What kind of daughter would she be to leave Mama behind and return to Atlanta?

The doorbell rang, followed by a few knocks on the front door. Tammy slid out from under Castle and opened the door.

Lorene skidded past Tammy into the house. Lingering traces of cigarette smoke made Tammy want to gag. This was the first time she'd noticed that stench coming from Lorene.

Tammy shook her head a couple of quick times. "Well, hi, Lorene. Come on in."

"You couldn't take a hint if it slapped you upside the head." Lorene lowered herself into Uncle Ellis's blue recliner and turned her face into the plush cushions. When she looked back at Tammy, tears lined her cheeks.

Tammy once again found herself swallowing a smart remark. She handed Lorene a box of tissues before she reclaimed the spot by Castle. "What do you mean?"

After she blew her nose, Lorene looked into the kitchen. "I wanted you to come by the shop today." Her gaze landed on Tammy before her lashes fluttered to the floor.

A cat yowled in the front yard. Lorene's hand went to her throat, and she nearly jumped out of the chair.

Tammy looked out the window and chuckled. A black and white cat stood with its claws out, while a gray one with fuzzed-up fur looked like it was ready to fight.

Tammy sat back down and glanced at Lorene. Her hands seemed to be trembling. Tammy wondered what made Lorene seem so nervous. "Why didn't you just ask me to stop by?"

"I did!" The incredulous look on Lorene's face almost made Tammy laugh. "Don't you remember me saying you needed to come by so I could show you how to curl your hair? I was afraid the killer would find out I said something."

Instead of blasting Lorene for not being straight, Tammy took a few breaths and decided to drop that subject. "What killer? I thought you said Uncle Ellis drowned."

"I wasn't going to say anything to you." Lorene's eyes shimmered, and her voice broke. "About Ellis's murder."

"Why not?" Tammy stared at Lorene.

She rubbed her forehead before she met Tammy's gaze. "Because I was afraid to get you involved. Ellis didn't want it."

A tremor passed over Tammy's body. "It's too late for that. Please tell me what you know."

After she hoisted to her feet, Lorene paced the floor. "Ellis found something out about an old friend who had drowned many years ago."

Tammy bolted upright, and her heart slammed against her ribcage. "Dennis Howard?"

Lorene nodded as Tammy walked into the kitchen. "I see you've been doing your homework already. You're good."

"I haven't been able to connect them more than drowning on Black River yet. Do you know what the connection is?"

"I don't have all the details." Lorene sipped from the bottled water Tammy handed her. "All I know is Obie was somehow involved with what Ellis was looking into."

A cold chill caused the hairs on Tammy's arms to rise. "How was the sheriff involved?"

"I really don't know." Lorene's lips bunched up, and she blinked multiple times. "Ellis wouldn't tell me every-thing. Maybe Obie was helping Ellis with something."

"It's vital you tell me everything you do know." Tammy leaned forward and clasped her hands together. "Do you believe the sheriff had something to do with Uncle Ellis's death?"

"No, I don't think so. Let me go home and gather my thoughts." She lowered her head into her hands and rubbed her temples. "My brain is so jumbled up I can't think straight. It'll be easier for me to write everything down for you."

"I can find some paper for you here."

"No, that won't do. My head is swimming, and I need to be home."

"Okay, but make sure you do it as quickly as possible." Tammy cocked her head. This conversation was not going the way she thought it would. "Before I forget, do you take a pill to help with anxiety?"

A question lit Lorene's eyes, and her forehead creased. "Actually, I do. How do you know that?"

Tammy told her about finding the pill by the refrigerator, and a sense of relief washed over Tammy to find that the pill could've belonged to Lorene.

"Is there anything else you want to share before you go home?" Tammy narrowed her eyes.

"No, not just yet." Lorene's hand moved to her neck, covering most of it.

Tammy stayed quiet as she observed Lorene's body language. If she had a polygraph machine, she'd bet Lorene would fail. But why? What would Lorene have to gain by lying?

Thirty minutes later, Tammy took a deep breath and rang Jace's doorbell. Within seconds, the door opened.

Jace didn't attempt to hide his shock. "Tammy? I sure wasn't expecting to see you."

"We need to add Lorene Pankey to the top of the suspect list." She pushed past Jace and stopped in her tracks. A beautiful woman in a robe came down the hallway. Her brow lifted when she made eye contact with Tammy.

The color drained from Tammy's face as she rushed out the front door. What a fool she'd been.

chapter thirty-five

ONCE A PIG, ALWAYS a pig, Tammy guessed. However, she had to admit she hadn't expected to see a woman like that at Jace's. She darted through the back door and slammed her purse on the kitchen island.

She breathed in a whiff of Uncle Ellis's Old Spice, which he always wore, and sighed. There needed to be more men like he was. Honest. Loyal.

Why was she so upset? She had no claim to Jace. They weren't together, and they weren't even friends, much less anything more. She stared into space for a moment and let that thought sink in.

Hadn't he tried to explain why he married Una? The Jace she'd known had always been one to keep his word, even when it was tough. One year, he'd promised Tammy and Nicole tickets to see Bon Jovi. He thought he figured out everything. He would take them both.

But when there were only two tickets left for the concert, he made sure Nicole and Tammy had one while he missed the concert.

For his favorite band.

Not that marrying Una could be compared to giving up a Bon Jovi concert. But at least she now understood Jace hadn't left her for another woman without a reason. At least a valid reason in his mind.

So why couldn't she move past it? Shouldn't she forgive him and allow him a fresh start? Yes, of course, she should. But something inside her still burned with anger, and she couldn't let it go. Or wouldn't.

Maybe because Jace took away the life she wanted. They could have children by now. Grandchildren even. He took that away by a promise he should've never made.

Deciding it would be a good idea to argue with herself, she thought about the men she'd turned down after moving to Atlanta. Couldn't she have married someone else and had those babies? There had been more than a few interested men along the way. What had stopped her?

The doorbell rang as she continued to argue with herself about her sanity. Or lack thereof.

"Tammy? Are you in there?"

Great.

Now, why would Jace follow her? Didn't he have another woman inside his home? She dragged her feet across the room and stopped at the door. "I am."

"Will you open the door?"

No. She narrowed her eyes, determined to win the staring contest she'd entered with the door.

"Tammy?"

Opening the door, she landed her best Ruby Anne Sharp southern smile on Jace. "Sorry about running off like that. I had something to do." The smile she plastered on would either convince Jace she was sincere or off her rocker.

His head tilted slightly to the side as he perused Tammy's face. "What was it?"

The fake smile quivered. She blinked her eyelashes a few times and threw her hands in the air. She reminded herself of a woman back in Atlanta who had shot and killed her elderly husband. That woman had stalled and led them on a wild goose chase with her innocent smile and friendly demeanor. In the end, the evidence pointed at her. She'd died in prison a year later. Sad, really.

As Tammy's mind worked to answer Jace's question, Mama and Castle came across the yard. Mama waved before she turned her gaze on Castle as he sniffed the ground.

Sometimes, it's better to remain silent. "Hey, y'all." Tammy squatted down and tapped her leg. "Come see me, Castle."

Castle bounded past Mama, only stopping when he got right in front of Tammy. He licked her ear and the side of her face before she raised back up.

The woman that had been at Jace's walked up the sidewalk. The matching purple Nike sweatsuit and purple and white Nike shoes made her look younger than Tammy thought she was. At least she had on more than a robe.

Tammy sized her up as she stopped right beside Jace. Beautiful hadn't been a good enough word to describe her. Exotic came to mind when the woman met Tammy's gaze. Her lips formed a perfect heart shape, large but not too large. Her eyes seemed to be greener than brown. Unusual against her dark skin, it worked for her. Too well.

Jace put his arm around the woman and squeezed her tight. Her eyes lingered on Tammy's ring finger. "Is this the woman you went to school with, Doda?"

Jace nodded. "Yes, Leotie, this is Tammy, her mama Miss Ruby, and that there is Castle."

Castle's rear end moved back and forth when his name was mentioned, and he moved closer to Jace. He rubbed Castle's head and nodded toward the woman. "Ladies and Castle, this is my daughter, Leotie, but everyone calls her Leo."

Mama beamed as she moved Jace to the side and wrapped Leo in a hug.

His daughter. Why hadn't Tammy figured that out when she saw her at Jace's? For goodness sake, she was supposed to be a detective. Maybe she needed to turn in her badge. Tammy stuck her hand out. "Nice to meet you."

Mama walked past Tammy and opened the front door. "It's a bit chilly out here. Y'all wanna come in?"

Leo glanced at her watch and scrunched her lips. "I'd like to, but I have a date."

Jace's head almost spun off his shoulders. "How do you have a date already? You just got here."

"We met online." She offered a smile before she crossed over to Jace's Mustang.

Jace held one finger up and hustled after her.

Mama wagged her head as Jace walked away. "I don't know why you haven't scooped that man up."

Scooped him up? Mama had lost her ever-loving mind. Well, maybe not entirely. How many men had the power to make Tammy's blood pump at the rate of a tornado?

Just one.

Leo pulled away in Jace's Mustang. He stood there a second and watched the car disappear down the road. He ran a hand through his hair before he turned back toward them. His lips lifted in a sad smile. Defeated, even. He must not want his daughter dating someone she met online. He looked like he needed a hug or some comfort.

It's not like a tiny part of Tammy didn't want to give him a chance. They still had chemistry. The attraction hadn't gone away, that was for sure.

After one last look at Jace, Tammy walked inside. "I refuse to be with a man who can't be trusted."

"Then why'd you kiss him the other night?"

Tammy's head swiveled, and she met the same chocolate brown eyes that had been forcing their way into her thoughts the past few nights. Who knew Jace's legs moved so fast?

A bloom of heat rushed through her neck and face. Determined to ignore it, she scooted past Mama and grabbed a bottle of water from the refrigerator. "Anyone want a water?"

Jace followed closely behind her. As he took the bottled water from her, his skin met hers, which caused the heat in Tammy's neck to intensify.

Jace rubbed the spot where they touched, seeming to feel it too. "We need to talk."

Tammy gulped air and nodded.

chapter thirty-six

For the third time, I drive past Lorene's Love Locks. What could be taking that woman so long? Her last customer had left an hour ago.

After Lorene's last visit with Detective Sharp, it was clear she ignored the messages I sent her. Pity. I truly do enjoy Lorene's company. She's witty, and her smart mouth has caused me to smile on more than one occasion.

She's a lot like Detective Sharp, allowing the desire for misplaced justice to cloud her vision. Ellis was dead. Didn't they know he would want them to do what it took to stay alive instead of focusing on finding a killer?

Even though Lorene brings me a bit of pleasure, emotional attachments can't stop me from doing what is necessary. It was, after all, for the greater good. Everything I have ever wanted is within reach. Finally! Letting emotions rule would mean I am weak, which will ruin everything.

And that will never work.

chapter thirty-seven

JACE OFTEN WONDERED WHAT it would take to earn Tammy's forgiveness. Standing in Ellis's kitchen, he couldn't help but immerse himself in the flood of memories that washed over him. The familiar sights and sounds reminded him of the countless meals and study sessions he and Tammy had shared during their teenage years.

It was in this very space that their bond had deepened, and now, as he stood there, Jace felt an overwhelming longing to somehow restore what they once had. The weight of seeking Tammy's forgiveness hung heavy on his mind, and he was determined to do whatever it took to make things right.

Tammy peeled the wrapper off her bottled water, seeming to want to look at anything but Jace. "What did you want to talk about?"

The urge to tug her hand away from the bottle almost overwhelmed Jace. He stuck his hands in the pockets of his Levi's. "Do you think we can continue to work together to solve Ellis's murder? Or are you still too angry?"

"I'd be lying if I said I wasn't angry." She huffed a breath out and met his gaze. "But I can move past it until afterward."

Until afterward? That meant she planned to walk out of his life. She'd find out that he would put up a fight before he let that happen.

For now, he'd play along. "All right."

She propped against the kitchen counter. "What do you know about lost gold?"

"Lost gold? From where?"

"Old Davidsonville, maybe? Or somewhere around this area."

She handed him her phone. He scanned the messages about finding gold. "Wow. It looks like I may have been right about Ellis's death being linked to stories about treasures from Old Davidsonville." He filled her in on his research into Old Davidsonville and the Spaniards who supposedly left gold and jewels behind.

"I just wish I knew what instructions they're talking about." She slipped the phone in her back pocket.

"I agree." He tapped his chin. "Do you have any voicemails or possible emails you haven't checked?"

"None." She shook her head, a look of exasperation etched on her face. "I've checked everything a message could be on."

"So, what do you want to do while we wait for the instructions to show up?"

"First, I want this kept between us." She looked around with a determination Jace appreciated. "Second, I have a gut feeling we're missing a clue about the gold somewhere in this house."

Miss Ruby walked out of Ellis's office and into the kitchen. "I know that look. What are you thinking?"

"We need to tear this place apart. Again. Uncle Ellis would've hidden it well."

Castle trotted to his bowl and slurped some water before he settled down at Tammy's side. Jace figured Castle sensed the urgency emanating from Tammy.

"Let's do this." Jace pitched the empty water bottle into the recycling bin. "Wanna each take a room or start on one together?"

Tammy opened her mouth, but Miss Ruby cut her off. "The two of you can take the office while I start on the kitchen."

"Hold up. Jace and I need to bring something to your attention about Sheriff Obie."

Jace and I? The lines of Jace's throat threatened to close in when Miss Ruby directed a glare at Tammy and then him.

She settled her arms over her chest. "What is it, Tammy Gail?"

Tammy squared her shoulders and met Miss Ruby's glare. The one who had the power to scare Jace half to death. "Evidence leads us to believe he could be involved in Uncle Ellis's murder."

How Miss Ruby could still cause Jace's pulse to quicken with fear was a mystery. For a moment, he thought back to the days when all she had to do was raise a brow to make him stutter. The first time she caught Tammy sneaking out at night, she had come close to throttling them both. Right now, she had that same expression on her face.

Something in Miss Ruby's eyes shifted, and her body visibly relaxed. "That's a bunch of baloney."

"No, it's not." Tammy's head wagged right and left as if she wanted to convey her point. "You need to keep your distance from him until after the investigation."

A curt laugh came from Miss Ruby. "Child, do you not think I know what I'm doing?"

Child? Jace had to bite back a laugh when he heard that. Tammy was definitely no child. He could think of a few other words to describe her: bull-headed, strong-willed, determined, stunning.

He scolded himself for allowing his mind to go there. Staying focused on solving the murder so he could get back to West Memphis had to be the top priority.

A bewildered expression flitted across Tammy's face. "I've worked more murder cases than Pocahontas has seen in a long time." She tilted her head to the right. "Probably ever."

Miss Ruby scrunched her face up. "Ever? I don't think so. Remember that Kizer man who killed a bunch of people then himself? And what about Ma Barker? We can't forget about that widow who married men just to kill them."

Tammy flung her head back and blinked her eyes at the ceiling. "At least keep your eyes open and be careful."

"I will, but I can promise you one thing. Obie was not involved in Ellis's murder. He may know more than he's saying, but he would never kill Ellis."

"Okay, Mama. I guess I have no choice but to trust your instincts."

The corners of Miss Ruby's lips curled as she pulled Tammy into a hug. After a few seconds, she stepped back and arched her brow. "You need to be worrying about that Sonny Perkins fella instead of focusing on Obie."

"I heard he ran off."

"Well, we still need to keep a watch for him."

A persistent knock at the front door interrupted their conversation. Tammy brushed past Jace and opened the door.

Leo walked inside and bent her knees low. She reached out to Castle with her hand and glanced at Tammy. "Will he come to me?"

Tammy nodded at Castle. "Come here, boy, and say hi to Leo."

Castle torpedoed through the kitchen and came to a fast halt beside Leo. She rubbed his side, and he plopped down beside her. "Hi there, Castle. You sure are a handsome doggie." After a few seconds, she pulled herself off the floor. Her eyes lingered on Tammy like she was Simon Cowell and Tammy was a horrible singer with a dream.

Jace cleared his throat. "I thought you had a date."

"Oh, that was a hard no." She rolled her eyes and blew her lips out. "I'm here to help with whatever it is you all are doing."

They explained the plan, and they decided Leo and Miss Ruby would start in the living room while Tammy and Jace tackled the back side of the house.

A few minutes in, and a yip of excitement sounded from the front of the house. Jace looked at Tammy, and they hoofed it down the hall.

The sofa had been moved away from the wall, and Leo and Miss Ruby stood at the end of it. Excitement beamed from both their faces. When Jace and Tammy reached where they stood, Tammy grabbed his arm.

A door had been built into the floor underneath the sofa. You had to look closely to see the lines around the opening. Whoever built this had ensured the door opening perfectly matched the wood floor. Another smaller box-like space opened to a combination lock and handle.

Tammy tried to lift the handle, but it wouldn't budge. Jace wasn't surprised. That's what the combination lock was there for. To keep people out.

What in the world had Ellis been involved in?

chapter thirty-eight

Two days. That's how long they'd worked on the combination lock and had made zero progress. Tammy wished she could take her gun and blow the lock apart but had no desire to end up back in the hospital.

They'd entered every date they could think of. Birthdays. Anniversaries. Phone numbers. To no avail.

Jace drained the cup of coffee he'd been nursing for all of three minutes and glanced at Tammy. "Do you want to go to Old Davidsonville today? At least we can stop by the bait shop and question some of the Rangers."

Tammy lifted herself off the floor and nodded. "Taking a break is probably a good idea."

Jace pushed the sofa into place before he took his cup to the kitchen. "Do you want to take my car or your Bronco?"

"Mine works." She paused and met Jace's gaze. "Hey, why don't you spend time with Leo today? You've been hanging out with me way too much."

"Leo and I have enjoyed dinner and a movie the past two nights." He chuckled as he dried his cup with a hand towel. "Believe me, she's spent more time with me than she wants to."

"I can relate." She bit her bottom lip to keep from laughing at his wide-eyed expression.

He clutched his heart and played like he was about to fall backward. "Now you've wounded me."

She grinned as she allowed a throaty laugh to escape. "Poor baby. I'm just gonna text Mama to keep an eye on Castle, and we can go before it gets dark."

An hour later, Tammy and Jace pulled up to Carter's Bait Shop. The rectangular white building brought back memories from Tammy's youth.

The strong pine smell failed to mask the scents of earthworms mixed with fish as Tammy stepped inside behind Jace. The shop had a gas station vibe on one side with cold drinks and rows of snacks, while the other side contained everything one would need to go on the lake fishing.

Lewis Carter greeted them. "Howdy, folks. What brings you in today?"

Even though he smiled and appeared happy to see them, Tammy had no doubt he felt the opposite. His eyes seemed to be full of animosity.

She ignored the alarm bells sounding in her head. "Hello, I'm Tammy Sharp, and this is Jace Eubanks. We want to ask you a few questions if that's okay."

"Of course. I remember you two." His lips slid into a frown as he wiped his hands on a towel hanging from his waist. "After your daddy passed, Ellis used to bring y'all in here all the time."

"That's right." Tammy looked around the shop. "I'd always get a banana flip and a carton of chocolate milk."

"Even after all these years, I still miss your daddy. We had some good times." Lewis came around the counter and faced Tammy. The way he stood, he almost pushed Jace out of the conversation. "What can I help you with?"

Tammy searched her memories. Lewis Carter had never liked Jace. That must be why he seemed upset. He still had something against him.

"I have a few questions for you about Uncle Ellis. First, have you noticed anything strange over the past few months?"

Lewis rubbed his chin. "I can't rightly say I have. It had been a few months since he'd been in here. Why do you ask? Didn't they rule his death an accident?"

"Yes, I'm just following up on a few things for my records," Tammy said as she perused the row of cakes and sweets.

"I was beginning to wonder if he found somewhere else to get his bait, but he passed before I had a chance to ask him about it. I sure wish I could be of more help."

After they took their leave, they headed to the Visitor's Center at Davidsonville Historic State Park. Tammy bit a chunk out of a honey bun before washing it with a swig of chocolate milk.

As they pulled into the campground, Tammy clenched her stomach. Being at one of the last places Uncle Ellis had ever seen brought mixed emotions. She swallowed what felt like a grenade and clamped her teeth down.

Had she taken the time to grieve the loss of Uncle Ellis? Truly grieve? She'd missed his funeral thanks to her stupidity in allowing herself to get shot, and other than focusing on solving his murder, she'd shut her mind off. Her neck twitched. Oh no. She couldn't do this in front of Jace.

He put his hand on her back and rubbed it. "I'm so sorry. I should've thought about how coming here might affect you."

When she heard his soft, comforting voice, a cry rose from deep within. Jace pulled Tammy into his arms, and she relaxed, allowing tears to flood her cheeks.

He handed her a wad of napkins from a discarded Taco Bell bag, and she blew her nose as she scooted into the driver's seat. "Thanks."

She studied Jace. The desire to lean close to him nearly overwhelmed her.

"There's no shame in grieving. Take it from me. It does more harm to hold it in."

"Thanks again." She closed her eyes, willing herself to get her act together.

"Let's walk down a trail. I think we could both use some fresh air."

They opted to park and walk to the Black River Trail. As they headed to their destination, the structures showing where buildings had been built at Davidsonville years earlier stood tall. Tammy smiled as she imagined the people milling around this exact spot nearly two hundred years earlier. She loved how she could walk the same path they used back then. Such history left her in awe.

Leaves covered the ground and crunched beneath their feet as they slogged to the trail's head. Blazes of orange and yellow melted together, giving them a gorgeous view. The cool breeze added to the experience and made Tammy wish to be on a hike for other reasons. She shook her head, determined to get rid of those thoughts.

As soon as they reached the entrance, Jace grasped Tammy's hand. She looked at their hands before she met his gaze. Could he be thinking along the same lines she had?

He kept a firm grip on her hand as he put a finger to his lips. He pointed down the trail. She followed his line of sight and mentally kicked herself. How had a trained detective missed the scene ahead? Because she allowed his presence to distract her. She hardened her heart as she took in the couple on the trail.

Sheriff Obie and another man stood deep in conversation. The man had a military stance. After a few minutes, the man handed Sheriff Obie a paper, and he looked at it before nodding.

The man said something, talking a lot with his hands. The sound of an owl hooting in the distance caused chill bumps to line Tammy's arm for some reason.

Jace motioned his head to a couple of trees with low branches that made a good hiding spot. Tammy took a step in the direction he nodded. Hopefully, the owl wasn't back there. Jace held her in place and led the way.

Leaves crunched as Sheriff Obie and the man walked up the trail. The man Sheriff Obie had met with walked past their hiding spot. Silence met Tammy as she craned her neck, but there was no sign of the sheriff.

His voice came from the other side of where they hid. "I know you're there, so you may as well come on out."

Jace mouthed, "Stay here," right before he approached the opening.

Tammy acted like she hadn't heard, following right behind Jace. The sheriff shook his head. "Tammy, I thought you was supposed to be a detective."

She narrowed her eyes. "I *am* a detective."

"Well, you ain't no good at surveillance."

chapter thirty-nine

TAMMY RUBBED HER FINGER under her nose as she and Mama stepped inside The Rest Easy Nursing Home. Even the entryway smelled of mothballs and illness. A man who looked a lot like Sheriff Obie displayed a toothless grin. He used his heels to zoom around in his wheelchair.

Speaking of the sheriff, she still couldn't believe how he made fun of her at Old Davidsonville the day before. Then, he had the nerve to walk away without answering her questions. When she got home, she moved his name to the top of her list of suspects. If he hadn't killed Uncle Ellis, at the least, he had information on what happened.

She'd been avoiding breaking the news to Mama about their encounter, but she knew she couldn't put it off any longer. Even though after Sheriff Obie left, Tammy and Jace had continued their hike along the trail, finding nothing of significance, Mama deserved to know her beau could be way more involved with what happened than she realized.

But for now, she'd focus on her discussion with Doris Howard.

Once inside the room, Miss Howard leaned forward in her recliner and clapped her hands together. Her near-translucent skin sagged on her arms. "Oh, Ruby, it's so good to see you."

After a hug, Mama smiled as she sat on the loveseat. "It's good to be here. I pray you've been well."

"As well as can be expected for a ninety-year-old." Miss Howard peered at Tammy. "You look just like your daddy."

"I'll take that as a compliment," Tammy said as she lowered herself to the seat closest to Miss Howard.

"It was one." Her face turned serious. "Ruby said you wanted to ask me some questions. What can I do for you, dear girl?"

"Did Uncle Ellis ever come to talk to you about your son, Dennis?"

Her pale blue eyes brightened. "Your Uncle Ellis and I spoke many times about my son."

"Do you mind sharing what you told him?"

"I told him how hard losing my only child had been. Not knowing who killed my son has been a burden I wouldn't wish on anyone. Ellis and I talked and prayed for hours about my pain, and he helped so much."

"I'm glad to hear my brother helped you, Doris," Mama said.

"He sure did." She wiped her eyes. "I gave him a key to the storage building where I keep everything."

"What did you have in the building?"

"My life." She looked out the window. Emotions and memories seemed to be on her mind. "I told Ellis he could have everything in there. There's no one left, you see."

This lead meant everything, but Tammy couldn't be insensitive. "Miss Howard, I am so sorry you've dealt with such pain and loss over the years."

"Thank you, dear. I have a feeling you're here to help with that." She twisted her hands together. "Ellis said you could solve even the toughest case. He was so proud of you."

A pang struck Tammy's middle. "I will sure try. Would you happen to have a spare key to the building?"

"I do." She dug around in her purse. "Ellis insisted I keep a copy here." Her head tilted. "The odd thing was, he said I could expect you to come here asking for it if anything happened to him."

As Miss Howard handed Tammy the key and the unit information, Tammy smiled, but her insides screamed for her to get up and run to the building.

Tammy stood and held up the key. "Thank you for this," she said, meeting Miss Howard's gaze. "I promise I'll do everything I can to bring your son's murderer to justice."

Miss Howard winced when she stood. "I believe you will. And I'm sorry to say this, but I think the person who killed my son was involved with what happened to Ellis."

"You're probably right," Mama said before she hugged Miss Howard on the way out.

On the way home, Mama got an emergency call from Heather, the pharmacist on duty. She had to leave, so Mama needed to work at the pharmacy.

"There's something off about several people around here, Mama." Tammy glanced in her direction right before she passed a pickup truck doing ten below the speed limit.

"Who?" Mama's incredulous, near-offended tone didn't escape Tammy.

"Lewis Carter, for starters. That man is prejudiced, and I think he's hiding something." Tammy tapped her fingers on the steering wheel. "Then we have Fred McCoy and his son Douglas."

"My goodness, Tammy Gail." Mama stared at Tammy with something close to sympathy. Sympathy? No, that couldn't be right. "Before too long, you and I need to have a talk."

"Okay, Mama." Tammy shrugged, and her lips bunched up. She pulled up next to the pharmacy. "Probably won't do you any good, but we can talk."

Mama got out and then poked her head back in. "Please wait for me to go to the storage unit. Or at least get Jace to go with you. It'll be dark shortly."

Tammy dialed Jace's number and showed her the phone. "Calling him now."

Mama nodded, her face full of relief.

As Tammy drove off, Jace's voicemail picked up. She shrugged and turned toward the storage complex. She technically hadn't said she wouldn't go alone.

Within a few minutes, Tammy's Bronco bounced over the gravel in the parking lot. She glanced at the key before making her way to unit nineteen. After jiggling the lock a few times, she raised the door to the storage unit.

Boxes lined against the left side of the room, while plastic bins and an antique cabinet took up the right side. She swiveled her head as she scanned the space for the best place to start.

She caught movement out of the corner of her eye. An older man hoofed it down the hall. He paused and glanced inside the unit. "Howdy."

Her heart lodged in her throat, and she itched to rest her hand on the gun strapped to her shoulder. "Hello."

He nodded his head and continued on his way.

She breathed a sigh of relief before she opened the first box, which contained tax packets and receipts from twenty years ago stacked to the top. She scanned a few documents before moving them to the side.

The next box held a few toys that looked to be at least seventy years old. She ran her hand down a wooden horse. She'd never know how it felt to buy toys for her child. Her life should've been different. It could've been if only she hadn't been so stubborn. Her mind drifted to a fantasy that always seemed to resurface, no matter how hard she tried to push it away. The same little girl with long dark hair was always playing outside. She'd call Tammy Mama, and they would laugh before Tammy chased her around the merry-go-round. This time, another person joined the daydream. Jace. They were a family.

A hard object pressed against her back. "Hello, Detective Sharp." An eerie whisper tickled her neck and caused chills to race down her spine. "Do not move, or I will be forced to use the gun in my hand."

She jerked her body to the right and smashed the wooden horse into her assailant's head. Quiet laughter met her ears just as the masked man brought the gun down on her temple.

The blow knocked Tammy to her knees. She fought to her feet and smashed her fist into his nose. He grabbed her arm and twisted until she cried out in pain. Her Glock 19 seemed to burn her side. She reached for it only to have the man put enough pressure on her arm she thought it would break.

The weight eased as the man used a zip tie to render her hands useless before he shoved her onto the floor. He moved her hair away from her face. Tammy bucked against the ties, jerking with all her strength. The man put his weight on her side right before something pinched her neck.

Tammy's eyes grew heavy. The last thought that entered her mind was how she had better let go of that stubborn streak before it destroyed her. She prayed she had another opportunity.

chapter forty

JACE'S BREATH CAME OUT in little white clouds as he ran down the trail. The cold wind nipped at his face. He hadn't felt so alive in weeks.

The homeless woman pushing a grocery cart seemed to come from nowhere. She lowered her head as they passed one another. The cart squealed, protesting being out in the cold.

Jace slowed down and backtracked to where she stopped under a bridge. Stringy dishwater blonde hair hung in her dirty face. She had to be pushing seventy. He couldn't tell if she carried extra weight or if she had on a few coats due to the weather. Either way, she needed help.

"Ma'am? Is there something I can do for you?"

She shook her head as she continued to eyeball the ground.

He handed her a twenty-dollar bill. She swallowed and seemed reluctant to accept the money. "It's too cold for you to be out here like this."

"I'm all right, young man," she replied in a haggard tone as she stuffed the money inside her stained coat.

He sniffed the air to determine if she had been drinking or using drugs. The only odor he detected came from her coat. It had a wet dog who desperately needed a bath smell. "If you come with me, I can put you up in a hotel for a week or so."

"Thank you, son, but I can't ask you to do that." She pushed past Jace and continued down the trail.

He followed her. "You didn't ask me to. Please. Let me help you."

"I could use a hot bath, but I ain't wanting you to go to no trouble. It's too much."

"Please don't take my blessing away."

Just as the sun dipped into the horizon, the woman nodded. "What's your name, young man?"

"Jace Eubanks, ma'am."

"I'm Bess Harrison. Thank you for your kindness."

By the time Jace got Bess settled at the local inn, half the moon winked at him from the sky as he drove home.

His phone buzzed. A quick glance at his dash revealed Miss Ruby as the caller. "Hello, Miss Ruby."

"Hi, Jace. Are you and Tammy still at the storage complex?"

Her words caused his stomach to flip flop. "No, ma'am. I haven't seen Tammy."

She gasped. "You have got to be kidding me. She's not answering her phone."

"What's going on?" Jace asked as he made a U-turn and headed to the storage complex.

She filled him in on their visit with Doris Howard, ending with Tammy picking up her phone to call Jace. "See why I thought she would be with you?"

"I'm five minutes away. How about I call you when I get there?"

"All right. I bet she's engrossed in whatever is in that unit."

"I agree. Her battery may be dead."

At the storage complex, Jace parked beside Tammy's Bronco. He eased his door shut and crept inside the building. Eerie silence blanketed the building as he made his way toward unit nineteen. He shined a flashlight toward the pull-down door. He secured his Glock 19 as he pulled the door up.

A few boxes lined the walls beside a China cabinet. He stepped inside and shined the light around. A body lay wedged between the boxes. Jace's blood went cold. The shoes belonged to Tammy. He dropped to his knees and checked for a pulse. Even though her skin felt chilled, her heart rate beat steadily. A bruise covered the left side of her face. After dragging her onto his lap, he cut the zip tie, binding her wrists.

Jace rubbed her cold skin. "Tammy?"

Her lids fluttered.

"I'm calling an ambulance," Jace said as he tapped his phone screen.

"No." Tammy croaked out and knocked the phone from his hand.

The phone clanked on the concrete floor. Jace watched it as he let what she said soak in. "Why not? You need to report this attack."

"No. Just help me up." Her words came out slurred as she tried to rise off the floor.

"Here. Hold on." Jace slipped his phone in his back pocket and lifted her into his arms.

She laid her head on his chest and snuggled close.

Once Jace deposited Tammy in the passenger seat of her Bronco and settled in the driver's seat, she gulped a leftover water from her cup holder. "Jace, I think whoever left that note for you was right about the police."

His forehead creased. He stayed alert to their surroundings. "What do you mean?"

"Whoever attacked me knew what they were doing. It could've been law enforcement." She laid her hand on his arm. "We have to investigate this ourselves."

Jace lost himself in Tammy's gaze. The vulnerable look on her face mixed with her soft tone nearly undone him.

Fast and hard knocks on Jace's window blasted into the car. Tammy screamed.

chapter forty-one

TAMMY'S HEART SPED OUT of control. Gleason Murphy stepped away from the window with both hands raised. "Sorry about that, folks."

"Mr. Murphy?" Jace rolled the window down.

"Howdy, Jace," Mr. Murphy said as he leaned on the side of the Bronco. "I was heading home and saw your cars out here. I thought I'd check on you."

Tammy massaged the scar on her chest. "I thought you were out of town."

"Got back this morning." He peered inside the vehicle. "Tammy, you look like you've seen a ghost."

"Yeah, you startled me." A nagging throb pulsed in her jaw.

"Gal, I thought you was a tough cookie. How you gonna let a little knock scare you?"

"Tammy has a bad headache," Jace said as he glanced at her. "Do you mind if I leave my car in the lot overnight so I can drive her home?"

Mr. Murphy slapped his hand against the car. "Absolutely. Leave it here as long as you need to. Tammy, I hope you get to feeling better."

She half smiled and nodded as Mr. Murphy backed away from the Bronco. If the older men in Arkansas didn't stop insulting her, she would scream.

Jace waved and jammed the gear in reverse. "If you don't go to the hospital, then I'm at least taking you to Nicole's."

"Fine." She propped her head on her arm and closed her eyes.

"I need to let Miss Ruby know you're okay." Jace picked up his phone at a stop sign.

Every bump Jace hit and stop he made vibrated throughout her skull. Every. Single. One.

When they finally made it to Nicole's, Tammy wanted nothing more than to take a sleeping pill and wake up three days later.

Mama slid into the driveway right behind Tammy and Jace. She raced out of her car and helped Tammy out. Amazingly, she remained silent, but the frost in her gaze gave away the fact that she held back her anger.

Nicole hoofed it off the porch. She favored Jace with a stare as he helped Tammy to the steps. "What's going on?" She said before blinking over to Tammy. "You don't look so good."

"I agree." Mama's lips thinned.

Nicole bounded down the hall and opened a door. "Bring her to the spare bedroom. I have my medicine bag in here already."

Jace removed her shoes, and Tammy flopped her legs on the bed. "Thank you."

"Jace, I need you to put on a pot of strong coffee," Nicole said as she tugged a comforter out of the chest at the end of the bed.

As Jace left the room, Mama moved out of Nicole's way. Her gaze bore into Tammy's. "What happened? I thought you called Jace."

"Miss Ruby, please let me check Tammy's vitals before you lambaste her." Nicole wrapped a blood pressure cuff on Tammy's arm. "Did you take sleeping pills or pain pills?"

Take? Tammy's brows furrowed as she worked to understand the question. "I didn't take anything."

"You're in my home, so there's no patient rights here." She cut her eyes to Mama. "You're displaying signs of drug use. What happened?"

"I'm fine, Nicole. I promise." Tammy shivered. She pulled the comforter to her hips. It helped to heat her cold limbs.

Nicole finished her examination without another word. She turned to Tammy as she put away her stethoscope. "Your heart rate is a little low but not enough to be alarmed. Miss Ruby, will you please bring Tammy a cup of coffee?" When Mama left, Nicole sighed. "Tammy, I know you're going through a lot with getting shot and then losing Ellis. I want to be here for you, but you need to tell me what happened."

"After I got shot, my doctor prescribed valium for my anxiety." Tammy's lashes slid closed. "I promise I'm not a drug addict."

Never in her life had Tammy been accused of drug use. She guessed she could thank Chip Reeker for this on top of everything else. No, it was time to lay the blame where it belonged. Tammy's lack of control had caused every problem in her life. This was her own doing.

"Please know I will do everything in my power to help with your anxiety." Nicole sucked air between her teeth when she tucked Tammy's hair behind her ear. "Where did you get this bruise?"

The door snapped closed behind Mama. "That's what I'd like to know."

"I'm going to let you two talk while I go grab an ice pack," Nicole said as she stood.

Mama handed Tammy the cup. "Drink some of this."

As she sipped the coffee, Tammy noticed tears pooling in Mama's eyes. She took a breath and filled her in on what had transpired. "Mama, I'm sorry I didn't wait for Jace to go with me." Tammy's voice quivered as she sought Mama's gaze.

"You could've been killed."

"Please forgive me." Tammy took another sip of the hot coffee. "I promise I won't act so impulsively again."

"We should call the police." She folded her arms across her chest. "You need protection, Tammy Gail."

"Not yet. I'll go to the police as soon as I feel comfortable."

"What about the hospital?" Mama asked, her lips pinned together. "You should get your head looked at."

Tammy drained the rest of her coffee and winked. "In more ways than one."

Mama's voice came out high-pitched, and her eyes drew together. "What is that supposed to mean?"

"Oh, nothing. I was trying to be funny."

"Well, it wasn't funny. If you keep this up, you'll be on the next flight back to Georgia."

chapter forty-two

ONCE AGAIN, TAMMY LET Mama talk her into doing something she hadn't planned. Dress up for a night out. Not that she minded spending the evening with Nicole and Mama at a play. Especially since she figured she'd better be more flexible before Mama made her leave.

People roamed about trying to find their seats in time for the production of Little Women at the Downtown Playhouse. Even though most people talked as quietly as possible, the crowd's voices blended. Laughter and excited sounds sprinkled the air, causing an unexpected excitement to swirl in Tammy's belly.

They had a table three rows back, which gave them a perfect view of the stage. A server brought their cold drinks, two slices of cheesecake, one for Mama, another for Nicole, and a piece of carrot cake for Tammy.

The black and white pinstriped suit Nicole wore seemed a whole size too big for her, but somehow, she made it work. Maybe it was the layers, with a white t-shirt and sneakers, that gave Tammy the cool tomboy vibe that pulled the outfit together.

Mama looked past Nicole, her gaze landing on a woman wearing a strapless dress two tables over. "I just don't like them. What are they called? Braless dresses?"

Tammy met Nicole's gaze, and they burst out laughing. "It's a strapless dress, Mama," Tammy said as she fought back tears.

"Well, it's too cold for that mess," Mama said as she tugged the cape on her black jumpsuit over her shoulder.

"True." Tammy glanced at the purple slacks and silver sparkly sweater Mama had bought her and almost grimaced. That is until her gaze landed on the shiny red three-inch heels, and she couldn't stop a smile from dancing across her face. Young Tammy had begged Mama for a pair of shiny red heels, but Mama wouldn't let her get them because they were too expensive. This outfit more than made up for it.

She squeezed Mama's hand and jiggled her foot around. "I can't believe you got me these heels."

Mama pursed her lips, and laughter sparkled in her eyes. "It was past time." She fanned herself with her hand. "And they do look fabulous on you."

Nicole leaned across the table. "I agree." Her face softened. "I'm so happy you're doing better. I can't even tell your face is bruised."

Tammy shrugged. "Thank you to Maybelline." A small giggle almost escaped until someone slammed a door. The laugh died in Tammy's chest as the echo from the door consumed her. Her hand flew to her chest and she sat straight up in her seat. The scar from the bullet tingled as her heart skipped a beat before it jolted into high gear.

A wide-eyed Mama leaned closer to her. "You okay?"

Tammy's hand clenched, deepening the pressure on her chest as she took a few deep breaths. Even though her stomach rolled, she waved as she eased back into her seat. "Of course, I'm fine, Mama."

A line creased Nicole's forehead as she eyeballed Tammy.

Mama narrowed her eyes. "Are you sure?"

She nodded and turned to the man who had walked onto the stage. As the place quieted, Tammy let out a sigh of relief. Mama twined their hands together before turning her attention to the speaker, who let them know the play would start in a few minutes.

Nicole groaned when she took her first bite of cheesecake. "This is fabulous."

Tammy grinned as she scooped a bite of carrot cake. "Here, try a bite of this."

They ended up sharing the dessert before the show started. The production was as good as any she'd seen and had the three of them in tears by the end.

On the way home, several stars littered the sky, forming what looked to be a protective layer around a light orange and pale blue circled moon.

After Tammy passed a car going ten miles below the limit, she turned to Mama. "I've been meaning to ask if you gave anyone my number."

Mama pooched her lips out and cocked her head. "No. Why would I do that?"

"I was just wondering," Tammy said.

Mama took a deep breath. "Wait a minute. I had the preacher put your number in the bulletin after you first got here."

Tammy's brow creased. "The bulletin?"

"Yeah, I wanted to make sure people could get ahold of you if needed."

An inward growl threatened to seep out of Tammy. "Mama. I saw a bulletin on the table in Lorene's shop where anyone could get it."

"I'm sorry, honey. I guess that was a bad idea."

"It's okay. Just ask him to take it out if he hasn't already."

After they dropped Nicole off, they pulled into Mama's driveway. A car eased in behind them. Sheriff Obie hopped out of the driver's seat while Vivian White exited on the passenger's side.

A most unladylike sound came from Mama as her hand settled on her hip. "Obie?"

"I found this one walking down the highway," he said as he gestured at Miss White. "She said she was heading over here, so I offered to bring her since I planned to drive by here anyway."

Mama's shoulders relaxed, and she turned into a hostess. "Well, come on in." She unlocked the door and held it open.

"You look mighty fine this evening, Ruby." Sheriff Obie took Mama's place and held the door open. "You do, too, Tammy. I like them shoes. You remind me a little of Dorothy in The Wizard of Oz."

Proud of herself for not slugging him, Tammy smiled. "Thanks."

Castle hopped off his bed when he saw Tammy. She let him outside as Sheriff Obie and Miss White settled in the living room. Tammy watched them, pondering their reasons for being out at almost eleven.

Mama headed toward the kitchen. "I'll get a pot of coffee going."

Tammy blocked her path. "You visit with your guests. I'll take care of the coffee."

"Alright, just don't make it too strong," Mama said as she claimed the spot next to the Sheriff. "Obie doesn't care for the strong stuff."

Tammy considered putting an extra scoop in as she stared at the filter. She bit her lip and looked inside the coffee tin. She tuned out the conversation coming from the living room until the name Sonny caught her attention.

After getting the coffee percolating, she let Castle in and took the seat on the other side of Mama. "What did you say about Sonny Perkins?"

"He's done run off in my car." Miss White lowered her gaze. "I'm sorry for what he did, and I sure hate to ask, but I need help finding him. That's why I'm out so late, Miss Sharp."

"It's too chilly to be out walking, you know." Mama crossed her legs. Her foot dangled next to the sheriff's leg.

"I know it is, but I was sitting home quilting when I got the feeling that something bad happened to that boy." Her bottom lip quivered, and she hugged her arms across her chest. "I tried to call you but didn't get an answer, so I figured I'd walk since it's not too awful far."

Sheriff Obie smoothed his mustache. The one that reminded Tammy of an old-school gangster. "The police are looking into it, Miss White."

Miss White landed a pleading gaze on Tammy. "I know that, but I was hoping to get a big city detective to help me."

Sheriff Obie grunted. "This here big city detective, as you call her, has no jurisdiction in Pocahontas, Arkansas."

He slapped his knee and got up like the conversation was over. "I do believe I'll get that cup of coffee."

Tammy grinned when he passed by. Enjoy your cup of mud, Sheriff.

Enjoy.

chapter forty-three

A LITTLE AFTER FIVE the following morning, Tammy punched in the alarm code and eased out the front door. The cold darkness slapped her like a wet rag as the door closed. Even though the moon disappeared behind the black sky, shards of light covered the street. Thank goodness the city had recently replaced the bulbs.

She couldn't shake the feeling that she was missing clues that were right in front of her. Thomas had found several articles about gold tied to Pocahontas but nothing that helped Tammy with her current situation. The jeweler, Henry Corey, had led nowhere. Why couldn't she figure this out?

She reached the bottom of the steps when the front door swung open. Mama pulled the shirt collar on her fluffy white pajamas closer to her throat and shivered. "Where are you going?"

Castle poked his head around Mama before he skipped around the house. Little punk. She knew she should've taken him with her, but his nails would've made too much noise on the floors.

Tammy shuffled her legs and squared her shoulders. "I'm going next door, Mama. Didn't want to wake you so early."

Mama's eye twitched as she took a step closer to Tammy. "Hmm. I noticed you ran off to bed after serving our guest a cup of tar last night."

A frown cut across Tammy's face, and she lowered her eyes, not meeting Mama's gaze. "That wasn't my finest moment," she said as she raised her face toward Mama. "I'll apologize to them."

"Miss White didn't have any, so you'll only need to speak to Obie." A gentle smile touched Mama's lips. "Why don't you like him?"

The chilly wind sliced into Tammy's nose, and she shivered. "Can we please talk about this after I get done at Uncle Ellis's? It's cold out here."

"Hold on, and I'll go with you." Mama disappeared inside a few seconds before returning, wearing fuzzy tan boots and a white robe that looked more like a mink coat than night clothes.

Tammy made a mental note to keep from taking any more punches or head knocks. If she didn't, she'd never get rid of her shadow. She was surprised Mama let her sleep alone last night.

A couple of hours later, Tammy fell onto the sofa and pulled a pillow over her face, screaming into it. They'd entered more random codes trying to get the secret door open than she cared to count.

Mama's phone buzzed, and she grinned as she tapped the keyboard. Tammy felt the urge to snatch the phone from her hands but pushed the ridiculous notion away. Besides, Tammy already knew the message had to be from the sheriff. Who else could cause Mama to grin like that?

"I'm gonna run home and throw on a sweat suit." Mama lifted herself off the floor and crossed to the door. "Be back in a few minutes."

Castle followed Mama outside as Tammy walked toward the office. She allowed her mind to rest while she waited for Mama and Castle to return.

Within fifteen minutes, a car door slammed out front and got Tammy's legs moving. She pushed the sofa into place and curled up on the recliner.

Mama and Castle walked inside. Sheriff Obie strolled in behind them, carrying two cups in his hand. He handed one to Mama and paused, seeming to contemplate what to do next. It didn't take him long to decide as he drifted near Tammy.

"Ruby says you love Pumpkin Spice, so I got you one of them lattes from the Busy Bean."

As Mama disappeared down the hallway, Tammy's eyes darted from the sheriff to the cup before she cracked a part grimace, part smile. "Can you promise me you didn't spit in it?"

His laughter rang out across the living room as he handed Tammy the cup. "I sure can." The laughs died down as he met Tammy's gaze.

She clutched the warm cup in her hands. "I owe you an apology, sheriff."

He flung his hands out and shook his head. "No need. I got a good laugh over that cup of horrible coffee."

"Really?" Tammy tilted her head before taking a sip of the coffee. Creamy pumpkin and cinnamon swirled around her mouth, and she sighed. "This is so good."

"I had them use heavy cream in it."

Either he was a good guy, or he was trying to throw Tammy off his trail. Regardless, the coffee had the best pumpkin flavor ever.

"Thank you, Sheriff."

Mama walked into the living room and grasped his hand. "Yes, thank you, Obie."

"You're very welcome. You ladies have a good day. If you need me, I'll be out hunting for Sonny Perkins." He lowered his gaze. "They found rope stashed at a house he was at in Walnut Ridge. It's a match for the rope used on your doors the night of the fire."

"Oh my goodness." Mama pressed her fingertips to her forehead and made small circles. "I pray he's found soon. Such a troubled young man."

"That he is." He almost made it through the door when Mama called his name.

He turned, and she pointed at the sofa. Tammy's breath hitched in her throat. What was Mama doing? Before she could stop her, Mama slid the sofa out from the wall, exposing the secret door. Tammy examined Sheriff Obie's face as the color left it. He knew about the door already. That scoundrel!

Mama didn't seem to notice anything amiss. "What do you think is down there, Obie?"

His throat visibly moved, and he released the breath he had to have been holding. "There ain't no telling. You have any idea what the code is?"

"We've tried everything we can think of." Mama's gaze met Sheriff Obie's. "Do you have any idea what it could be?"

"I sure don't." He backpedaled to the door and twisted the knob. "Will you keep me posted?"

"Sure thing, Obie. I hope you find that young man."

Tammy's eyes narrowed as she considered Mama long and hard. She was up to something that Tammy didn't like. Instead of confronting Mama, Tammy decided to wait and watch a few more days.

After throwing an internal hissy fit, Tammy dropped down next to the sofa and examined the combination lock. Castle nipped her hand as he inserted himself between her and the door. She scratched behind his ear and sighed as her gaze landed on the table, focusing on a framed photo of her and Castle. "Uncle Ellis sure did love you, boy. He was with me the day we found you curled up by the dumpster in that alley."

What Tammy called a smile crossed Castle's face. He'd come so far from the skinny, half-starved puppy she'd adopted that cold day in October. That night, after feeding and bathing Castle, Uncle Ellis had patted Castle's head and told Tammy that day would be a date to remember.

Tammy's lungs jolted as air invaded her chest. Why hadn't she thought of that date before now? "Mama, I think the code is the day I found Castle." She crawled around Castle and held her breath as she typed in 102220.

"October twenty-second?" Mama got out of the recliner and focused her gaze on the keypad.

The light turned green as the lock clicked out of place. Mama gasped as Tammy bolted off the floor and out the front door.

She had to get Jace.

chapter forty-four

JACE STARED AT THE pictures of Sheriff Obie and Lorene Pankey. He and Tammy had agreed to move Obie to the top of the suspect list, but he was reconsidering that notion. Something felt off about Obie killing Ellis. Maybe the man knew something, but Jace didn't think he'd been the one to murder Ellis.

He bit into the sausage pancake on a stick and grimaced. The icy cold sausage told him he hadn't left it in the microwave long enough. He popped it in for another thirty seconds and took it and a fresh cup of coffee back to the living room.

Someone knocked on the front door like the police about to raid his house. His forehead creased as he set his coffee cup on the table. Who in the world would be at his door this early? Based on the rapid knocks, they must have something important to tell him.

When he opened the door, a flash of excitement crossed Tammy's features. Her gaze drilled into his as she pointed toward Ellis's house. "We figured out the code. The door is open!"

His pulse quickened with the thought of finally getting inside the room. He grabbed a sweatshirt and pulled it on as he stepped outside. "What's in there?"

"I don't know." Tammy's voice came out ragged as she almost ran across the lawn. "I came to get you before going inside."

If Jace's pulse picked up at the thought of seeing what the room held, well, it skyrocketed when he found out Tammy hadn't gone inside without him. His brain fizzled with the idea of grabbing her hand and pulling her close. If only he could swing her into his arms. His eyes widened as he struggled to get his thoughts straight.

Miss Ruby hovered above the door, tapping her foot as they entered. "I thought y'all would never get here." She clutched the built-in handle and started to tug the door up. "Let's get this door opened."

Tammy unholstered her gun. Castle let out a low growl as he eyed the weapon in Tammy's hand. She slipped it back into her holster before she touched Miss Ruby's shoulder. "Hold on a minute, Mama. You pull it up, and I'll go inside first."

Jace itched to move them aside but figured Tammy wouldn't appreciate the gentlemanly notion. Instead, he watched Tammy inspect the solid wood spring door and nod at Miss Ruby before she descended the steps to the hidden room.

Miss Ruby waved a hand and bunched her lips together. "Go ahead, Jace. I'll bring up the tail with Castle."

Light flooded the room when they entered. They must be motion-activated since Jace didn't see a light switch anywhere. Built-in bookcases free of books lined one wall, so stark white they almost blended in with the paint. A magnetic board displaying several newspaper clippings hung directly across from the bookcase. The rest of the furniture comprised of a sleek black desk and matching chair on one side and a comfortable looking blue sofa and loveseat on the opposite side.

All three of them headed straight for the newspaper clippings. Jace wasn't surprised to see old stories about Davidsonville and various stories about Dennis Howard. Tammy snapped pictures with her phone as she perused the board. After they read the articles, Jace traded a glance with Tammy as they stood almost in awe of the space. Jace could tell Tammy was at a loss for words by the way she sucked her lower lip between her teeth.

Miss Ruby marched past Jace and pulled open a desk drawer. That's all it took for Tammy to find her voice. "Mama, please don't handle things in this room without gloves."

Miss Ruby stepped away from the desk. "Whose fingerprints do you think you're going to find? If I was a betting woman, I'd bet my last dollar Ellis was the only one down here."

"I'm sure you're right, but we have to put safety first at any rate." Tammy slipped a pair of blue disposable gloves on and took the spot Miss Ruby had just vacated.

Jace's lips twitched. Of course, she carried gloves in her pocket.

Miss Ruby mumbled something about Ellis not leaving anything dangerous behind as Tammy reached inside the desk drawer. She laid a brown leather-bound journal and a black one-inch binder on the desk before peering inside the other two drawers.

Jace moved closer to get a better look as Tammy flipped to the first page in the journal. She looked at Jace with her brows raised. "The first page has a checklist."

"What does it say?" Miss Ruby leaned over Tammy's shoulder, with Jace following suit.

Lines creased his forehead as he read the list.

1. *Hide Dennis's letter and treasure map.*

2. *Get close to her.*

3. *Discuss treasure with Pat.*

4. *Leave clues for Tammy.*

Tammy stood and picked up the items from the desk. She rested her eyes on Jace. "Can we go to your place so we can update the murder board?"

Since a picture of Miss Ruby's beau was on that murder board, as Tammy called it, Jace had no desire to take her with them. He scratched the back of his neck and darted his eyes in Miss Ruby's direction.

Understanding dawned on Tammy's face before she started up the staircase. She paused midway up and looked over her shoulder. "On second thought, maybe we should lay everything on the kitchen table here."

Once they'd all claimed a chair, Miss Ruby let out a breath. "I wonder if Ellis was talking about Dennis Howard?"

"I would imagine so. I mean, that would only make sense," Tammy said.

Jace rubbed his forehead. "Do you know who the woman is that Ellis referred to on the second line?"

"Not at all." Miss Ruby tapped the journal. "And look, Tammy Gail, he knew you'd be the one looking for clues."

Her face paled, and she brought a trembling hand to her throat. "This must mean Ellis knew he would possibly be killed."

The corners of Jace's lips tugged downward. "I think he knew there was danger. At least that's the feeling I got when he asked me to come here."

Tammy closed the journal and slipped it inside her purse. She filled Jace in about Sonny being the one who set the fire before turning to Miss Ruby. "Mama. Please stay out of this. No more sticking your nose in this investigation. Period."

"He was my brother, and I owe him – "

"You know what you owe Uncle Ellis?" Tammy's tone left no room for argument. "You owe him your safety. If he'd wanted you involved, he would've told you about it when he was alive."

Tears pooled in Miss Ruby's eyes as she rose from the table. "You're right."

Tammy crushed her mama close and whispered words of comfort. Castle barked at the front door, interrupting the moment.

They exited Ellis's at the same time Sheriff Obie slid into the driveway. He thundered in their direction, stopping only when he reached Miss Ruby.

She wiped her eyes and landed a half smile on him. "What's wrong, Obie?"

"Sonny Perkins is dead."

chapter forty-five

THE NEWS OF SONNY Perkins's death had Tammy's mind whirling. Pocahontas had always been a safe haven—a place where bad things rarely happened.

Mama gripped Tammy's arm, and her face blanched. "Dead? How?"

Sheriff Obie cleared his throat, and a look of pure exhaustion crossed his features. "You remember Gleason's ex-wife?"

"Yes, of course. I remember Gleason's grief when she left him for another man back when we were in our twenties." Mama wiped her face with a handkerchief Sheriff Obie handed her.

"That's right, you would remember her." He coughed and looked past Mama, his eyes focused on her house. "I almost forgot about you and Gleason cozying up after their divorce."

Say what? Did Mama date Gleason Murphy? How had Tammy gone her entire life without knowing that bit of information? That could be a vital clue. She'd have to figure out how Gleason fit into the scenario with Mama and Uncle Ellis.

"We didn't cozy up, as you put it. He and I were both alone, and we spent a little time together, but nothing ever got serious." Mama looked at the sheriff with dark eyes. "Anyway, what does Margaret Murphy, or whatever her name is now, have to do with this?"

"Well, she listed the land she owns toward Maynard with Stephanie Whitcomb." He coughed and cleared his throat. Again. "Stephanie went there this morning to check the property out, and she found him shot to death in one of the old barns."

"I feel so bad for Sonny. Poor thing destroyed his life when he got hooked on drugs."

Poor Sonny? Yes, Tammy felt terrible that his life ended, but Stephanie would be the one dealing with the trauma of finding a dead body for the rest of her life.

Tammy filed away two things. One, Gleason may be more involved than she'd initially thought. Two, Sheriff Obie seemed nervous, like he was hiding something. Her eyes linked with Jace's. They were thinking along the same lines.

"I wanted to let you know before news traveled through the grapevine." Sheriff Obie patted Mama's back. "I need to work through some things, so I'm going to get. I may not see you again until tomorrow or late this evening."

"I understand, Obie." Mama followed him as he climbed into his squad car. "Be careful."

As soon as Obie backed out of the driveway, Mama turned to Tammy. "This investigation will have to go on hold for today."

"On hold? Why?" Tammy shielded her eyes from the sun's sudden appearance. "Sonny Perkins' death has no bearing on what we're doing."

Mama gave Tammy a look that brooked no resistance. "You're gonna help me make a couple of casseroles to take to Vivian and Stephanie."

Tammy's eyes doubled in size as she swerved around to look at Jace, who was no help. A cockeyed grin took up half his face, and he shrugged. Yeah, he wouldn't take Mama on for anything.

Jace cocked his head, and his eyes sought Castle. "Why don't you let me watch Castle for you?"

Guess she would be baking casseroles and visiting people with Mama like they used to years ago. A break could give Tammy time to look at things from a different perspective.

Two and a half hours, two casseroles, and a loaf of cinnamon bread later, Tammy stood outside Miss Vivan White's tiny home. It looked like more Christmas lights had been added since Tammy had last stopped by.

Once inside, Miss Vivian sobbed into the tissue she held before she motioned for them to sit. Mama put the chicken and broccoli casserole on the table and glanced around the kitchen and living room combo.

Tammy lowered herself onto the end of a firm brown sofa while Mama pulled a painted green kitchen chair beside the blue recliner Miss Vivian claimed.

Mama patted Miss Vivian's hand. "We're so sorry for your loss."

Miss Vivian nodded as she blew her nose. "I just wish that boy had never laid eyes on drugs. His life could've been so different."

After she scooted to the sofa's edge, Tammy lowered her normal speaking voice an octave. "Yes, we're so sorry. If you don't mind me asking, what happened to him?"

Mama cleared her throat, her lashes flying high.

Miss Vivian didn't seem to notice as she shook her head. "I don't mind. The sheriff said it looked like a drug deal went wrong."

A little later, the preacher and his wife stopped by, so Tammy and Mama took their leave with the promise to return the next day.

By the time they delivered the other casserole to the realtor, darkness covered the area.

"Don't forget to stop by the station so I can give Obie this bread."

"On the way there now."

Mama's phone rang, and after hearing the one-sided conversation, Tammy headed home instead of the station. Sheriff Obie leaned on his car when they pulled in.

He followed them inside and stood beside the door. "I don't know how to tell you this..."

"What is it, Obie?" Mama's hand landed on the base of her neck. "Please tell me no one else has died."

"Not that we know of. This hasn't been released to the public, and I'm only here because of how I feel about you."

That got Tammy's attention. "Just say it."

He squared his shoulders and met Mama's curious gaze. "The car found in the barn with Sonny Perkins's body belongs to Lorene Pankey."

chapter forty-six

NEVER IN HER LIFE had Tammy thought she'd play a game called Exploding Kittens. Yet here she sat, holding a handful of cards with various kittens on them and doing everything she could to beat Jace. After Mama, Harry, and Nicole had all exploded, it was down to them two.

Mama had been sad and reserved after the news about Lorene's car. Tammy figured having a few people over would distract her, and she'd been right. Mama's spirits seemed lifted.

Tammy held her breath, nearly praying for Jace's next card to be the exploding one. The side grin told her it wasn't, as he stuck the card with the rest in his hand. She groaned as she slid the corner of the next card up. Of course, she'd be the one to get the exploding card. She turned it over and stuck her tongue out at Jace.

Harry stood and glanced at Jace before he grabbed his jacket. "You've managed to win again. Nicole and I will take our leave." He rubbed Castle's head on the way to the door.

Nicole hugged everyone before she took her jacket from Harry. "Thank you for having us over. It was fun," she said before biting her bottom lip. "Hey, Tammy, can I talk to you in private for a minute?"

"Sure thing." Tammy led Nicole to her bedroom.

"Did you have a good time tonight?"

"I did. Thank you for coming over." Tammy cocked her head as her fingers trailed over a bump on her hand.

"Hey, I'm here for you if you are still struggling." Nicole took both Tammy's hands in hers. "Call me if you have an urge to take pills and need someone to talk you down or if you simply want to talk."

Tammy crinkled her nose. "Nicole, I promise you I am not on drugs. I am not taking anything that would cause harm."

"Just know I love you, and you can call me day or night." She clasped Tammy's hands to her chest as if she wanted her to feel her heartbeat.

"Thank you," Tammy squeezed Nicole's hands before raking her fingers through her hair. "And I love you, too." She needed to tell Nicole about Uncle Ellis before she planned a full-blown intervention.

After Harry and Nicole left, Jace turned to Mama. "One more game or no?"

Mama giggled as she swirled her glass of ice water. Tammy mouthed thank you to Jace as she gathered the cards.

Mama sat there for a few minutes before she yawned and glanced at her watch. "I think I've reached my limit of exploding kittens this evening. But you two should play one more to see who can claim the champ's title."

Tammy raised a brow as Mama walked away.

Jace slipped the deck of cards out of Tammy's hands and shuffled them.

It would be best to keep the conversation light. What better way than talking about someone's kid? Tammy watched Jace deal them each ten cards. "How's Leo?"

He laid the rest of the deck in the middle of the table and picked up his cards. "She's doing well. Getting ready to move and start a new job."

Tammy organized her cards in pairs. "Really? Where to?"

"She's moving out of our house in West Memphis to an apartment in Marion this weekend," he shrugged and made a sour face. "I offered to help her move, but she asked her cousins."

Tammy drew a card. "Why is she moving out?"

"She said something about being independent." Jace air quoted the last word.

"That makes sense." She grinned when she drew a card that would save her from exploding in the game. "What line of work is she in?"

He looked up from the cards in his hand. "She's a crime scene investigator."

"Wow, that's impressive."

"Yeah, and she's always wanted to get away from West Memphis."

"I can understand that desire," she said with a chuckle. "For a while, I considered moving to New York, but in the end, I stayed in Atlanta."

He took a break from staring at the cards in his hand to probe Tammy's eyes. "Was there someone or something in New York that made you want to move there?"

"Oh, no." She bit her bottom lip and tied her hair into a messy bun. "I just...well, it's silly."

"What?" He rested his elbows on the table, his eyes glued to her face. "Now you have to tell me."

As she glanced through the dining room window, she focused on the streetlight as she pondered telling him about her secret crush. "Did you ever watch that TV show with Detective Beckett and Rick Castle?"

Jace scooted back in his chair so fast it screeched against the floor. "I knew it! Is that who you named Castle after?"

"Guilty as charged. When I started watching the show, I couldn't stop myself from dreaming about having my very own good-looking writer following me around." Her collarbone turned hot, and she grinned. "You know, he would be my shadow, helping solve murders."

His voice turned husky, and his hand lingered on the card on top of the deck. "Would an investigative journalist do?"

Tammy's mouth fell open, and she gaped at Jace. A month ago, she would've gladly punched him in the face for having the gall to ask that question. But now? Now, her mind raced for words. She opted to ignore the question. Instead, she continued to focus on winning the game.

Jace raised a brow but drew a card without another comment. He scowled and laid the exploding card on the deck. "Good job, champ." The sparkle in his eye, coupled with the way he brushed his teeth over his bottom lip, told Tammy he had more to say.

Thankfully, Mama padded through the dining room, humming. She didn't even glance their way as she made a beeline for the refrigerator. She stood there no more than thirty seconds before she backtracked to where they sat. "I would love some roasted marsh-mallows." A smile gleamed across her face. "Is there any way I can get you two to fire up the pit?"

Even though Tammy contemplated handcuffing Mama and sending her to bed for her meddling, she couldn't stop her insides from dancing a jig. "We can as long as Jace agrees." Tammy latched her gaze onto Mama's. "But you're staying outside with us. You hear?"

"Of course, I hear. I wouldn't dream of leaving you two alone outside at night. You may try to sneak another kiss." Mama winked at Tammy, slipped her coat on, and escaped down the hall. Jace and Tammy gawked after her.

chapter forty-seven

Thinking about embracing Tammy caused Jace's heart to pound. Instead of doing something that would get his face slapped, he batted his lashes and gave her a cockeyed smile. "I'm game to sneak a kiss if you are."

The cockeyed smile turned into a face-splitting grin when a shot of crimson flamed her cheeks. "No, thank you," she said as she moved away from Jace and headed after Miss Ruby.

Castle cocked his head and stared at Jace before he curled up on the couch. Laughter rumbled from Jace's chest as he followed Tammy out the back door. By the time they made it out, Miss Ruby had hunkered down by the fire pit, striking a match. Newly strung outdoor lights draped around the wood pavilion shined brightly. The lights and the bright moon made Jace think of outdoor seating at a fancy beach restaurant.

Tammy sat in one of the iron chairs near Miss Ruby. "I thought you needed me and Jace to get the fire going," she said.

"How do you think I start a fire when no one is here?" The fire crackled to life as Miss Ruby found her feet. She shrugged, snagged a fold-up chair, and pulled it close to the flames. "Honestly, I just wanted the company."

Jace pulled another fold-up chair on the other side of Tammy. "We're happy to spend time with you, Miss Ruby."

She grinned, and Jace sensed she wanted him and Tammy to have another chance at things. Warmth filled his bones as his gaze moved to Tammy. She pulled her hair out of the bun, and the long locks cascaded over her shoulders. That and how the fire caused her face to glow had his heart pumping into overdrive. He sat on his hands for fear he'd reach out and touch her hair. He didn't want to get in trouble, so he'd better quench that desire and fast.

Miss Ruby leaned her elbows across her knees. "I wanted to talk to you both about the investigation. Tammy, you were right to keep looking into what happened."

Tammy shook her head. "Mama. You're not to be involved in the investigation."

"I believe I'm sixty-three years old. Lord willing, I'll be turning sixty-four in a few months." A spark of determination ignited Miss Ruby's eyes. "As long as I'm doing what the Lord would have me do, nobody else gets to boss me around."

"But–"

When Miss Ruby cut her off, Jace angled his head to look at Tammy. She wagged a finger in Tammy's direction. "Not even you, Tammy Gail. My brother was murdered, and I will do everything in my power to bring his killer to justice. You hear me?"

"I do." Tammy's spine stiffened about like the concrete Jace recently laid in his driveway. She said what Miss Ruby wanted to hear. But as Jace took stock of Tammy, he had no doubt she'd do her best to keep her mama clear of danger.

Either Miss Ruby didn't notice the glint in Tammy's eyes, or she chose to ignore it. She clasped her hands together and lowered her voice. "I've been thinking, and I believe the person on line three in Ellis's journal has to be the history teacher, Patrick Wood."

The whites of Tammy's eyes nearly glowed when Miss Ruby pulled the journal out of the inside pocket of her coat. "Mama! How did you get that?"

"It was in your room. But that's not what's important." She flipped to a page halfway through the journal. "Look at this."

Jace and Tammy moved closer to Miss Ruby. The page she'd turned to had pencil markings across it and revealed what had been written on the missing page.

Look for clues. There is a map only you will understand, Tammy. I love you and pray for you daily. Please be careful.

Uncle Ellis

Tammy ran her hand across the page and bit her lip. So many emotions crossed her face. The type that caused Jace to want to comfort her. If only he knew how.

"Now turn to the back page and check it out," Miss Ruby said.

Jace leaned closer to see what Miss Ruby was talking about. *0864* had been lightly penned in the top right corner.

"Mama, will you make a list of significant dates in Uncle Ellis's life? Maybe something can be tied to these numbers."

Miss Ruby nodded as she pulled out a pocket notebook and started writing in it.

"We also need to find Lorene."

"We sure do. Why do y'all think her car was in that barn? Is she in on it?" Miss Ruby shuddered. "Or, God forbid, is she dead?"

A sinking feeling settled in Jace's stomach. "I thought she was out of town visiting family."

"I haven't had a chance to say anything, but I called her family today." Tammy blew out a breath and laid her hand on Miss Ruby's. "She never showed up."

Miss Ruby sucked in her breath and shook her head back and forth. "I knew it! Lorene's been kidnapped."

Tammy drew her brows together. "Kidnapped? Don't you think that's a stretch?"

"It has to be tied to whatever Ellis had going on."

Jace tapped his leg before he got up and threw a piece of wood on the fire. "I agree. Lorene's disappearance is too big a coincidence. It has to be connected."

"I just wish we had more details." Tammy turned to Miss Ruby. "Can you think of anything about lost gold you've heard over the years?"

"Nothing that I've not already told you about."

"I mean, it's ridiculous that someone thinks I know where lost gold is." Tammy blew out a deep breath.

Miss Ruby nodded. "I bet Ellis planned to leave more clues." She lowered her gaze, and Jace thought she had tears on her lids.

He patted her hand before reclaiming his seat. "He probably thought he had more time."

"It's on me to find it." Tammy's face hardened. "I can't let anyone else die because of this."

Jace longed to comfort her. If only she'd allow him to pull her into his arms. He'd give anything to find the killer – to help her have peace of mind.

A scraping metal sound came from the front yard, followed by an almost otherworldly howl. What in the world?

Tammy met Jace's gaze right before two shadowy figures crept around the house.

Tammy heaved herself up, her hand ready to pull the gun strapped to her hip. She didn't want to shoot someone in front of Mama but would if it came down to it. Jace stood directly beside Tammy, his hands clenched into fists.

Nicole and Harry charged around the house, Nicole's arms flailing. Harry seemed uncomfortable but going along for Nicole's pleasure. Nicole roared with laughter before she held both hands out, palms up. "We're sorry, but we couldn't resist."

Harry put his hand over his mouth and coughed a few times. "We came back to get Nicole's purse, and she saw a golden opportunity."

Jace closed the space between him and Nicole and put her in a headlock. He scraped his knuckles over her head. "I see how you are, little sister."

After she maneuvered out of Jace's grip, Nicole shoved Jace toward Tammy. "Remember how you used to scare Tammy and me half to death?" Her laughs died down, but her face still held amusement.

Jace moved closer to the fire, and a trace of a smile graced his lips. "I remember Daddy would make us a fire to roast marshmallows."

"Yeah, I think you and your daddy were in on it together." Tammy walked past Jace and elbowed him in the side on the way. "Let's go grab your purse, Nicole."

A message pinged Tammy's phone a little after Nicole and Harry left for home.

Lorene Pankey is at Walmart in town.

Who is this?

Get here fast before she's gone.

She filled Mama and Jace in, and they all, including Castle, piled into her Bronco and drove to Walmart.

By the time Tammy crawled into bed at almost midnight, her mind raced. Lorene Pankey had been nowhere to be found at Walmart. Had she even been there? Tammy didn't think so.

She determined she would focus on finding out the identity of the person texting her. With a plan in place, her mind drifted to the conversations between her and Jace. She couldn't believe he offered to kiss her. Not to mention the part about Castle and him following her like Rick followed Kate had almost been her undoing.

Castle nudged the bedroom door open and jumped on the bed.

Tammy puckered her lips. "Where have you been?"

That earned her a lick across her arm.

"You better get some sleep. You have a playdate with your doggie friends, and I plan to go see the history teacher early in the morning."

Thankfully, Mama planned to work until noon at the pharmacy since the other pharmacist on duty had a doctor's appointment in Jonesboro.

Tammy rolled her eyes at Castle's bland expression. Even though he seemed unimpressed, he curled up in the crook of her knees.

chapter forty-eight

THE MOONLESS SKY AND foggy night conceal the beat-up black Camry I'd borrowed from my nearest neighbor. Of course, she had no idea, but she was old and sound asleep when I left. About like Lorene Pankey had no idea I'd borrowed her car and left it with Sonny. If she ever returns to town, she'll have to answer to the police.

I smile. I'm satisfied that the dark car wash is the perfect spot to park and walk through the streets of Pocahontas.

The chilly black night seeps into my bones, but none of that matters. The only thing on my mind is getting into that hidden room at Ellis's place. Thanks to Detective Sharp for letting me know the code, I can finally get inside. How stupid Detective Sharp is! She thought she had everything figured out. Getting her and Jace to leave had been a breeze. They didn't even question going to Walmart to look for Lorene.

I will admit that Detective Sharp seems to want to be a good person. She seems to care about others. Just not enough. If she did, she'd be following instructions. I wonder if she'd ever had despair blind her to what is right and wrong. If not, could she truly understand what desperation could cause some people to do? Desperation mixed with love had to be the most dangerous combination a person could ever face. That combination could cause one to do the unimaginable. The unspeakable.

I would know.

A thud hit the side of the box in my hands, and I can't wipe the gleeful smile off my face. This had to be the best idea ever. A slithery surprise would await the detective inside the room. I cannot wait to savor the moment she opens the box.

chapter forty-nine

Early the next day, Tammy glanced at the school secretary. "I only need to see Mr. Wood for a minute."

The plump secretary looked at Tammy over black-rimmed glasses. "He's at a workshop out of town, but I can give him the message for you." When she turned, ash blonde hair with a chunk of teal on the right side fell across her shoulders.

"I like the teal in your hair." Tammy surprised herself by this admission. She usually didn't like bold colors like that.

A pleased smile crossed the woman's lips. "I'm an Ovarian Cancer survivor. That's why I have teal in my hair. I got it in September to bring awareness, and it kinda grew on me, so I kept it."

If Tammy liked it before, its story made Tammy love it. "Well, it looks great, and I'm so happy to hear you're a survivor."

After her conversation with the school's secretary, Tammy contemplated her next destination. She wanted to go to the public library, and since Castle wasn't with her, today would be the best time. She left the school with a lifted spirit and a brightened mood.

Time got away from Tammy at the library. She'd found a book on Randolph County History that had mesmerized her. Her watch buzzed with a text from Jace at almost one o'clock.

You might want to come home.

Why?

Miss Ruby and the sheriff just went into Ellis's.

ON MY WAY!

By the time Tammy slid sideways into the driveway, Jace stood on the front porch. "Have you gone inside?"

"Was waiting for you."

"Come on, then." Tammy aimed her steps at the not-so-secret door. After she hollered for Mama, Tammy pressed her lips together and entered the code—the one that she would be changing before the day was out.

When the door flipped open, a ticking sound vibrated up the steps. What could Mama and Sheriff Obie be up to?

Jace grabbed Tammy's arm and moved her behind him. He pressed his finger over his lips and eased down the staircase. They'd made it close to the bottom when Tammy linked eyes with Mama's.

Mama squatted on top of the desk, a look of terror on her face. "Get back up the stairs, Tammy. Right now!"

Tammy peered around Jace and stopped in her tracks. Sheriff Obie held a walking stick, facing off with a rattlesnake.

chapter fifty

THE RATTLES GOT LOUDER as the snake reared its head back, prepped to strike. Jace would've been worried if not for the stick in Sheriff Obie's hand. Just as Jace figured, the sheriff used the walking stick like a baseball bat and knocked the snake against the wall with a thud.

When the snake's limp body landed on the floor, Sheriff Obie rushed over to Miss Ruby. He picked her up and deposited her on the stairs directly in front of Jace. "Y'all go on up. I'll be there in a minute."

Without so much as a word, Tammy pivoted on her heel and hightailed it upstairs with Miss Ruby behind her.

Miss Ruby collapsed on the recliner and met Tammy's gaze of fire. "Tammy Gail, did you take everything out of that room?"

Tammy claimed the corner of the sofa. "No, Mama, I didn't. You sure Sheriff Obie didn't sneak down there and remove all the evidence?"

A hush fell over the room as the sheriff stood at the top of the stairs, his eyes on Tammy. He took the last step and set a box he carried on the kitchen table next to where Jace sat.

He pulled off a pair of blue gloves and threw them in the trash before he addressed Tammy. "I've been more than patient with your childish dislike of me, Tammy. But

I will not put up with you accusing me of something like this."

Jace almost complimented the sheriff on his self-control but kept his two cents to himself. Instead, he looked at Tammy and waited for her response.

"It's not a childish dislike, sheriff." Tammy stood, closed the space between them, and lifted her chin to stare into his eyes. "I'm trying to figure out who killed Uncle Ellis, and you just so happen to be in the way of my investigation."

Before Tammy got the last word out, Miss Ruby squeezed her way between her and the sheriff.

"Your investigation?" Sheriff Obie stepped around Miss Ruby. He shook his head as a chuckle vibrated from his chest. "I'd be interested in knowing when you were hired as an investigator in Arkansas."

"This is my uncle's murder we're talking about. It doesn't matter to me one way or the other where I'm an official investigator. Nothing will stop me from bringing his killer to justice."

"Ellis was my best friend for more than twenty years." His face took on a worn, distant look. "Have you considered you're hindering *my* investigation?"

Tammy stared at Sheriff Obie. Miss Ruby took her hand and led her to the sofa. "Honey, Obie is a good man."

"But he's hiding something." She craned her neck to look at the sheriff, who stood beside the secret door. "I know he is."

"You bet I am." Sheriff Obie's voice thundered throughout the room. "I'm working on a case and will not apologize for keeping it confidential. Now that Lorene's gone missing, it ain't just about Ellis. Her life could depend on me keeping my mouth shut."

That seemed to suck the anger from Tammy as she lowered herself onto the sofa. Her face softened to one of consideration. To one of so much beauty that it took Jace's breath away. Not that she wasn't beautiful when angry, but when she allowed her face to relax, it changed her.

Jace guessed that's what anger did to people. He'd spent many years angry at Mato for taking his life with Tammy away. Even though he'd tried to hide it from Una, she had called him out on more than one occasion in their first couple years of marriage. That's when he decided to let the anger go before it consumed his life.

"You knew about the secret room before Mama showed you. Why didn't you say something?"

"Of course, I knew about the room," he said as he twisted his fore and middle fingers over one another. "Me and Ellis was thick as thieves. Close kinda like male versions of Thelma and Louise. He told me about the room. Said he was working on something he'd need my help with, but he wanted to get a few facts straight."

Miss Ruby looked from Sheriff Obie to Tammy, her gaze intense. She had to be waiting for Tammy to explode, about like Jace.

"You could allow me to help you." Tammy crossed her legs. "Instead, you're blocking me every step of the way. Help me understand."

"Listen here, gal, don't you know how you getting shot nearly killed your mama? I had a front-row seat after you sent her home." His tone became harsh, as if he wanted to scold Tammy. He grasped Miss Ruby's hand. "If you think I'd do anything to jeopardize your health, you're wrong. Ruby means the world to me."

Tammy lowered her eyes as she rubbed a spot beside her thumb. "You're right, Sheriff Obie. I've treated you unfairly, and I apologize."

"Apology accepted." He ran his fingers over his thick mustache. "What do you say we work together from here on out? I'll share what I can with you, but I want you to take a more behind-the-scenes role."

Tammy tilted her head and stared at the sheriff. "I'd say that sounds like a good plan. Let's start by talking about the room and the snake."

"Somebody knew about the room. Have you told anybody else?"

"Not a soul," Tammy said.

Sheriff Obie nodded at the box. "I'll take the rattler and this box to my pal in Jonesboro this week to see if he can find any prints." He handed Tammy an index card. "Any idea who wants you to find gold?"

Tammy read the card and turned it around for Jace and Miss Ruby to see.

FIND THE GOLD OR THE NEXT BOX WILL HOLD FAR WORSE

"I have no idea, but I know this has something to do with Uncle Ellis being killed."

Jace's stomach gurgled so loud that he figured Nicole and Harry had heard two streets over. "Who's up to grab a bite to eat? We can compare notes and see what we come up with."

Tammy grinned. "I have a little over an hour before I need to pick Castle up, so we can run down to Dora's if that works."

"That sounds mighty fine." Sheriff Obie helped Miss Ruby out of the recliner.

On the way out the door, Tammy's phone buzzed. She bit her lip and stepped back inside. Her tone turned firm when she answered. "Detective Sharp."

Within a couple of minutes, she returned, visibly paler than before. Miss Ruby furrowed her brow as she moved next to Tammy. "Who was that?"

Tammy rubbed the bridge of her nose. "That was my captain. The man who shot me escaped. He's on the run."

chapter fifty-one

After the call with her captain, Tammy contacted Thomas as they all drove to town in her Bronco. Thomas assured her they'd find the shooter and told her to worry about nothing but healing. Ha. If only he knew she'd found herself investigating the most personal murder ever.

She glanced at Jace. He looked good behind the wheel of her Bronco.

"How did that boy who shot you escape?" Mama leaned across the seat, her brow furrowed, letting Tammy know she meant to have answers and wouldn't stop until she was satisfied.

"How does anyone ever escape?" Tammy lifted her left shoulder. "He had some medical issues that put him in the hospital, and someone wasn't watching him."

"You have got to be kidding me." Mama's brow furrow got even worse, if that was possible. "That burns me up."

"I can camp out on the couch until he's caught." Jace put his two cents in.

"What?" Tammy threw her head back into the headrest. "No. It's fine."

"What are they doing to apprehend him?" Sheriff Obie asked.

"Look, my partner, Thomas, assured me they don't think he's coming after me. He's a kid. He's probably scared to death somewhere, doing his best not to get caught."

Mama's brow eased up a tiny bit. "So you don't think you're in danger?"

"No, Mama. I don't." Tammy put her arm into the back and grasped Mama's hand, hoping she would stop making a big deal out of it.

"Okay, then. Let's go on in and get some lunch." Mama said.

The glass door at Dora's Sale Barn Cafe snapped shut behind Tammy. An aroma of greasy burgers and spaghetti surrounded Tammy. Not a bad greasy smell, but the one that let you know the burger was going to be good. Only three tables held customers since the lunch hour was over.

Cow art lined the walls, playing into the fact that a livestock auction occupied the other side of the building. Mama greeted a hefty woman wearing an apron. She looked to be in her mid to late eighties but buzzed around the room like it was nothing. After Mama and the lady whispered about who knows what, they hugged. Mama slid into a booth in the far back right corner, followed by Sheriff Obie.

That left the other side for Tammy and Jace.

Jace stopped in his tracks and stared at the green, maroon, and tan wooden booth. Tammy wondered if memories of their time together plagued him like they did her. As teenagers, they'd shared many root beer floats at Dora's. Nostalgia made her fingers itch to reach out to Jace and pull him close. To lay her head on his shoulder like old times. To snuggle close and breathe in his scent.

What was wrong with her? She shouldn't have allowed those thoughts to invade her mind. These feelings were not only unexpected—they were unwelcome. She headed to the bathroom. Maybe an ice-cold splash of water would get her head back on straight. Her focus was not on Jace Eubanks.

She couldn't continue thinking about how, on some days, he smelled like pine mixed with a leather saddle and, on others, like a spice store. Or how the tiny laugh lines around his eyes made him look better than she could've ever dreamed. What good would that do her?

None.

Especially since she had no plans to act on those thoughts.

Back at the booth, after everyone ordered burgers and fries and introductions were made, Tammy leaned her elbow on the table and locked her eyes on Sheriff Obie. "Before we go any farther, I need to know who you met at Old Davidsonville."

Sheriff Obie crunched a piece of ice, seeming to study Tammy before he answered. "Have you met the history teacher?"

"Not yet. I left a message for him to call me, but I haven't heard from him." Tammy kept her eyes on the sheriff. "Why?"

"That's who you saw me with at Old Davidsonville." He tipped his head forward. "Why are you trying to get ahold of him?"

Tammy, Jace, and Mama took turns telling Sheriff Obie about what they'd found and how the name Pat was on a page in Uncle Ellis's notebook.

Sheriff Obie rubbed his mustache with his thumb and index finger, and his head bobbed with approval. "I'm working off a hunch that Pat knows something. Ellis met with him several times the month before he drowned."

Tammy and Jace exchanged glances before he cocked his head. "Sounds like we're on the right track." She narrowed her eyes at the sheriff. "If you and Uncle Ellis were so close, why do you think he didn't tell you what he was up to?"

"I knew about the room and that he was working on something. I just hadn't seen it yet. He promised he'd fill me in as soon as he had more to go on. Said he didn't want the police involved just yet."

"He probably didn't want Obie to get in trouble," Mama interjected.

Sheriff Obie nodded.

Tammy slid her phone across the table. She tapped the screen. "Scroll through those pictures."

"Will you share these with me so I can take a closer look when I get home?"

Tammy took the phone and added the photos to a message to the sheriff. "Do you have any other clues that could lead us to the lost gold?"

"Not at the moment. It would be nice if we could find things as easily as the folks in that one treasure-hunting movie." He rubbed his beard. "Oh, what was it called?"

"Are you talking about National Treasure with Nicolas Cage?" Jace flipped a sugar packet over in his hands a few times.

"That's the one." Sheriff Obie nodded.

"I agree, Obie. More importantly, do you have any idea where Lorene is?" Mama asked.

"I wish I did, Ruby, but she's vanished."

The owner, Miss Martha, headed their way with their order on a tray.

Sheriff Obie took Mama's hand and kissed her palm before he grinned at Tammy. "I hope you're ready for the best burger in Arkansas."

She stared at his hand and fought the ridiculous urge to knock it away from Mama. Instead of making a scene, she pasted on a smile.

Amusement burned bright on Miss Martha's face. "If I didn't know better, I'd think you was trying to get a free meal again, Sheriff Obie."

A look of shock crossed his features, and he held his chest. "Now, Miss Martha, you oughta be ashamed. I'd never!"

She wagged her finger and raised a brow. "You wouldn't be telling me a story, would you sheriff?"

The shock on his face deepened, and he chuckled. "I could never lie to you. I need your vote next election!"

Laughter filled the table after Miss Martha pinched Sheriff Obie. "Just eat your burger and hush. You folks, let me know if you need anything."

"I love this place." Mama's lips trembled almost like she held tears at bay. "Not only is the food delicious, but they donate their leftover food to the women's shelter in town every day."

Another reason Tammy needed to move back home was the people. "I didn't know. That's awesome."

As soon as Miss Martha disappeared through a swinging door at the back of the room, Tammy turned the subject back to the case. "I want to know why Lorene's car was in the same barn as Sonny Perkins's body."

"That's one of the mysteries we're working to solve." Sheriff Obie closed his eyes and took a whiff of his plate. "Let's pray over the food and continue this talk afterward."

The talk, as Sheriff Obie called it, left Tammy with no more clues than she'd started with. He pussyfooted around every question like a star detective would. She hadn't decided whether to tell him good job and take him off the suspect list or leave him at the top.

Miss Martha cleared their empty plates and set the ticket down. Right in front of Sheriff Obie. He removed the toothpick from his mouth and pulled out his wallet.

Jace laid three twenties on the table and waved his hand at Sheriff Obie. "I got it this time."

They argued back and forth, but in the end, Jace won and paid the bill.

Miss Martha strolled back to their booth as Tammy picked up her purse. She set a drink on the table, followed by two straws. "Here's a root beer float for you two."

Jace averted his gaze. Instead of looking at Tammy, he thanked Miss Martha.

Mama kicked Tammy under the table and bunched her lips up. "Obie, can you run me to the pharmacy for a minute?"

Sheriff Obie scrambled out of the booth and got his legs moving. Mama took off behind him without another word to Tammy or Jace.

As the door clicked shut behind Mama, Tammy noticed the restaurant had cleared out. She and Jace were the only two customers. And Miss Martha? She abandoned Tammy just like Mama had.

That float may as well have been poison. Because Tammy would not touch it.

No, thanks.

After he removed the lid from the float and wrappers from both straws, Jace pushed the drink toward Tammy. His eyes almost implored hers. "Will you try it? For old time's sake?"

She ogled the float. It was just root beer and ice cream. Right? And since he asked so nicely, what could be the harm? It would be a shame to let it go to waste.

She sucked on the straw, allowing the chilled cream to coat her mouth. A grin sprung across her face when her throat cooled off. As she took another taste, she found herself unable to wrench her gaze from Jace. His eyes brimmed with warmth as he twirled a lock of her hair around his fingers and tugged her close.

Her lids drifted closed. She had to slow her heart down to a steady pound. If only she could breathe and think about something else. Anything else. When her eyes fluttered open, she found Jace studying her. His tender look caused all thoughts to vanish as she leaned closer.

Miss Martha yelled something about a cow being at the front door. Tammy turned and met the brown eyes of a bull. A white streak ran down his head and both legs while the rest of his coat shined like a black Lamborghini. He had his face against the door, staring inside like he knew they had his cousin in the freezer. Laughter bubbled from Jace as they scooted out of the booth.

After the bull's owner loaded him up, Tammy slid into the seat across from Jace. This could be so easy. Being silly with Jace. She lowered her head.

"Tammy?"

She needed to keep things strictly professional. "Let's just drink this in silence. Okay?"

The light went out of Jace's eyes, and he scooted to the edge of the seat. "Whatever you want, Tammy. Whatever you want."

chapter fifty-two

MY MIND IS ON my childhood as I float down the Black River. Mother used to stripe me when I didn't behave. Other kids got spanked. I got beat like a common criminal. I still had scars on my legs from the time she beat me with a metal bar she found leaning against the house. She never wanted me. She loved my sister more. My beautiful sister with her blonde curls that always bounced after Mother spent so much time making her favorite child look perfect.

My poor Mother had a heart attack a week after my sister died a few weeks after giving birth. Sister's husband lost his life before he even knew sister was pregnant. Poor stupid man.

So, I was lucky enough to be there when the baby was born. Me. I can still remember the pure joy on my sister's face when she looked at her newborn. I wanted that joy. My sister had been happy her whole life. It was my turn.

Who could blame me for what I did?

I force my mind to the present. A blue tent is up ahead. Someone was camping. A woman with red hair waved at me. I wave back. From a distance, I believe this is Lorene Pankey. Could it be my lucky day? When I get close, a surge of anger nearly overcomes me as I see it's not Lorene.

Lorene is gone because of Detective Sharp. After a few deep breaths, I feel calmer. I'll find a way to make Detective Sharp pay.

"How are you doing?" She waves again.

I know her name is Abigail Hunt. I've seen her around town several times. Rumor has it she likes to stir up trouble. She dated a married man one time. She has to be a loose woman. Maybe I should stop. That would be the neighborly thing to do, right? She doesn't have to know how I feel about her. I am good at pretending, after all.

"I'm just out here trying to catch a fish or two. How are you doing, Miss Abigail?"

She glances behind her, and I can tell she's looking past the tent into the wooded area. She looks back at me and shrugs. "Facing my fear of the woods."

"That's awfully brave of you." I pause a moment. Just long enough for her to bask in the compliment. "Please tell me you're not out here alone." I smile. I've been told my smile puts people at ease.

She waves a hand in the air, dismissing my concerns. "I have pepper spray, so I should be fine," she said, her lips twisted into a smirk.

Another person blatantly ignoring my advice. Why? Did she not think what I said was important enough to listen to? She reminded me of how Mother had been—dismissive and arrogant.

Abigail Hunt was laughing at me. She thinks I'm unworthy of her attention. Unworthy of being loved. Even by a loose woman with no morals. How dare she laugh in my face!

It takes all my willpower to stay in the boat. I smile again before I leave. "Well, all right then. I better get back to my fishing. You take care."

"You, too." She waved again before she disappeared into her tent.

I turn my anger into opportunity. This is perfect. The air smells fresher than it did before I saw Abigail Hunt. Happiness almost blinds me as I continue down the river. I've wanted a reason to use the crowbar I buried in my yard. Now, I have the best reason ever. Abigail said she fears the woods. I can't wait to show her the true meaning of fear.

Tonight.

chapter fifty-three

No matter what she did, Tammy struggled to take her mind off the third almost kiss with Jace. Tammy picked up her pistol and looked through the barrel from back to front. The way her luck had been, a bullet would end up in the chamber or be stuck in the barrel.

Sunlight beamed around the backyard, giving Tammy a beautiful setting to clean her weapon. She poured cleaning solvent on a pad and wedged it inside the stripped barrel, running it through.

Castle sneezed, gave her a dirty look, and trotted toward Uncle Ellis's. He must miss the extra morning attention he usually got from Mama.

Heather had called in sick, and her other pharmacist, Melinda Seevers, was on vacation, so Mama would be at work the rest of the week. Which was good, in Tammy's opinion. It would give her some time away from Sheriff Obie. They needed a bit of separation.

Besides, Tammy had no doubt the sheriff was up to something. How else would Uncle Ellis's secret room have gotten cleaned out so fast? Nothing else made sense. He had to have known or at least had a good idea of the combination.

A car door slammed, and within seconds, Nicole skidded around the side of the house. With her fuzzy green Santa pajama pants, oversized sweatshirt, and Ugg boots, she looked like she just rolled out of bed.

Nicole waved her phone in front of Tammy. "Have you watched the news?"

Tammy's lips edged down at the corners. "I haven't. Why?"

After she tapped the screen, Nicole handed the phone to Tammy. "Just watch this."

A red "Breaking News" tag scrolled across the bottom of the screen. A man wearing a green sweater stared into the camera. His short black curls and face, which belonged on television, could get anyone's attention.

Wait. He stood in front of Lorene's Love Locks. Tammy's stomach vacated her body as she watched the man prepare to speak. It seemed like minutes had passed before he started, but the video showed it had only been seconds.

"We are live in front of Lorene's Love Locks in Pocahontas, where the owner, Lorene Pankey, has mysteriously disappeared."

He took a breath and waved his arm toward the beauty shop. "Miss Pankey's sister, Edith Pankey, came to us, desperate for answers. She says the police have been little help, even after Miss Pankey's car was found in an abandoned barn earlier this week."

His face took on an even more serious look. "But that's not all that was in that barn. Folks, you're hearing this first on Channel Twelve: Miss Pankey's car was found in the same barn as a dead body."

He paused. "Our team discovered the deceased was a local named Sonny Perkins. He'd just been released from the hospital after being shot at the home of Ruby

Sharp, the owner of Sharp Pharmacy here in Pocahontas." Another pause. "Tune back into Channel Twelve for the latest update at five."

Tammy pressed her mouth into a flat line, her teeth locked. If not for bringing whoever killed Uncle Ellis to justice, she'd go back to Atlanta and take Mama with her.

A swoosh of air came from Nicole as she claimed the seat across from Tammy. "This is ridiculous. Can they use your mama's name like that?"

Tammy shrugged but kept her teeth smashed together. She didn't trust what she'd say at the moment.

"That has to bug you," Nicole said.

"Yep, but nothing I can do...." Tammy stopped midsentence and drew a lungful of oxygen through her nose. "Nicole, you are a genius."

"What do you mean?"

Tammy finished cleaning her gun, leaned close to Nicole, and lowered her tone to a whisper. "I think Mama's and Uncle Ellis's houses have been bugged."

Nicole mouthed, "What?"

"Wanna help me find a bug?"

"Normally, that would be a hard no, but I'm intrigued," Nicole said as her eyes widened. "Does this mean you're finally going to tell me what you and Jace have been up to?"

Tammy shrugged before she rustled around in her bag and grabbed a radiofrequency scanner.

"What's that?" Nicole took a step closer to the device.

"A bug scanner. Ready?"

It didn't take long for the scanner to detect a listening device hidden in Mama's smoke alarm. Tammy gritted her teeth as heat flashed through her neck and face—another miss on her part. She slipped on a pair of gloves and deposited the bug inside a plastic baggie.

Confusion colored Nicole's cheeks. "Who would put a bug inside your mama's house? And why?"

"That's what I need to figure out. First, let's finish here and then check Uncle Ellis's."

"Lead the way," Nicole said.

After Tammy cleared the rest of the house, they headed across the yards. Nicole put her hand on Tammy's forearm. "Hey, I want to ask a question."

"Go ahead." Tammy sped up, hoping to stall Nicole.

No such luck. Nicole high-stepped it right along with Tammy. "Is it true you and Jace had a romantic moment at the diner the other day?"

A bark of laughter came from Tammy as she let herself inside Uncle Ellis's. "He just bought us a float."

Thankfully, the machine detected another bug and took Nicole's mind off her line of questions. Tammy added it to the bag with the other one before she moved around the rest of the house.

"What will you do with the bugs?" Nicole cut her eyes to the table and lowered her voice.

Tammy nodded toward the door. Once outside, she blew out a breath. "I'll give them to Sheriff Obie."

"That's a good idea." She rubbed her chin, her face a mask of confusion. "I wish you trusted me enough to share what's been going on."

"It's not that I don't trust you."

A car horn blasted from the roadway. Tammy and Nicole smiled at the man who lived a few blocks over as he waved out the window.

"A lot has happened to you and Miss Ruby the past few weeks."

"You're right about that."

"You know you can trust me, right?" Nicole's gaze probed Tammy's.

Tammy's reluctance to share had nothing to do with trust. It would be selfish to pull yet another person into the investigation if she didn't have to.

"Of course, I know that." Tammy bit the side of her lip as she covered the pros and cons of filling Nicole in. "I promise it's not about trust."

A car pulled up at Jace's, making the decision for her. Leo went inside but stepped back out within a few seconds. She glanced around before she marched to where Tammy and Nicole stood.

Without so much as a hello, she looked at Nicole. "Have you seen Doda?"

"He and Harry went fishing. What are you doing back?"

Tammy could almost feel turmoil emanating from Leo. "Are you okay?"

"Mind your own business." Leo glared at Tammy before she turned her attention back to Nicole. "Please take me to him."

"Why are you being rude to Tammy?"

"I'll explain in the car." Leo trudged to Nicole's car and got in the passenger's seat.

Nicole grasped Tammy's hand. "I'm so sorry."

"I appreciate that, but you didn't do anything."

Leo cocked her head and scowled at Tammy through the window until she walked away. Tammy had no doubt she would not want to be in the middle of whatever conversation Leo planned on having with Jace.

chapter fifty-four

JACE PULLED HIS TEAL hoodie over his head and laid it on the back of the chair. The sun beat down, heating his neck and now bare arms. The day had turned out unseasonably warm and perfect for a fishing excursion at Davidsonville Historic State Park.

He couldn't remember the last time he'd fished from the shore—it had to have been more than twenty years. He needed to clear his head. Being around Tammy for the past few weeks had messed with his mind. It was time to decide if that was a good or bad thing. He didn't like feeling out of control. And that's what she did to him. Made him lose control.

"I can't believe we haven't even had a bite," Harry said, adding a fresh worm to his hook and throwing the line into the water.

"It sure is peaceful out here, though," Jace said.

A faraway look crossed Harry's features right before he sighed. "With the way my life has been going, a little peace is what I need."

Jace whipped his head around. "What do you mean? Is something going on with you and Nicole I need to know about?"

"No, brother, it's nothing like that. Nicole is as close to perfect as a woman could get."

A light laugh left Jace. Harry would change his tune if he'd lived with Nicole as a teenager. She'd been a menace. "I'll take your word for it."

A minivan pulled up at the playground, and two women got out, followed by four kids. Excited shrills and laughter came from their direction. Oh, to be four or five again without a care.

Other than the kids yelling, Jace and Harry sat in comfortable silence for the next fifteen minutes or so. Jace could tell Harry had something on his mind. Since he and Nicole married, Jace and Harry had grown fairly close. Maybe Harry needed this time to gather his thoughts. Jace figured he could do the same.

Now that Sheriff Obie had been removed from the top of the suspect list, he had to consider moving Lorene Pankey back to the top. He mentally listed everything going against her.

1. *She was the closest person to Ellis, besides Miss Ruby, that Jace knew of.*

2. *She'd left town over a week ago, never arriving at her destination.*

3. *Her car was in the barn with Sonny Perkins's dead body, but she was not.*

4. *She was hiding something. Her actions gave her away.*

What else did they need to tie her to the murder? Something more concrete. Even though she'd acted cagey, he wasn't completely positive she killed Ellis. And his gut? It told him she had information but had not been the murderer.

"Where's your mind, brother?"

"Sorry. I was thinking about Ellis."

Harry shook his head before taking a swig from his coffee thermos. "I still can't believe you think he was murdered. What could be the reason?"

"Money is at the top of my list," Jace remarked.

"Are you close to figuring out who did it?"

"Not really. But I want to know what's going on with you. You seem to have a lot on your mind."

One of the kids yelled so loud that Jace figured he wanted the Park Rangers to hear. Jace and Harry eyeballed the playground area to ensure he wasn't hurt. After they determined he was just a kid having fun, they focused their attention back on the water.

Harry propelled himself to his feet when his line bobbed. He reeled in a nice-sized bass and then released it into the water. He laid his pole down and looked at Jace. "I have committed a colossal mistake."

Jace remained silent, giving Harry the time he needed to explain further.

"I attended a conference late last year in Memphis. In our downtime, we decided to go to the casino." A haunted look crossed his face. "As it turns out, I very much love gambling, but it does not love me."

"What are you saying?"

Harry took a breath and sighed. "I've spent a fortune gambling over the past few months. I continue to do it because I know I will win it back."

"Have you?"

"No, I have not, and I need your help figuring out a way to tell Nicole."

"The best thing to do is be honest," Jace said.

"We leave in the morning for our anniversary trip. Do you think I should tell her while we're away?"

"I would." Jace rubbed the bridge of his nose. "Do you have money for this trip?"

"We already paid for the trip, and I have our spending money saved back." Giddiness replaced the sadness on Harry's face. He leaned forward, seeming to be ready to jump out of the chair. "I have a lead where there's plenty of money to be made."

Jace didn't like the sound of that. His forehead creased. "A lead? What kind of lead?"

Before Harry answered, Nicole's car pulled into a parking spot. Nicole and Leo stepped out. Leo? What in the world was she doing here?

Nicole sat down at the picnic table closest to the parking lot. Leo marched toward Jace. Nicole hollered for Harry, and he wasted no time scrambling to his feet and leaving Jace behind.

When Leo got close, a pang struck Jace's middle. Something was wrong. Instead of the usual smile and hug, she greeted him with an expression that bordered fury. He crept forward, only to stop when she held up her hands.

"What's going on, Leo?"

"I have a question, and I need you to be completely honest." She balled her hands into fists, and they dropped to her sides.

"Of course. Ask me anything."

In Jace's experience, the question they planned on asking would not be easy anytime someone said they wanted honesty. Even so, Jace was not expecting what came out of Leo's mouth.

"Did you murder my mother?"

chapter fifty-five

Tammy carefully maneuvered her car into the space between a shiny red Camaro and a white Ford Fusion at Black River Overlook Park. As she stepped out, a refreshing cool breeze gently kissed her cheeks, carrying with it the earthy scents of the park. With Castle, by her side, she took a moment to savor the picturesque surroundings. It had been years since she'd last set foot in the peaceful park.

They stopped in front of a statue of Pocahontas, and Tammy paused. "Dear Pocahontas, what would you think of the world today?"

Castle tilted his head with curiosity and made his way towards the playground. As he reached the edge of the river, he paused and gazed at the water before lowering his head to sniff the ground beside the love lock fence. The fence was adorned with locks of different shapes, sizes, and colors, each one bearing the names of couples in love.

Tammy furrowed her brow in slight disgust and carried on, her boots crunching on the loose rocks as she strode past Castle on the paved walkway. Not one to be overtaken, Castle swiftly maneuvered around Tammy and came to an abrupt halt near a man playing catch with a gray labradoodle. A smile formed on her face as she admired his immaculate black sweatpants, matching hoodie, and pristine white and black Jordans. She appreciated a man who took care of his appearance.

What were the odds of encountering Patrick Wood out here? She had studied his features meticulously on the online school staff page. Although he seemed to have put on a few pounds since the photo, she was certain that it was him.

He eyed Castle before settling his gaze on Tammy. "Is he friendly?"

After taking another moment to size him up, Tammy nodded. "He sure is."

"I'm Pat Wood, and my buddy there is Winston."

"Tammy Sharp and Castle." She closed the space and stuck her hand out. "Nice to meet you."

He planted a kiss on her hand, his deep brown eyes glowing. "I've actually heard a lot about you, Miss Sharp."

"From Uncle Ellis?" After warmth settled on Tammy's cheeks, she regretted leaving her gloves in the car. She stuck her hands in the pockets of her emerald green puffer jacket.

Pat blinked a few times and looked at the ground. "Yes. I thought the world of Ellis. He helped me out when I first moved to Pocahontas."

"That doesn't surprise me," Tammy replied, her lips lifting into a small smile.

Castle and Winston seemed to be having the time of their lives, zipping around the grassy area. Pat watched them for a second before pointing at a bench toward the river. "Want to sit with me while they get acquainted?"

After they made small talk about things of little importance, Tammy bit the side of her jaw and squinted her eyes. "Do you know of anything that could've gotten Uncle Ellis killed?"

His eyes widened, and he shifted his body to face Tammy. "Killed?"

"Yes."

"I can't imagine..." He stopped midway through the sentence, and something of a sadness overtook his features.

Tammy's hand gripped the bench. "What are you thinking?"

"When I moved here, there was a man who was very vocal about my skin color. He didn't want a black man teaching his granddaughter." He paused and stared into the distance.

Tammy hated the circumstances, but this could be the break she'd been waiting for. "Go on."

He leaned his elbows on his knees and swiveled his head to meet Tammy's eager gaze. "Ellis stepped in, and even when things got ugly, he stood by me."

Her eyes shot open. "What do you mean by ugly?"

"I started getting threatening phone calls suggesting I move to another town." His lips tugged downward. "The family even went to the board and filed complaints."

"I'm so sorry."

He sniffed, and his eyes narrowed. "That's not the worst part. They lied and tried to have me arrested."

"Arrested for what?" Tammy asked, fiddling with the zipper on her jacket.

"Penny Carter accused me of assault," he said as his lips tugged downward.

This conversation could be what Tammy needed to further the investigation. A few feet ahead, a husky puppy zoomed by with Castle and Winston in her sights. The owner spoke as he rushed after her. Tammy scooted an inch closer to Pat and lowered her voice. "Assault?"

"She tried to say I lured her to my house." Pat's tone lowered to match Tammy's as he watched the man with the husky.

"Wow," Tammy said as her back smushed into the bench. She hated how Pat was treated because of his skin color.

"They didn't know I had left my car at home on the day in question, but I was in Jonesboro with Ellis," Pat said.

"That's good." The hair on Tammy's arms stood upright when the name Pat said struck her. "Wait, did you say the girl's last name is Carter? Is she kin to the people who own the bait shop on the way to Old Davidsonville?"

He nodded. "Yes, Lewis Carter is her granddaddy."

"That makes sense. He's always treated my, um, friend, Jace, differently," Tammy said, rubbing her arms over her puffer jacket. "I guess because he's Native American."

"I believe it."

"Did they try to pursue it after Uncle Ellis came forward?"

"No, they dropped the accusation when they found out I had a solid alibi." His jaw ticked, and he shook his head. "Penny claimed she was upset over a bad grade."

The man snapped a leash on his husky before they continued walking. Castle and Winston bounced toward Tammy and Pat brimming with uncontainable excitement. He threw a tennis ball near them, and they both dove for it. Winston nailed it and ran in front of them with Castle nipping at his heels.

The side of Tammy's mouth quirked upward. Castle seemed to be having the time of his life. "Is Penny Carter still in school here?"

"I can say I'm thankful she's not. Her parents moved to Poplar Bluff, Missouri, I guess, around a month after Penny got caught in the lie."

"That sounds drastic." The wind picked up, and cool air bit Tammy's nose. She had a feeling it looked red and puffy.

"Her daddy took a job somewhere else. It always seemed fishy to me, though." He gave a lopsided grin. "Truthfully, I was just happy to see them go."

"Yeah, the timing is suspicious." Tammy rubbed her finger across the back of her neck. "I went to school with Anthony Carter but didn't run in the same crowds. Do you believe any of the Carters are capable of murder?"

"After how they treated me, I wouldn't put anything past them."

"Has Lewis Carter bothered you since then?"

"Not at all. He acts remorseful, but I think he's putting on a good show since he's a volunteer constable. Everyone else has been welcoming, and I've enjoyed being here." He stared at Tammy with sparkling brown eyes. "Especially after meeting you."

Two girls who looked to be around twelve skipped over to Pat. The skinny, dark-haired one stopped at the bench while the pudgy one ran after Winston and Castle. "Hi, Mr. Wood! What are you doing?"

"Nothing much, Baylee. What about you two?"

She shrugged and started skipping toward her friend. "My parents brought us here. Can we play with your dogs?"

"Sure, they're both friendly."

Baylee's parents waved at Tammy and Pat before claiming an unoccupied picnic table near the playground equipment.

An emptiness mixed with a longing Tammy couldn't shake nearly curdled her stomach as the girls jumped around with Castle and Winston.

Pat nodded toward the girl playing with Baylee. "That little girl has had a hard go of it."

"What do you mean?"

"Baylee's parents are fostering her. She has no family other than a grandmother who doesn't want her."

Tammy stared at the little girl. Her voice came out hoarse as she spoke. "What's her name?"

A slight smile crossed his lips. "Her name is Alvie Leigh."

She cleared her throat as she watched Alvie and Baylee through hooded eyes. "Would you introduce me to her?"

He nodded.

After twenty minutes of chasing the girls, Castle and Winston, Tammy collapsed on the bench beside Pat. Her fingers curled around the bench seat, and she swallowed her emotions before smiling. "Thank you for introducing me to the girls. And for talking to me about what you've been through."

Smooth laughter vibrated from his chest as Pat capped his eyes on Tammy. "I enjoyed myself."

She lowered her gaze. "Is there anything else you think I should know?"

His lips curved into a smile that reached his eyes. "Only that I'd love to take you to dinner tonight."

Pat stared at Tammy until she felt the need to squirm. Instead, she matched his stare and admitted she could go to dinner with much worse. Besides, it would only be a fact-finding meal.

"All right. We can continue our discussion over dinner."

"Absolutely," Pat said.

Pat may have agreed, but his intense look told Tammy he had more on his mind than fact-finding.

chapter fifty-six

TAMMY'S MIND RACED THE entire drive home. Alvie and Baylee were sweet little girls. If Tammy had made better choices, she could have her own Alvie or Baylee right now. A deep frown creased her forehead. She passed the building where Taco Casa used to be, and her face fell even more. That had been her favorite restaurant growing up. Now it was closed. Just another sad part of her life.

She rolled her shoulders. There was no way she could allow her mind to take over. It was time to focus on the here and now. On what she could do something about. Anthony Carter would've had easy access to Uncle Ellis's boat. Had he been so upset about Patrick Wood's race that he meticulously planned a murder over it?

It would've been easy to drive from Poplar Bluff, kill Uncle Ellis, and be home the same night. The move could've been the only way Anthony knew how to secure a solid alibi.

She'd worked on many cases where people had been murdered after people allowed anger and hatred to take hold of their hearts. This could be it. She needed to fill Jace and Mama in on their new suspect.

Had they been looking in the wrong direction the entire time? Maybe. Maybe not. The best course of action would be to continue to follow the clues. That meant she had a trip to Poplar Bluff on the agenda. She should also spend time getting to know Patrick Wood. He was cute, after all, and clearly interested in her. But was he cute enough to take her mind off the one person she dreamed of? He could be.

She took a gulp of air as her life played over in her mind. After Jace left her, she pushed away every man who attempted to get close. Grief and what could've been consumed her mind. By the time she moved past Jace, her life had taken a shape of its own. Her job replaced the grief that once owned her thoughts.

The fact that she had no husband, children, or love life had been her own doing. She couldn't lay that at Jace's feet. Yes, he hurt her, but the decisions she made afterward had nothing to do with him. She needed to change, or she would die alone. The time had come to allow her heart to feel more than a passing attraction. The revelation and decision to change unleashed a laugh full and free.

Castle awoke from his nap, and she didn't try to stop the lick he bestowed on the side of her face. The laugh gave way to a rash of mirth as she and Castle raced up the steps.

She hung her jacket in the closet and bounced into the kitchen. A whiff of fried potatoes caused Tammy's stomach to gurgle. "Hi, Mama. How was your day?"

Mama tossed Tammy the side-eye before she flipped the potatoes. "How in the world did you end up having dinner plans with Patrick Wood?"

"How do you know about that?"

"He called me. He said he forgot to get your number from his house before he took off," Mama said with a raised brow.

Tammy popped a piece of fried potato from the end of the spatula Mama held into her mouth. "Okay, now I'm confused."

"Sorry, he needs to reschedule. He got a call his daddy had a heart attack."

"Oh no. I hope you asked him to keep us updated."

"Of course I did." Mama pointed the spatula at the refrigerator. "Now make yourself useful and put a salad together."

"All right. Let me grab my phone out of the car first."

As Tammy opened the front door, raised voices came from across the lawn. Jace stood outside Leo's car, waving his hands in the air. Part of Tammy wanted to get her phone and mind her own business. The other part, the part that she always listened to, wanted to get involved. At least to try to calm the situation. Her legs moved as she crossed the yards.

Jace swung his frame toward Tammy, his gaze mixed with anger and hurt. "Tammy."

"Hey, I wanted to make sure everything was okay."

Leo skewered Tammy with a hot gaze. "I thought I told you to mind your own business."

"As Jace's landlord–"

Leo cut Tammy off. "You're full of it. I know you want to be more than his landlord."

Jace leaned his shoulder on the door frame. "Leo, please. Tammy has nothing to do with this."

"Yeah, right." A bitter laugh accompanied the nasty look Leo landed on Jace. "Have I ever told you how many times

I overheard you and Mama talking about Tammy Sharp, the so-called love of your life?"

One look at Jace's face, red with embarrassment, and Tammy knew she had no business butting her nose where it didn't belong. She took a few steps backward and shifted her eyes to Jace. "Look, I think Leo is right. This is none of my business."

"One time, Mama actually thanked him for sacrificing so much for us." She stared straight at Tammy. "I listened to her cry as she talked about how she knew his love for you would always be a part of him."

A hollow feeling settled in Tammy's stomach. What could she say to Leo? Before she had a chance to respond, Leo started the car.

"I'm going home." The car rolled back a few inches.

Jace walked with the car, his arm on the doorframe. "You know better than to think I would ever..."

"There are three things I know. One, you have always been in love with that woman." She pointed at Tammy. "Two, my mama, your wife, was killed. Three, you're here with her instead of at home helping figure out who killed Mama." The look of raw pain and anguish that crossed Jace's face as Leo rolled the window up caused Tammy's stomach to constrict.

Leo didn't seem to notice the pain she caused her daddy. The window lowered, and her gaze met Tammy's. "By the way, I hope you know you have the hots for a wife murderer."

chapter fifty-seven

A CHILL BLANKETED THE air and settled in Jace's bones as Leo's tail lights disappeared into the sunset. Unshed tears stung his eyes, and his chest ached. After being accused of murder by his own daughter, he'd rather face off with Hulk Hogan than look at Tammy.

"Jace?" Tammy's voice came out in a near whisper.

He stole a glance her way, fully expecting to see anger. Instead, moisture lined her lashes. "I'm here if you need to talk."

He shivered as his gaze dove into hers. He couldn't seem to put a sentence together. All he could think about was Una's body lying in a pool of blood. How could Leo accuse him of such a horrific act? A rush of heat hit Jace in the face as Tammy led him inside the house. He sat on the sofa, and Tammy claimed the spot beside him.

They sat in silence for a few minutes before Tammy pecked on her phone. She looked at the screen and slipped it inside her jacket.

The knot in his throat wrenched up and down. After a forceful swallow, he met Tammy's gaze. "Una was killed in our home a few years ago. There were no prints or clues left behind."

"I'm so sorry."

"I've spent the past three years searching for her killer." He gulped past his dry throat. "When Ellis called me, I jumped at the chance to come here. I figured I needed to step away to see things clearer."

Tammy went to the kitchen and brought a cup of water back. He nodded his thanks before he downed the contents in a long drink.

She took the cup and met his tortured gaze. "I can understand you wanting to take a mental break. But why did your daughter accuse you of murder?"

He barked a laugh. "Leo's best friend is a dispatcher at the station in West Memphis where Una was killed. Looks like the police think I did it."

"Surely Leo doesn't believe you killed Una. Her emotions must be running high right now." Tammy would avoid the elephant in the room at all costs. She needed time to process what Leo said about Jace always loving her. A lot of time.

"She was upset when I left West Memphis before the case was solved. I told her I desperately needed a change of scenery." He laid his head in his hands. "I had to take a break from the constant guilt. Not to mention, the new detective asked me to take a step back."

"She'll cool down and rethink things."

"I thought she understood the detective asked me to leave." He lifted his head and met Tammy's concerned gaze. "But when she found out I bought the paper, she said I was giving up on bringing Una's murderer to justice."

"That was the anger talking." Her mouth sank into a sorrowful smile. "Believe me, I understand how easy it can be to say hurtful things when you're angry."

"I haven't told her my plans because I don't want to disappoint her."

"Plans?"

"I have every intention of using my connections with the newspaper here to help figure out who killed Una."

"Maybe you should go back to West Memphis and think about that later." Tammy bit her bottom lip, and her brows melted together. "You need to clear your name."

His stomach revolted, and the water he'd drank threatened to come back up. He grasped Tammy's hand. "I deserve to go to prison."

"What do you mean?"

His grip tightened on her hand. "I may not have killed Una, but Leo is right. I need to pay for never fully giving her my heart."

Even though her eyes shot open, Tammy kept her expression guarded. "That's not the same as murder. I know you loved Una."

"Loved her? Yes. I grew to love her. Una was a good woman, and I owed her my affection."

"See there?" Tammy looked at their hands and tried to pull hers away. When Jace's grip stayed firm, she gave up.

His eyes tangled with hers as quakes hit deep behind his ribs. "Tammy."

She jerked her hand away and lifted herself to stand in front of the painting of his grandfather. Her shoulders moved so quickly that Jace could tell the beats of her heart matched his.

He gripped her shoulders and forced her to look at him. "The only person to ever truly consume my mind, body, and soul is you."

"Jace, you need to stop this."

"Don't worry, Tammy. Even though I love you from the deepest part of my being, I know we can't be together. As soon as we solve this case, you'll never have to see me again."

Seconds could've been minutes as each stared into the other's eyes. "We will see each other again. How else will I be able to help you solve Una's murder?"

A sob started in his stomach and clawed its way through his body until it escaped. Even to his own ears, the cry sounded hauntingly sad yet full of hope. What an odd combination as the tears he failed to stop wet his cheeks and dripped onto the same teal hoodie he'd worn fishing with Harry. He clenched his eyes together. If only he could blink and go back to that moment. If only he could change Leo's mind about him. If only he could bring Una back.

Yes, he would bring her back without hesitation. He would trade his life for hers.

If only.

He reluctantly pried open his eyes when warmth encompassed his upper body. Tammy's face pressed against his neck, and she offered comfort he desperately needed. Time paused as they clung to one another, and Jace felt Tammy needed this moment as much, if not more, than he did. Their tears mingled as Jace allowed himself to mourn what could've been, what wasn't, and what was as he released years of pent-up regret and sorrow.

chapter fifty-eight

SECONDS FELT LIKE HOURS as Tammy held onto Jace. She pressed her face into his neck and breathed in lavender mint. This was what she'd missed her entire adult life. Holding him now seemed so much better than she remembered. So much more. They took a step back at the same time. Tammy ran her hand across her neck as she headed outside. She needed air.

She glanced across the lawns. Sheriff Obie and Mama sat on the swing.

Tammy tore her eyes away from the pair when Jace joined her on the porch. "Mama's cooking supper. You're more than welcome."

He took her hand, and his brown eyes implored her. "First, I need to know that you forgive me."

Tammy waved a hand. "You had no control over Leo –"

"No, I mean for how I handled things with you and Una. Please forgive me."

That potato Tammy had swiped from Mama's spatula threatened to come back up. Her first instinct was to stop Jace in his tracks. Shut him down, like always. Instead, she took a deep breath and met his gaze. "I forgive you."

A choking sound left Jace. "You have no idea how much that means to me."

She lowered her gaze to stare at her hand. "Honestly, it's way past time. Can you come over to Mama's? I have something I want to talk to you about."

Jace nodded, his face full of emotions that caused Tammy's insides to churn. They fell into step beside one another and stayed silent until they made it through Uncle Ellis's yard. Sheriff Obie got in his car and waved as he drove by.

Tammy waved back before meeting Jace's gaze. "Have you considered hiring a private investigator to look into Una's death?"

"I have considered it but didn't know how I'd feel about getting a stranger involved."

"Do you remember my cousin Sherry Langston?"

"Yeah, I think so. Isn't she your great aunt's daughter or something?"

"Yes, we share the same great-grandma." Tammy opened the front door to Mama's. "Anyway, her husband is a private investigator out of Memphis. We could give them a call tomorrow if you wanted."

"Thank you. I'm willing to try anything."

Mama strolled into the living room. She laid a hand towel on her shoulder and cocked her head. "Y'all better get your hands washed before supper gets cold."

The dining room table had already been set for three people. "Where was the sheriff going?"

"He said he needed to follow up on a lead," Mama said as she sat a pitcher of tea on the table.

"A lead? Why didn't he tell me?"

"Surely you don't expect Obie to run everything by you."

"Maybe not everything," Tammy said. "Did he tell you where he's going?"

"Old Davidsonville. I'm sure he'll fill us in if he finds anything."

Jace pulled a chair out and nodded at Tammy, then the seat. She plopped down with a huff. He claimed the seat across from her. "Miss Ruby, this chicken smells delicious. It all looks so good."

"It sure does, but I need to tell y'all what Nicole and I found earlier. Guess we can tell Sheriff Obie later," Tammy said.

"Well, don't leave us hanging, Tammy Gail."

Tammy filled them in on how she and Nicole found the listening devices.

Jace tucked a piece of hair behind his ear. "Where are the bugs now?"

"I hid them in town." She blinked over to Jace. "You need to check your place as well."

He ducked his chin in agreement.

Mama rubbed her forehead. "What is going on here? Why is all this happening to us?"

"I don't have the answers yet, but I promise we will get to the bottom of this."

Mama blew out her breath. "All right. I guess we better eat. I just thought of this. We should've invited Harry and Nicole."

"They're getting packed for their anniversary trip," Jace said after swallowing a mouthful of chicken.

"Where are they going?"

Jace tugged at the collar of his hoodie. "They leave for Hot Springs in the morning."

Mama didn't seem to notice her line of questions made Jace uncomfortable. "Well, I hope they have a good time."

A wrinkle cut across Tammy's forehead as she slathered ketchup on her fried potatoes. Jace must be having a hard time dealing with Leo's accusations. Turmoil swam in his eyes.

As soon as Mama went into the kitchen for a loaf of bread, Tammy leaned across the table and whispered, "I'll be going to Old Davidsonville early in the morning. Do you want to come?"

Even though his eyelids stretched wide, Jace dipped his chin in agreement.

Tammy spread butter on a soft piece of honey wheat bread and handed it to Mama. "Will you watch Castle for me tomorrow?"

"Sure. What do you have planned?"

"Jace and I want to go on an excursion tomorrow morning."

"Really? Where to?"

Heat traveled from Tammy's neck to the top of her head, and her eyes grew to the size of the slice of bread she held.

Mama's brows rose, and a grin tugged at her lips. "Nevermind. You two enjoy yourselves. Castle and I will have a day out."

Later that night, Tammy tossed and turned so many times she felt like a ceiling fan. She didn't care one way or the other if she saw Jace again. Then what would cause the tingles of nerves to flow through Tammy's body? Surely not anticipation of the day ahead. Castle moved to the end of the bed. Tammy kicked the cover off and rolled onto her back. Castle huffed and jumped off the bed.

She didn't blame him.

chapter fifty-nine

EVEN THOUGH THE SUN beat down, the wind had a chill to it on Black River. Jace could tell Tammy kept a lid on her emotions. After his early morning call with Leo, he knew the feeling. She had apologized for calling him a murderer but also said he needed to go back to West Memphis to work on Una's case. She even accused him of chasing a ghost of a relationship with Tammy.

A tiny jolt cut through the left of his heart. Could Leo be right? No, his relationship with Tammy had improved over the past month. At least she had stopped acting like she hated the sight of him.

Tammy ran her hand down the seat cushion in Ellis's fishing boat. She picked up an orange life jacket and hugged it to her chest.

"Let me know where you want to pull over." Jace raised his voice so Tammy could hear him over the boat motor and wind.

She gave a thumbs up.

Jace studied her side profile as she scanned the river bank. He would never understand how she was still single. It must be by choice. Or maybe it was his fault. Had he made her so bitter she refused to give love a shot?

He slowed the boat to a snail's pace and followed Tammy's gaze as he killed the motor. Trees of various colors lined the rocky shore. Some green with hints of brown, a few cherry red, and several orange ones. Jace wondered what kind of animal made the tracks on the muddy banks. Even though the bank held plenty of mud, Jace could see shadows of boulders on the bottom of the lake near the shore.

"I can't believe Castle is scared of water," Jace said.

Tammy shrugged. "I figure he had a bad experience with water before I found him."

"Found him?"

Tammy's face glowed with happiness as she recounted the story. "Uncle Ellis is the one who spotted him behind a dumpster one year when he'd come for a visit. We'd driven to Savannah to sightsee."

"Was he a pup when y'all found him?"

She dipped her hand in the water and turned it in circles. "Yes, a sweet little baby, skinny as a rail and scared to death."

Jace started the motor and eased down the river. They went around a slight bend, and he stopped the boat. Something white caught in a pile of wood floated near the bank. Jace rubbed his eyes and took another look. The tiny hairs on his arms stood at attention as he narrowed his gaze to make out the object.

Tammy said something Jace couldn't make out. His mind centered around whatever had been snagged by the wood pile. "Take a look at that pile of wood. I thought I saw something out of place."

She let out a whoosh of air. "Get closer. I think that's a body."

"A body?" His breath caught in his throat.

"Yes." Tammy pulled her phone out. Her lashes flew high right before her mouth set in a grim line. Within seconds, a man from emergency services answered and dispatched an ambulance and police.

Jace killed the engine next to the body. "This is as close as we can get."

She slipped on a pair of gloves and gently tugged at the body until she could check for a pulse. "She's gone."

"She?"

"Yes." Tammy turned to Jace, her face two sheets whiter than normal. "Jace, I think we just found Lorene Pankey."

His heart dropped to his stomach. "Is she recognizable?"

"No, but her hair is the same color as Lorene's." Tammy bit her bottom lip. "For some reason, she's wearing a red nightgown."

"I'm so sorry." Jace longed to rush to the other end of the boat and wrap Tammy in his arms.

She tossed her phone to Jace. "Look at the messages I got right before I called 911."

Jace looked at the screen, his heart in his throat.

Her death is your fault.

The second message caused a fear Jace hadn't felt in many years to settle in his stomach. He scanned the area for movement and saw nothing but peaceful calm, which couldn't have been more of a contrast to his insides that churned like a raging sea during a hurricane. He looked at Tammy and then reread the message.

Until you find my gold, more bodies will come.

chapter sixty

ONCE THE POLICE FINISHED questioning Tammy and Jace, they went straight to Mama's and filled her in on everything. Tammy thought it best that Mama knew the whole story in case anything else happened. Together, they came up with the craziest plan imaginable.

As soon as the town died down and no one roamed the streets, they put their plan in motion. Tammy took a deep breath and shimmied inside the only unlocked window at Lorene's trailer house. Her hand slipped, and she cracked her elbow on the metal around the glass. That's probably less than she deserved.

"You all right?"

Even though Jace whispered, his voice caused Tammy to bump her head on the top of the window. "Ouch," she said as she landed on the carpeted floor. "I'm fine."

After she took inventory of the space, Tammy tiptoed to the back door and unlocked it for Mama. At least she hoped the person in all black, including a ski mask and gloves, was Mama.

Their lookout guy, also known as Jace, jogged across the yard and disappeared. Mama headed down the hall-way, leaving Tammy to catch up.

Mama opened a door and disappeared inside. Light flickered across the bedroom from her flashlight. Tammy froze in place when the light landed on a person wearing a pink gown with enough sequins to furnish an entire beauty pageant lineup. The person turned out to be a mannequin. The rest of the bedroom followed suit, with pink everywhere.

By the time Tammy finished examining the place, Mama had gone through an entire dresser. "There is nothing but clothes in here," Mama announced.

Tammy rummaged through the white side table. It held a stack of letters, face moisturizer, and toenail fungus cream. She shined the light on the letter on top of the stack and gasped.

Mama trotted across the room. "What is it, Tammy Gail?"

Tammy gritted her teeth. "Somebody has been threatening Lorene's sister. Read this."

Your sister looked nice today. I wonder if her pink sweater would look good smeared in blood?

Tammy laid the first page aside and read through the rest. Her phone buzzed, but Tammy couldn't tear her eyes away from the papers.

Keep your mouth shut, or your sister will pay the price.
I bet Ellis wishes you'd stayed quiet. Have you seen your sister lately?
Go to the police, and you'll get to watch your sister die.

Mama gripped Tammy's forearm like she was about to fall off a cliff, and Tammy's arm was the only thing that could save her. "What in the world have we stumbled into?"

"I'm not sure, Mama. At first, I thought Uncle Ellis had gotten involved in something that got him killed, but now I think it was Lorene who drug him into her mess."

"Are you certain that was Lorene in the river?"

"Certain? No. The woman in the river had the same color hair as Lorene, but that's it." Tammy scanned underneath the bed. "The more I think about it, I believe the woman in the river was younger than Lorene."

"Oh, I sure hope it wasn't her." Mama paused. "Not that I'm wishing death on someone else."

"I know that, Mama." Tammy used the bed to pull herself off the floor.

Chirps from a wall clock sounded in the hallway. Mama's shoulders jerked, and she let out a nervous laugh. "What next?"

"Let's finish looking for clues to where Lorene went."

The front door closed, and heavy footsteps came in their direction. Tammy met Mama's wide-eyed gaze and nodded toward the bathroom. Right before Tammy pulled her gun, the bedroom light came on, and a familiar voice floated into the bathroom.

"I know you're in there, Ruby," Sheriff Obie said.

Mama opened the bathroom door and shrugged. "What are you doing here, Obie?"

Laughter poured from Sheriff Obie when he laid eyes on Mama. "Y'all remind me of that one robber from Home Alone." He sat on Lorene's bed as tears flowed from his fit of merriment.

Mama's eyes tightened at the corners, and her hand flew to her hip. "This is not funny."

He dabbed his cheeks with a handkerchief and gave Tammy a look layered with amusement. "What hair-brained scheme have you done got your mama involved in?"

Tammy's gaze bounced from Sheriff Obie to Jace, who leaned against the door frame. Heat ran up her neck, and she frowned. "We're looking for clues. If you were half the sheriff you were supposed to be, you'd be doing the same thing."

That seemed to sober the sheriff from his fit of laughter. "Now listen here –"

"I apologize. I have no idea what you've been doing, so that was uncalled for," Tammy cut him off.

The relief in his tone couldn't be missed. "I appreciate that. Now, would you three like to explain why you broke into Miss Pankey's house here or down at the station?"

Mama sucked in a deep breath and marched close to where Obie sat. "What do you mean?"

He chuckled. "I need you to understand you can't just break into people's homes, Ruby. It's against the law."

"I know that. But you're not taking us to the station." Mama prissed across the room. She stopped by Jace and put her eyes on the sheriff. "Now, get on up and take me to the house. We'll fill you in over a cup of coffee."

Sheriff Obie glanced at Tammy as he linked his hand through Mama's. "That's fine as long as Tammy ain't the one making it."

chapter sixty-one

As it turned out, Sheriff Obie made the coffee while Mama changed clothes. Afterward, they sat around the kitchen table. Tammy shared pictures of the letters they found at Lorene's.

"Tammy, you oughta know better than to break into somebody's house." Sheriff Obie tapped his finger on the side of the green coffee cup.

She had the grace to blush. "You're right."

"Is there anything else you're keeping from me?" He looked from Jace to Mama and then stopped at Tammy.

"Just that I've been getting threatening text messages about finding gold." She stared intently to see his reaction.

He set his coffee cup down and sighed. "Ruby, you know how dangerous this situation is. Please don't keep anything else from me. If Tammy don't tell me, I need you to."

"I will, Obie." Mama cast her eyes downward. "I promise."

He nodded, seeming to accept Mama at her word. "Let me read the messages. I'll run a trace on the number."

Tammy pulled her chair close to his and scrolled to the first message. "Each message has come from a different burner phone."

"Y'all ain't got a lick of sense. I expect to be kept in the loop, Tammy." The tone of his voice hardened. "I don't want Ruby, or anyone else, in danger."

The look in his eyes left little doubt that he cared for Mama. A lot. "I give you my word. I'll keep you updated." She sipped her coffee. "As a matter of fact, we're going to Poplar Bluff Library tomorrow for a book signing event."

The Poplar Bluff library smelled of flowery perfume and books. Tammy glanced around the room and took it all in. Tables full of writers selling books lined the walls at the Author Fair, where Regina Carter was featured as a local author. Most authors already had small crowds bustling around them.

The woman who stood in line beside Mama put her hand on Mama's arm. When she moved, Tammy got another whiff of the perfume, and now her mouth tasted like it.

Tammy missed the first half of what the woman said, but the last part had Tammy's radar going off. "My daughter is Regina Carter." She beamed. "This is her first local author event."

"Oh, I know her." Mama clasped her hands together, seeming to be poised to give the performance of her life. "She's married to a sweet young man from my hometown."

The woman's mouth fell open. "You're from Pocahontas?"

Mama nodded, a big grin splitting her face. "We sure are."

"I went to school with Anthony. I thought that name sounded familiar when Mama asked me to come to this event."

"I'm Diana Prichards. Did you good folks come all this way just to attend the author event?"

"Mama is a big reader, and we thought it would be fun."

"I'm looking forward to reading another one of Regina's books," Mama said as she scrambled backward to keep a little boy from knocking her down. She raised a brow but kept her focus on Miss Prichards. "I love supporting local folks."

A man raced toward the little boy and scooped him up. He stopped in front of Mama. "Bryson, tell this nice lady you're sorry for almost knocking her over."

The boy looked at his hands as he twisted them together. "I'm sorry, ma'am."

"That's okay. Thank you for apologizing."

Miss Prichards watched them leave the room. "We're thankful Regina was able to come. Did you know about the bad wreck they had a couple of weeks after moving here?"

"No, what happened?"

"A man swerved to miss a dog and hit their car instead. Poor Anthony had to have back surgery. Regina and Penny were hurt, but thankfully, not as bad."

By that time, the crowd around Regina's table had disappeared. As they made their way over, a sense of *deja vu* attacked Tammy's senses. She licked her lips and picked up a book about a lost prince as Mama and Miss

Prichards dominated the conversation for the first few minutes.

"This is my daughter, Tammy," Mama said, pointing a book in Tammy's direction.

"Oh! The one who moved off to Georgia?" Regina Carter held her hand out. "It's nice to meet you, Tammy." She glanced at the book in Tammy's hand. "Are you a reader?"

"Mmm, not particularly." Tammy shook Regina's offered hand. Apparently, Mama had told Regina about Tammy moving off. No telling what else. "I just finished reading a Jane Austen novel of Mama's, though."

Excitement practically emanated from Regina as she bounced on her toes. "I love Jane Austen. She's the inspiration behind The Lost Prince."

For a moment, Tammy got lost in Regina's enthusiasm and almost forgot why they were there. From the look on Mama's face, she did, too. "Really? What's it about?"

"A woman writer from the nineteenth century who finds a lost prince close to death on her parent's land." She bit the bottom of her lip, and her eyes turned misty. "It's about her journey as a spinster who finally falls in love with a man who's the last person she should've even met, much less loved."

"That sounds good." Mama handed Regina the book in her hand. "I'll take a copy as long as you sign it."

"Of course." Regina's lips curved into a smile.

"Tell them about the bad wreck that almost killed poor Anthony." Miss Prichards put her hand on her hip, pinning Regina with her gaze.

Before Regina answered, a man in a wheelchair stopped directly beside them. "Miss Ruby, Tammy

Sharp?" Anthony Carter's head cocked, and he smiled. "I thought that was you."

After a hug, they spent a few minutes discussing the accident. Anthony's lips slid into a frown. "I've learned a greater appreciation for life, that's for certain."

"When did you say it happened?" Tammy tucked a fly-away hair behind her ear.

"Almost four months ago."

"I'm glad everyone is okay," Tammy said, ruling out their family as suspects. She'd verify the dates, but there would've been no way a man with a broken back could've killed Uncle Ellis.

"Have you seen your daddy lately?" Mama tucked a curl behind her ear as she noticed the man at the next table ogling her.

"You mean Lewis?" Anthony's cheeks reddened. "He came up here a few weeks after the wreck. Why do you ask?"

"Just wondering," Mama replied, ignoring the man from the table next to them, who had walked closer to where she stood.

Two hours and seven author tables later, they headed home with five novels, several bookmarks, and a t-shirt. Mama even scored a set of Bigfoot earrings.

At least the day hadn't been entirely wasted.

chapter sixty-two

As the door swung shut behind Tammy, she stepped into Dora's Sale Barn Café. The tantalizing scent of freshly brewed coffee and sizzling bacon filled the air.

The café bustled with hunters dressed in camouflage, eagerly seeking a hearty breakfast before their day in the woods.

She peeled her white puffer jacket off, glanced at her black slim-fitting Nike joggers, and smiled. She may never wear blue jeans again. Ha. Of course, she would. She loved the feel of blue jeans against her skin.

Jace turned, and his gaze lingered on her hoodie. He grinned and said, "That's fitting."

She shrugged. Last Christmas, Thomas and Sybil bought Tammy a hoodie that said, "I catch killers for a living. What's your superpower?" Even though she'd never buy it herself, she loved it.

A middle-aged woman with salt and pepper hair that hung past her shoulders buzzed by, talking as she walked. "I have you guys a booth getting cleaned. Give me a few minutes."

A group of older women caught their attention as they waited for their table. Vivian White waved them over.

After they exchanged greetings, Miss Vivian smiled at Tammy. "I wanted to let you know the police found my car."

"That's good. Where was it?"

Miss Vivian's eyes darted to the door when a group of men entered. Tammy followed her gaze and inwardly groaned. Douglas and Fred McCoy stood in line for a table with Lewis Carter not far behind them. Even after Tammy smiled in greeting, Douglas gave her the stink eye. She needed to find out what his problem was.

"Pardon?" Miss Vivian fiddled with her hair, her gaze locked on the three men.

Understanding dawned on Tammy. Miss Vivian must have a crush on one of them. Tammy took another look. Fred and Lewis were both decent-looking older men. Douglas wouldn't be unattractive if he'd learn how to smile.

"I just asked where they found your car."

"Oh." Miss Vivian's lips pinched upward. "It was parked at an old house in Walnut Ridge. At one of them places where Sonny got his poison."

"I'm glad they found it." Jace nodded at the ladies before he touched Tammy's back. "I'm gonna go ahead and go to our booth. It's ready."

Lewis Carter cleared his throat as he took Jace's spot beside Tammy. His eyes traveled over each woman at the table and lingered on Miss Vivian. "Morning, ladies."

The women at the table seemed to be in a competition for who could smile and bat their eyes the longest. Miss Vivan blushed.

A couple of minutes later, Tammy excused herself to join Jace. The corners of her mouth edged upward as she leaned across the booth. "I think Miss Vivian has a crush on Lewis Carter."

He cast a glance at the table of older folks. "I think you may be right."

Their waitress, a teenager with streaks of purple layered throughout her blonde hair, set two cups of coffee down and took their orders.

While waiting for their food, Tammy filled Jace in on the trip to Poplar Bluff. He agreed to keep Anthony Carter off the murder board.

Lewis Carter slid into the booth behind them. He nodded at Tammy and picked up the menu. His gaze darted to Miss Vivian's table. Tammy grinned. It looked like he might be interested in one of the ladies. Hopefully, it was Miss Vivian. At least somebody could get some romance going.

Tammy added sugar and cream to her coffee. She took a sip and cringed. After she added another sugar packet, it tasted nearly perfect. She lowered the cup and met Douglas's stony gaze. He looked away and picked up a newspaper.

"I don't think Douglas McCoy likes me," Tammy said.

Jace's shoulder twitched. "From what I've seen, I don't think he likes anybody."

Tammy's head tilted to the left and back straight. Jace was probably right. Mama was the only person she'd noticed Douglas smile at. "Mama said Sheriff Obie plans to leave for Jonesboro this afternoon."

"That's good." Jace shifted in his seat. "I hope his friend finds something to lead us to the person who left the snake at Ellis's."

"Yeah, I doubt it, though."

The waitress brought their plates over. The stack of pancakes with a side of bacon made Tammy's mouth water as she drizzled maple syrup on top of the creamy butter.

Jace licked his lips, slathered his toast in peach jelly, and piled a fried egg and hashbrowns on top of it like a sandwich. "I still can't believe Castle was pouting last night when we got to your mama's."

Tammy eyeballed Jace as peach jelly and egg yolk dripped down his lip. "Yeah, he hates being left alone."

He washed the bite down with coffee. "What did you do with him in Atlanta while you worked?"

Tammy bit the side of her lip to keep from laughing at the food on his face. "Doggie daycare."

Another bite, and then, "That's a thing?"

The pancake delivered a taste of maple and creamy butter. "Yeah, it is. I actually found one here, too."

"Seriously?"

"Yep. It's home-based, but Harry vouched for her, and she has excellent reviews." Her lips twitched as Jace took another bite of his homemade sandwich.

"What do you keep smiling at?"

Instead of telling him, she snapped a picture of the trail of food and turned her phone around. "I'm sorry. I've been laughing at your expense," she said as she embraced the laughter, demanding to escape her chest.

He wiped his mouth and gave a fake, stern look. "You should be ashamed."

She cracked a grin that came close to a smirk. "Well, I'm not."

His eyes took on a stormy look before he laid his hand on hers. "You're beautiful."

The touch of his hand, combined with his words, caused heat to pump through Tammy's heart.

Before she commented, their waitress buzzed by and turned the television up so loud that people who drove by could probably hear it.

Breaking News flashed across the screen as a local reporter stood in front of Black River. "The body found by a couple who were out fishing earlier this week has been identified as Abigail Hunt. We spoke to her parents, who said the twenty-seven-year-old had taken a week off work at the First Trust Bank to hike and explore."

Douglas McCoy stood so fast that his chair fell backward. He laid a bill on the table and rushed out the door with Fred McCoy right behind him.

Tammy's gaze remained on the door as it drifted closed.

chapter sixty-three

THE FORD TAURUS IDLES as I wait for the red light to change to green. Sheriff Obie had gotten a few cars ahead, which was perfect. I didn't want him to notice he had a tail.

If the sheriff thought the snake or box would provide answers, he would be better off taking a desk job and letting somebody else be sheriff.

An impatient person in one of the cars lined up at the light honked when I didn't move fast enough through the intersection.

Jonesboro drivers could be ridiculous.

About like Detective Sharp.

That woman meddled more than Ellis ever had. Too bad for her. She'd soon be reminded of what happened to people who failed to mind their own business.

Now, her focus needed to be on finding where Ellis hid the gold instead of who killed him. It's not like finding out would bring him back.

So why bother?

I'd never understand why people focused on the dead. I knew how to let people go. Mother taught me that.

At least I found something to admire about Detective Sharp. The way she found the listening devices was impressive. That had earned her the right to live.

After she hands me the gold, whether she kept that right was yet to be seen.

chapter sixty-four

SNORES SOUNDED FROM THE foot of Tammy's bed. Tammy raised her head and stared at Castle. He had both her legs pinned down with his body. She wiggled until he moved over a few inches.

After laying both paws over his face, he snuggled into the fluffy comforter. Almost seven, and she couldn't believe he hadn't woken her up yet.

The doorbell rang before footsteps sounded down the hallway. She slipped out of bed and pulled on a robe. A cup of coffee called her name right about now.

"Tammy!"

Whoever was at the door must've brought news Mama didn't like. Tammy tripped over Castle's rope toy and stumbled across the room. She glared at him as she limped to the door.

The front door closed, and Mama met Tammy in the hallway. "That was Officer Rayburn. Obie's in the hospital." She speed-walked past Tammy and disappeared into her room. "He may not make it."

A pang struck Tammy's middle as she followed Mama. "What happened?"

A hanger flipped out of the closet when Mama snatched an oversized sweater. "He didn't come home last night. Somebody found him wrapped around a tree outside of Bono."

"Didn't you talk to him last night?" Tammy picked the hanger up and hung it in the closet.

Mama slipped on a pair of skinny jeans and thigh-high black leather boots. "I guess we spoke around seven. He said he was staying in Jonesboro for dinner with friends. That's the last I heard from him."

"Oh, Mama, I'm sorry."

"Don't be sorry just yet." She pulled a brush through her hair. With a sigh, she stopped and stared at Tammy. "Why are you standing around? Get dressed. I need you to drive me to Jonesboro."

"Of course. Give me five minutes."

"Make it three. I'll ask Jace to watch Castle while you're getting ready."

Fifteen minutes later, Tammy nursed a Nutmeg Latte from the Busy Bean while Mama prattled on about Tammy needing to hurry.

Tammy put her coffee in the holder and peered at Mama. The woman who never left the house without her makeup on and hair done sat there makeup-free, wearing a baseball cap.

Maybe Tammy shouldn't say never. When Tammy was twelve, she cut her arm open when she crawled under an old lawn chair. Uncle Ellis had screamed for Mama, and they'd rushed her to the clinic. Mama had just gotten out of the shower, so her hair was soaking wet, and her face was free of makeup.

"I think you like Sheriff Obie more than you've let on."

"What makes you say that?"

"Well, for one, you're about to tap a hole in my floor-board. Two, you left the house without a shower or even a smidge of makeup."

The only response Tammy got was a grunt. Tammy took the hint and gave Mama her time to pray or think the rest of the way to Jonesboro.

They passed Fat City and a Starbucks that Mama polite-ly told Tammy she could not stop at. Tammy kept quiet as she pulled into a parking lot full of cars at the hospital.

As soon as they walked through the double doors, the preacher, Todd Herrera, waved them over to the waiting area. He stood and limped up to Mama and gave her a hug. "Miss Ruby, I pray you're doing okay."

"Better than it looks like you are. What's going on with your foot?"

"My gout flared up last night, so I'm having a hard time walking, but I'll be just fine."

"I'm sorry to hear that." Mama led him to the seats, and he waved his hand to decline to sit. "Is there any news on Obie?"

The preacher glanced at the floor, and he wore an expression like he found something distasteful in his line of sight. "He's still in surgery. It looks like he will be for a while."

"Okay, then we wait and pray," Mama said.

"Most certainly. Here comes Obie's son, Erwin. Hope-fully, he has an update."

Mama's face paled as a man who looked to be in his late forties stopped beside the preacher. He wore his dark brown hair in a combover in an attempt to hide his bald head. He narrowed his eyes as his gaze traveled up and down Mama.

"I know who you are. You're that Ruby Sharp woman who's after my daddy." He reminded Tammy of an old-school, slimy car salesman when he spoke.

Mama's spine visibly stiffened as she attempted to plaster on a smile.

Before Mama could respond, Tammy dropped her purse on the ground and closed the space between herself and the rude man. She met him eye to eye. "How dare you speak to my mama like that."

The preacher swallowed and shook his head. "Miss Ruby is a good woman, Erwin."

Erwin's left eye twitched as he and Tammy continued their staring contest. "Apologies. I'm a little upset right now, and that came out wrong." His lips curved into a half smile.

When Erwin smiled, most people would probably feel at ease. His smile seemed genuine. Caring and apologetic, even. But as Tammy's eyes linked to his, she had no doubt he had a sick, maybe even perverse side that he hid well.

Mama's eyes glistened, and she moved closer to Erwin. In the process, she blocked Tammy from his view. "That's completely understandable. How is Obie?"

He opened a piece of peppermint candy and popped it in his mouth before he answered. "I don't know for sure. All they've said is that one of his legs was crushed in the wreck, and they have a lot of work to do on him."

Liar. "That's all you've been told?" Tammy gritted her teeth to keep from saying something more that she'd come to regret.

"Oh, they said something about him being unconscious because of a poison or something."

"Caused by the wreck?" Mama's voice raised an octave.

"No, I don't think so. They said cyanide poisoning likely caused the heart attack and crash."

Mama squeezed Tammy's arm. "Heart attack?"

Erwin's phone rang, and he excused himself before he answered Mama's question.

Tammy's mind raced. Cyanide poison? Where could Sheriff Obie have contacted cyanide?

Her phone buzzed with a text. She dug it out of her purse, and the air in her lungs stilled as she read the message.

> *Follow the instructions, or more people will suffer for your inability.*

> *What do you mean?*

> *Don't be stupid. Find the gold. Or else.*

Tammy walked down the hall by the cafeteria. She dialed the number, not expecting an answer. She gasped when a robotic voice sounded on the other end. "Detective Sharp. I sometimes think you're smarter than you let on."

"Who is this? What do you want?"

"Then you ask questions like that, and I realize you're rather slow. Who I am does not matter. What I want is the gold. Find it, Detective Sharp. Before it's too late."

chapter sixty-five

THE HOSPITAL CAFETERIA BRIMMED with several people patiently waiting in line. The delicious aroma of gravy and steak sauce wafted through the air, making Tammy's stomach grumble as she stood by, waiting for Mama to decide what she wanted.

Sheriff Obie had made it through surgery but was still unconscious. The doctor said the pain medication would help him to sleep for at least a few hours.

Even though he hadn't woken up, Erwin had the nerve to ask them to leave. Said he wanted time alone with his daddy. Mama had understood, or at least she said she did. At any rate, Mama needed a break.

After they decided on medium rare ribeyes and all the fixings, they made their way to a corner table. Tammy took a few minutes to observe Mama as they ate in silence. Her normal bouncy curls drooped on her shoulders, and her face looked almost haggard and worn.

"Mama, I think we should go home so you can get some rest."

Mama's glass of sweet tea clanked on the table. "I can't rest right now. Obie needs me."

"He wouldn't want you wearing yourself down. You know that," Tammy said.

Mama changed the subject. Tears brimmed on her lids. "I still can't believe that was Abigail Hunt you found on the river."

Tammy swallowed the bite of steak and laid her hand on Mama's. "I know."

"Her poor parents are just devastated. Will you go with me to the funeral?"

"Of course, I will," Tammy said as she pinched the bridge of her nose. "I just wonder where Lorene is."

"I hope she's okay, wherever she may be." Mama pushed her half-full plate to the side and went for another drink of sweet tea.

"I have a feeling she holds the clues to finding out who killed Uncle Ellis."

Mama's eyes flared with anger. "I fear you may be right, Tammy Gail."

Tammy pondered whether she should share the conversation from earlier with Mama. Mama had too many worries already, and Tammy couldn't bear to add another. She'd tell her after Sheriff Obie woke up.

Someone called Tammy's name from across the cafeteria. She looked up and met Pat Wood's hawkish gaze. "Hello Tammy, Miss Sharp."

The heat of a blush settled on Tammy's cheeks as she tore her gaze away from his. She'd never experienced feeling like a person's favorite dessert at a sweet lover's convention. Until now. It wasn't a feeling she appreciated. Pat Wood had a good-looking face, that was for sure, but he didn't make her heart flutter as Jace did. Life would be much simpler if only she could somehow get her heart to cooperate.

The thought of Jace caused a surge of blood to stampede through her veins. Mama and Pat's words sounded like they came from the end of a cell phone in the middle of nowhere. Somehow, Pat ended up sitting directly beside Tammy. She swiveled in his direction. "Hello, Pat. I wasn't expecting to see you here."

A trifle of a smile crossed his lips. "I've been here with my dad, and I'm happy to say he's getting released today."

Duh. "I'm so sorry. With everything going on, I forgot."

"No worries." An expression of concern creased his forehead. "How's the sheriff? I heard he had a bad wreck."

"He's in a room, but we don't know exactly what will happen," Mama said.

Erwin walked into the cafeteria, his shoulders hunched over, and he eyeballed people like they trespassed on private property. He strolled up to their table and openly gawked at Pat before he addressed Mama. "Daddy's awake, and he's asking for you."

Mama sprang to her feet. Her face brightened with happiness. She kissed Erwin's cheek before she charged out of the cafeteria.

A surprised look passed over Erwin's features as he sloped his head to the right, seeming to watch Mama. He nodded at Tammy before his footsteps carried him deeper into the dining room. Tammy found it odd that he never removed his left hand from the pocket of his blue jeans.

Pat stood, his hand on the back of Tammy's chair. "I hope to see you soon for our dinner date."

As he left, Tammy eyed him through a low-lashed gaze. Pat Wood had been in Jonesboro all week. He had time and opportunity to poison Sheriff Obie. But what motive would he have? The gold? He *had* spent quite a bit of time with Uncle Ellis before he died. Maybe he and Uncle Ellis met that night, and Pat killed him before he realized the gold wasn't there. Tammy inclined her head in his direction as her mind worked out possible scenarios.

Before Pat fully exited the cafeteria, he turned toward Erwin, and they exchanged a stare that Tammy would call nothing but deadly.

Erwin would've known Uncle Ellis because of his daddy. Could he be the one looking for the gold? Tammy tapped her chin as she continued to ponder the situation.

Looks like she had a few changes to make to the murder board.

chapter sixty-six

JACE SHOVED THE DOOR of his rental closed and pointed at Castle's water bowl. They'd spent the morning at the newspaper office before Jace took Castle on a walk-turned-run. Castle had more energy than a puppy. "You about wore me out, Castle."

The doorbell pinged. On the other side stood Jace's friend and lead Homicide Detective from West Memphis, Arnold Davidson. Arnold's parents must've loved the Terminator movies and named him after the main character. With Arnold's massive height and bulky, muscled physique, the name fit him perfectly.

After the situation with Leo, Jace considered slamming the door in his face.

Arnold held both meaty hands up. "Look, I know you're probably mad, but can I at least explain?"

Jace moved away from the door and pulled his hair into a ponytail. "Mad? You told my daughter I killed Una. I would say I'm more than mad."

Arnold glanced at Castle before he pushed the black leather coat down and off his shoulders. "Look, we were tossing around naming you as a suspect to put the killer at ease. Leo's buddy at the station overheard part of the conversation." He paused. "The wrong part."

"Obviously."

"I heard what happened with y'all, and I'm really sorry, man." He jabbed a thumb toward the sofa. "You may want to sit down for what I'm about to tell you."

A surge of hope teetered through Jace as he lowered himself onto the recliner. "Have you found her killer?"

Steel gray eyes met Jace's, and Arnold nodded. "Jace, we got him."

Even though Jace sat in the recliner, he lost strength in his legs. "Who was it?"

His lips slid into a thin line. "Do you remember Slate Sanders?"

Jace's brows twitched together, and at the same time, his pulse skyrocketed. "The Slate Sanders that Leo dated?"

Castle whined and laid his head on Jace's leg. He rubbed Castle's neck, desperately needing the comfort Castle so willingly provided.

Arnold let out a long breath. "Yep. I drove here when we got done booking him into custody."

"What made y'all think Slate Sanders killed her?" His foot seemed to be dead set on tapping a hole in the floor.

"We tied him to a small gang that rose to power in the Memphis area the year Una was killed."

"So the home invasion was for sure gang-related?" Bile pooled at the base of Jace's throat.

"It was. What sealed the case against Slate was one of our newly recruited CIs confirmed Slate murdered Una as an initiation into the gang."

As his bowels trembled, Jace itched to punch something. Anything. "My wife was murdered so Slate could join a gang. I can't believe this. He said he had to work. I should've been there."

"You couldn't have known this would happen." Arnold's steady gaze anchored Jace.

Jace glanced at his phone. "I need to call Leo."

Arnold stood and picked up his coat. "I'll leave you to it. Holler if you need anything."

Jace rose and extended his hand. "Thank you for coming. I appreciate it, man."

Later that afternoon, Jace pulled the blinds away from the window. They clinked against the glass as he walked away. Tammy should be home by now, and he needed to tell her about his decisions.

A few minutes later, he opened the front door and stared outside. He had so much he needed to sort out, yet his brain seemed to want to shut down. Tammy's Bronco eased down the street as if she read his mind. Jace pulled a deep green hoodie over his t-shirt and whistled for Castle to follow him.

Castle bounced down the steps and lit into high gear when he saw Tammy. Within seconds, Castle danced around Tammy as sweet laughter left her lips. Jace imagined her reaction if he ran up to her like that. She probably wouldn't laugh and look at him with the same love she bestowed on Castle, that's for sure.

Yet, he had to be thankful their relationship had improved over the past few weeks. After all these years, she'd finally forgiven him. He felt she looked at him as a friend. Maybe more. He just hoped she wouldn't hate him for what he had to do.

Miss Ruby waved before she disappeared inside the house. Tammy motioned for Jace to follow.

"I was so thankful to hear about the sheriff waking up." Jace sank onto the couch.

Tammy claimed the seat farthest from Jace. "Yes, that was the best possible outcome." Tammy cocked her head. "What's wrong?"

He squared his shoulders and met Tammy's concerned gaze. "They made an arrest in Una's murder."

She moved to sit directly beside him and wrapped his hand in hers. "I'm so happy for you, Jace. Does Leo know?"

He nodded as his eyes focused on their hands. "Yes, we spoke earlier. She's devastated."

Tammy's grip on his hand loosened. "Why? I mean, I understand this must be a lot to process for her. And you."

"It's not just that. The person they arrested for Una's murder is Leo's ex-boyfriend."

Her mouth dropped open. "Oh wow. I'm so sorry."

"I have to go home, Tammy. Leo needs me now more than ever."

She stood and walked across the room. "That makes sense."

"I hope you understand." Jace closed the space between them and pulled her hand into his.

"I do understand." She tugged her hand away and waved it in the air. "If I had a child, I'd do the same thing."

"Tammy..."

"Look, it's okay. I'll be going home to Atlanta as soon as I find Uncle Ellis's killer anyway."

The fried bologna sandwich he had eaten for lunch threatened to come back up. "You're leaving?"

"It's for the best." She stuck her hand out like they were business partners shaking hands as they parted ways.

Jace swallowed a few times and grasped her hand in his. "So this is goodbye?"

"This is goodbye. Look on the bright side…at least we're parting on good terms this time." A half smile graced her perfect lips. "I truly wish you the best, Jace."

With those last words, Tammy padded down the hall with Castle on her heels. The thud as the door closed made things seem so final. Flames of heat ravaged Jace's chest as his hand dropped to his side. He raced out of the house before he allowed the sobs to overtake him.

chapter sixty-seven

IF TAMMY HAD LEARNED anything over the past few months, it was how things could change in the blink of an eye. It seemed like yesterday she had been working side by side with Thomas, doing everything in their power to bring killers to justice.

All it took was a bullet smaller than her finger to change her entire life. If she was honest, her life had changed for the better and the worse. She'd grown closer to Mama and rekindled a relationship with Jace. If only she'd known how much of a weight forgiveness released, she would've sought Jace out years earlier.

On the other hand, losing Uncle Ellis had widened the hole she'd carried in her heart since Daddy died. A hole that would never completely close. But maybe, just maybe, it could be patched.

She kissed Castle on the side of his head before she grabbed his leash. "What do you say we go for a walk and look for gold?"

A few minutes later, Tammy clicked the blinker left to head out of the neighborhood. She desperately needed to figure out where Uncle Ellis would've hidden gold. It wasn't at his house. Could he have a safety deposit box she didn't know about? Or a storage unit? If she couldn't find the gold, then maybe she needed to offer money to the person who kept messaging her. She could set him up. Money seemed to be his top priority. Did it have to be gold? She'd sell everything she owned to keep anyone else from dying. This would warrant looking into.

A cool breeze tickled her hair from the open window. She glanced down the street and turned her blinker off. Nicole and Harry had made it home from their trip. It wouldn't hurt to say hi and welcome them back.

Nicole bustled through the front door and slammed it. "Stay away from me."

Harry followed her outside, waving his hands in the air. "I said I'm sorry. What more do you want?"

Tammy rolled the window up and slipped out the door, purposely leaving Castle inside. "Hey, you two. What's going on?"

Splotches of red lined both their cheeks, giving Tammy the impression they'd both been crying. Nicole rushed up to Tammy. "Will you please take me somewhere?"

Harry threw a hand in the air. "Go ahead, Tammy. Take her somewhere so she can be away from me." He turned red-rimmed eyes on Nicole. "I'll be here when you are ready to discuss what I have done."

As the door shut behind Harry, Nicole settled in the passenger seat and buried her face in Castle's neck. She didn't stop the sobs until Tammy got on the road heading toward Davidsonville Historic State Park. "He lost everything."

Not sure if she heard her right, Tammy glanced at Nicole, dread lining her stomach. "I didn't understand you."

"He lost all the money we had saved betting on those stupid horses." Nicole wiped her nose on a Sonic napkin. "Every last penny and then some."

"Oh. Wow, I'm sorry, Nicole."

"He's the sorry one." Her eyes widened, and she gasped like she remembered something worse. "Look at me going on and on about my life when poor Abigail Hunt lost her life on the river, and the sheriff almost died in a car wreck."

"A lot is going on, that's for sure." Tammy glanced at Nicole, who had Castle hugged tight. "But that doesn't discount what you're going through."

Tears glistened on her lashes as she loosened her grip on Castle. "How could he do this?"

"I don't know, but I understand that gambling can be very addictive."

"Why are we at Old Davidsonville?"

Tammy parked in an empty space. A man looked up from the grill outside his RV and waved. She waved back before she gave Nicole her full attention. "I've been trying to remember where we used to camp with Uncle Ellis. Do you mind? Maybe you can gather your thoughts before going back to see Harry."

The nip in the air smelled of earth and green plants. Trees of various sizes stood everywhere around them. Several had fallen or had limbs and brown leaves scattered around them. Tammy had a sudden urge to shimmy to the top of one but shook it off. That line of thinking was what got people hurt. She would've had no problem climbing one when she'd been younger. Uncle Ellis would have laughed and told her to get down before she hurt herself. This place had gotten her through many hard times as a youth. It held a freedom she'd desperately needed back then.

Nicole's voice interrupted Tammy's walk down memory lane. "I remember coming out here with y'all. You and Jace used to sneak off."

"No, we did not!"

"Did, too. Jace was always trying to figure out ways to get you alone."

"Do you feel like walking around the woods? I'd like to see if anything looks familiar."

"Yeah. Maybe you're right, and it'll do me some good," Nicole said as she and Castle fell behind Tammy. "I've decided to take a leave of absence from work. I'm going to Oklahoma to stay with Mama for a while."

A few vibrant red mushrooms littered the path ahead. Tammy leaned down and snapped several pictures of them. She cocked her head to meet Nicole's gaze. "What about Harry?"

Nicole sighed. "Some time apart will do us both some good."

Castle stopped sniffing the ground and stared back toward the parking area. A low growl started in his chest as he took inventory of their surroundings. Someone moved behind a tree several feet away.

Tammy pushed Nicole behind her and undid the button on her gun holster. "I know you're there, so come on out."

Fred McCoy took a few faltering steps toward where Tammy and Nicole stood. "I didn't mean to startle you two ladies."

"What were you doing hiding behind that tree?"

"I saw you walk out here and was hoping to have a word with you about Ruby." His Adam's apple bobbed so hard it looked like it might fly out of his throat.

"What do you mean?" As Tammy stared into Fred McCoy's eyes, she had no doubt he was not the hermit his son made him out to be. He was up to something. But did it have anything to do with Uncle Ellis's murder?

"I just was, uh, wanting to know how Obie's doing." He rubbed his chin and shuffled from one foot to the other.

"You can call the hospital. I don't know how he is." Tammy's lips formed a thin line as she and Fred McCoy took part in a staring contest.

"I'll do that, Detective Sharp." The smile he'd kept plastered on slid off his face. "I hope you ladies enjoy the rest of your day."

The look in Fred McCoy's eyes titillated every nerve in Tammy's body. It was time to narrow the suspect pool down. But instead, the list continued to grow.

chapter sixty-eight

THE RYDER FUNERAL HOME parking lot seemed to hold more cars than the last pop concert Tammy attended with Thomas's family back in Atlanta. Tammy couldn't remember the name of the Indie group, but she'd enjoyed the show more than she'd thought.

She and Mama had arrived early for the memorial, so they opted to sit in the car for a few minutes.

As Tammy got ready for Abigail Hunt's funeral, she took a closer look at her life. She'd spent too much time focusing on herself. It was time to get back to doing what she loved.

Finding killers.

It wasn't so much finding the killer that made her heart thump with joy; it was the look on people's faces when the person who murdered their loved one was brought to justice.

She'd slacked on finding who killed Uncle Ellis. If this had been a case back in Atlanta, she and Thomas would've likely already made an arrest.

Uncle Ellis's murder hit too close to home. Maybe that's why she felt she could be doing more to find his killer.

It was time to dive in head first. Finding the killer would be Tammy's top priority. Then she'd go home.

With a decision made, she sighed as she placed both hands on the steering wheel. "Mama, are you sure you want to spend the next few nights at the hospital?"

"Erwin has a work emergency that's taking him out of town."

"I think Sheriff Obie will be fine without you staying there."

"I've already told Erwin I'd be there this afternoon." Mama gripped the door handle and left the passenger door cracked open.

"But you'll be super uncomfortable sleeping on the hard little couch."

"I'm not leaving him alone in that hospital. And that's final. I do wish you'd come with me, though."

"That's not happening," Tammy said before folding her lips shut.

"We could have dinner with Obie in his room and play cards." Mama's eyes crinkled with a smile.

"At least he's awake now. And you don't need to worry about leaving me here. I've lived alone for the past twenty years."

The stern look on Mama's face morphed into one of relief. "I'm so thankful he's awake. Tammy, I do believe I love that man."

A sharp breath left Tammy. Right along with the ridiculous notion of returning to Atlanta. Mama need-ed Tammy now more than ever. "Love? I thought you were just trying to figure out who killed Uncle Ellis."

"At first, yes." Mama turned her head toward the passenger window. "Our mutual love and respect for Ellis brought us together. I think Ellis would be tickled."

That left Tammy speechless. She probed Mama's eyes before she opened the door. "We better get inside."

The heat hit Tammy's face when she got out of the car. It had been fifty degrees yesterday, and today, it had to be at least eighty.

Mama looked at the sky on her way into the funeral home. "I hope it doesn't storm," she said.

A few minutes later, Tammy entwined her arm in Mama's and focused on the song playing over the loudspeaker.

Amazing Grace, how sweet the sound...

Mama glanced at Tammy before she pulled her close. Could she tell Tammy had considered leaving when she found Uncle Ellis's killer, only to change her mind because of Mama's relationship with the sheriff?

A little voice inside Tammy's head whispered that she was being selfish. Mama deserved love and happiness. She shut the voice down and listened to Abigail's best friend speak about their lifelong friendship.

"Even when Abigail and I bickered over who would win Douglas's heart, she and I always put each other first. In the end, he didn't pick either one of us." She wiped her eyes as a small smile crept across her face. "I remember how we laughed for hours over how stupid we'd been, almost letting a man come between us..."

The rest of what she said became a blur as Tammy sought Douglas McCoy out. He sat midway back, his spine rigid against the wooden bench. His face matched his back. Hard, uncaring even.

Her watch buzzed against her wrist. She almost decided not to read it. But it could be significant.

Still, she shielded the screen from Mama as she read the text.

> *Let the dead bury the dead. You should be looking for the gold.*

chapter sixty-nine

Before five o'clock, the light outside the windows faded to darkness. A boom of thunder rattled the house as Tammy climbed onto her bed and patted the space beside her. Castle jumped, his spine shaking with emotion over the upcoming storm.

She rubbed his side a few times and whispered words of comfort as she peered out the window. After she stared outside for a few minutes, she picked up a notebook and listed each suspect. A sigh left her as she read through her research on lost gold. It still dumbfounded her to know she couldn't even find Uncle Ellis's clues, much less the actual gold. Uncle Ellis said he was leaving clues, so there had to be something she was missing.

A downpour beat against the side of the house. She bit her lip as she listed all her assets on another piece of paper. It was time to gather all she could to stop the killings.

Another round of thunder boomed. Tammy's brow furrowed as she pulled up the Weather Chasers social media page. Sure thing, the map looked like a homemade Valentine's Day card, full of red.

Jace's name and number flashed across the screen. Her heart jolted. She took a deep breath and answered. "Hello."

"Tammy, are you and your mom okay?"

"Mama is at the hospital with Sheriff Obie, but I'm fine." Another round of thunder boomed. "I think."

"Listen, I just wanted you to know I'm here at the house, packing a few things. Leo and I fly out for Oklahoma tomorrow night."

"Thanks for telling me. I'm glad to hear you and Leo are getting along."

"Yeah, me too. My stepdad has a birthday this weekend, so we'll be there for that."

"I hope you're not planning to leave in this mess."

"No, I'll be staying put until it passes. The radar shows some bad weather coming through."

"Good deal. Oh, my Captain called me yesterday. They found Chip Reeker camped in Florida. He's back in jail, where he belongs."

"That's good news."

"Yep."

After a few awkward moments of silence, Jace cleared his throat. "Holler if you need anything."

"You, too. Oh, Mama's beeping in. I better get it."

"Bye, Tammy."

The phone call with Mama had Tammy on the move, looking for a rain jacket and boots. One of Mama's employees, Heather, was stuck in traffic in Little Rock, and her sixteen-year-old daughter, Ashley, was home alone. She'd asked Tammy to pick her up.

By the time Mama texted Tammy the address, the rain had slowed to a mere drizzle. When she stepped outside, a deep purple and gray sky greeted her. Her stomach dropped. This couldn't be a good sign.

Jace stood out on his front porch, his head angled toward the sky. He glanced in Tammy's direction before he jogged across the yard. "Hey, you're not going out in this, are you?"

She filled him in on the situation with Heather, and he insisted on going with her. They, including Castle, piled in her Bronco and headed across town.

The sky shifted to a greenish-black color, making Tammy's skin crawl. "The sky looks scary."

"Yeah, we need to hurry. That's a wall cloud in the distance," Jace said.

With five minutes left to go, quarter-sized hail pinged the windshield. Tammy pressed the gas pedal. Officer Rayburn would have to let her speeding slide.

Heather's yellow house stood out among a street full of basic white ones. Tammy ran to the porch and knocked. The door swung open. Ashley, wearing a blue rain jacket, held a tiny gray kitten in her arms. Her eyes darted from Tammy to the Bronco.

"Ashley? I'm Tammy. I see you're ready to go."

"I know who you are. I looked you up on Instagram. I'm not leaving without Skittles."

"Okay, bring him. Let's run."

Rain slapped Tammy in the face. After she helped Ashley into the back, she scrambled to get in the driver's seat. Her veins pumped with adrenaline as she backed out of the driveway. Castle swiveled his body and stared at the kitten. Jace ruffled Castle's hair, and he let out a huff and turned back around.

A piece of tin flew across the street in front of the Bronco. It hit a mailbox and knocked it to the ground. Jace laid his arm on the dash and peered out the window. "We need to go to Ellis's."

"What's that sound?" Ashley's voice rose with the last word.

Before Tammy could ask what sound, it hit her. The last time she'd visited Helen, Georgia, she'd hiked up to Anna Ruby Falls. The two waterfalls were breathtaking and so loud. That's the sound Tammy heard right now. Massive waterfalls except tripled. Tammy would bet her last dollar that a tornado had to be near.

She pushed the gas pedal to the floor. They had to make it to Uncle Ellis's. The secret room was underground. That had to be why Jace said to go there. Within minutes, Tammy slid into the yard and stopped right outside the door.

"Give me the keys and stay here." Jace took the keys and shielded his face as he ran to the door.

Within seconds, he came back and hollered for Tammy to go. Jace used his jacket to shield Ashley and her kitten as pieces of hail hammered them.

Castle refused to budge. Tammy started off the porch. Jace grabbed her arm and shook his head. He ran to the Bronco and carried Castle in like a baby. Castle cut his eyes over to Tammy, and she could've sworn he looked smug.

The wind roared to the point that the house seemed to breathe. Even so, Tammy felt peace as she closed the trap door behind her.

Jace wiped the water from his eyes. "I'm gonna go upstairs and get some towels, blankets, and pillows. Be right back."

An hour later, the storm hadn't let up. Soft snores came from the sofa where Ashley, Skittles, and Castle lay bundled up.

Tammy blinked at Jace, who sat on the other end of the loveseat. "Thank you for being here. I don't know what I would've done without you."

He chuckled. "I have a feeling you would've been just fine without me."

Tammy's voice came out as a mere whisper, and she lowered her gaze. "I'm beginning to wonder about that."

Jace leaned closer to Tammy. "Could you possibly mean…"

She closed the space between them and breathed in musty rain and spice before she turned her face to his. Jace's eyes widened as he wrapped his hands in Tammy's hair and tugged her close. Her thoughts jumbled together as she lost herself in Jace's gaze.

Ashley coughed and rolled onto her side.

Tammy and Jace smiled and put some space between them. Jace ran the tip of his fingers down Tammy's face. She caught his hand and hugged it to her heart before she lay her head on his chest. The storm that raged outside could not compare to the one inside Tammy. She felt, no, she knew, in the last few moments, her life had taken a turn, and it would never be the same.

chapter seventy

With Mama in Jonesboro and Jace in Oklahoma, Tammy had plenty of time to look at the case with fresh eyes. She plopped down at the kitchen island with the notebook from the previous day. She looked at each suspect's name and wrote the reason for each one.

1. *Lorene Pankey was dating Uncle Ellis, knows more than she lets on, and is missing. Was she kidnapped, or did she run?*

2. *Sheriff Obie knew about the secret room. He was close to Uncle Ellis. Could he have killed him over the gold?*

3. *Erwin Wilson could've been in on it with Sheriff Obie. He looks like a weasel.*

4. *Douglas McCoy is just shady. He's up to something. But does it have to do with Uncle Ellis?*

5. *Fred McCoy lurks around for no good reason. Could he and Douglas be in on it together?*

6. *Patrick Wood was more involved with Uncle Ellis, so he could know more than he was saying. Uncle Ellis*

could've asked for his opinion on something... the gold?

7. *Since Anthony had been cleared, Lewis Carter may have held a grudge against Uncle Ellis for siding with Pat Wood over his family. He lives close to Black River, so he could've had easy access.*

"What do you think, Castle? Should I take the sheriff's name off the list?" He licked her hand.

"I'll take that as a yes." She tapped her chin with the ink pen. "But for now, I'll just move him to the bottom of the pool."

At the bottom of the page, she wrote: **WHERE IS THE GOLD?!?**

This was useless. She needed to go back to the crime scene. Black River. For that, she'd need warm clothes and fishing gear. After she spent thirty minutes gathering what she needed, she dropped Castle off with Heather and Ashley and headed to the storage building to swap vehicles.

Her poor Bronco would need to have the hail damage fixed, but that would come later. Another item on Tammy's list was to install a garage. She couldn't live somewhere her baby had to stay out in the elements. No way.

As Tammy picked up the bait and maneuvered the boat into the water, a chilly breeze gently nipped at her cheeks. The setting sun cast a mesmerizing dance of light and shadows across the rippling water, while a fish playfully popped in and out, adding to the serene beauty of the scene.

Memories of Uncle Ellis flooded her mind. No matter what, she had to bring the murderer to justice. To do that, she needed to figure out what gold they expected her to find. A sigh of frustration left her. Who in the world knew how to simply find gold? If it was that simple, wouldn't everyone be doing it? She'd give anything to know where it was. Right now, she felt clueless. She didn't even know what gold to look for. Should she focus on the gold the Kizer man supposedly buried? The gold many people thought was hiding around Old Davidsonville? How did one find lost gold? There had to be clues from Uncle Ellis. But where?

A piece of yellow crime scene tape clung to a log where she and Jace found Abigail's body. Tammy scanned the area and prayed no one else would be there.

She could picture Uncle Ellis throwing a line into the water and handing a young Tammy the pole. He'd tease her about getting the hook caught in underwater bushes. When they'd bring Jace, he always said she fished like a girl.

"Oh, Uncle Ellis, I miss you so much." Her voice seemed to echo in the crook of the river.

An eagle flew across the sky. Tammy turned the motor off and floated near a bunch of trees with their roots hanging into the water. This is the spot where Uncle Ellis liked to park and fish. As a kid, she never noticed the beauty surrounding them. Now, it nearly took her breath away.

She strung a worm on her hook and threw the line into the water. Although she supposed fishing was a pointless waste of time right now, it reminded her of Uncle Ellis.

When dusk kissed the sky, she wrapped the line around the pole and squirted sanitizer on her hands. A boat came around the bend and stopped directly beside Tammy's.

A woman with a platinum blonde updo grinned. "Howdy, Tammy."

The woman's voice had Tammy blinking. "Hi." She took a closer look and gasped. "Miss Vivian? You changed your hair."

"Yes. I sure did. It was time. Have you found what you're looking for?" Miss Vivian met Tammy's gaze. She exuded confidence that Tammy had not noticed before this moment.

A grin tugged at Tammy's lips as she thought of Miss Vivian flirting with the men at the diner. That had to be the reason for her apparent makeover. "I've been fishing. What I caught, I put back. What are you doing out here?"

"Same as you. Just fishing to pass the time." Miss Vivian's gaze traveled over the contents of Tammy's boat. "Where's your cute dog?"

"He's not a fan of water, so I didn't bring him." Tammy moved to the seat by the motor. "I was just about to head back."

"All right. I'll tag along then since it's getting dark fast. Maybe I could get you to help me with my boat?"

Tammy nodded. She almost asked who helped her unload it but didn't want to sound mean. When they got to shore, Tammy glanced inside Miss Vivian's boat. Something was off. But what?

Miss Vivian pointed at the parking area. "My old beater is just up there. Would you be a dear and help me up this hill?"

"Sure thing."

An older Chevy with a boat trailer on the back, Uncle Ellis's Ford, and another car had the parking lot to themselves. Tammy stopped beside the Chevy and laid eyes on the only other car. A Ford Taurus. Her blood went cold, and her stomach sank with dread. Miss Vivian's boat had been empty. No pole. No fish. She whipped about.

Miss Vivian held a tire iron in her hand. Before Tammy could act, the iron cracked into her skull. Someone caught Tammy from behind as she lost her balance.

A loud voice in her ear caused Tammy's head to throb. "Why'd you hit her so hard? We ain't trying to kill her just yet, woman!"

The person with the loud voice stuffed a greasy rag in Tammy's mouth and dragged her across dead leaves and bumpy ground. She tried to make out who it was that held her, but her vision jumped all over, and all she made out was a blur.

"Pop the trunk before somebody comes."

Tammy landed in the trunk with a thud. She cried out against the rag when her knee twisted almost backward. Someone jerked her leg out from underneath her and tied her feet and hands together. Her knee and head played a tune as the throbs jumped from one to the other.

She should've never left Castle behind.

chapter seventy-one

THE ECHO OF A gunshot rang throughout the air and sent Tammy's mind spiraling back to Chip Reeker's apartment. Her chest burned like the bullet that changed her life had returned. Each erratic breath cringed in her lungs as despair threatened to overtake her.

Something heavy landed on her chest, causing her to spring into action. With a series of jerks, she managed to shift the weight. Then, without warning, the burden lifted, and a heart-wrenching cry, so piercing that it seemed to resonate within Tammy's very bones, emanated from above her head.

A few seconds later, the weight returned, and hair tickled her face. After maneuvering to the left, she craned her neck and scanned the area. A masked man stood in the distance, holding the tire iron. He sprinted into the woods. As Tammy jerked against the ties, she vowed she would make him pay.

She dragged in a labored breath. The burden on her chest wasn't something. It was someone. She caught a whiff of Red Door perfume. Dread pooled in her stomach. This had to be Vivian White. That scent seemed too familiar.

The dirty rag the man had stuffed in her mouth nearly choked her, so she squeezed her eyes shut and waited. After the gunshot, rangers would come to investigate.

Within seconds, someone lifted the body off Tammy. She opened her eyes. Lorene Pankey pulled the rag out of Tammy's mouth. "Lorene?"

Lorene's eyes widened as she scanned Tammy's face. She cut the zip tie, binding Tammy's ankles together. For once, she didn't seem to have anything smart to say. "Let's get you out of here."

Tammy landed on both feet, and her left leg buckled. She locked her molars to keep from crying out as a sharp pain hammered through her knee. "What are you doing here?"

"I'm sorry, honey. Ellis would be fit to be tied if he knew this happened to you."

Flashing blue lights shined in the distance. Help will be here soon. "How?" Tammy's thoughts muddled together.

"I have to go, but I will see you soon. Please don't say anything about me being here to anyone. The police are in on it."

"In on what?" Tammy attempted to lean her head into her hands, but the binding on her wrists stopped her.

Tires screeched at the same time the lights nearly blinded Tammy. Lorene disappeared into the woods. In her place stood a park ranger Tammy recognized as Amber Travis, someone she had met on more than one occasion.

Amber held Tammy steady before she cut the binding around her wrists. "Here, lean on me."

"Thank you."

A second park ranger performed CPR on the person Tammy confirmed as Vivian White. He shook his graying head. "It's no use. She's gone." He moved his gaze to Tammy. "I don't guess you know who shot her?"

Tammy shook her head as she stared into Miss Vivian's haunted gaze. Her brain fogged over, and she struggled to remember what had happened. "I think there was a man here."

"A man? Can you tell us who?"

Tammy closed her eyes and attempted to shake her head.

Amber kept Tammy's arm steady. "The police are on their way."

That's the last thing Tammy heard before she leaned on the back of the car. Waves of nausea started in the pit of her stomach, and her mouth watered. Things around her moved in slow motion, and the voices echoed as if they came from a tunnel across town.

Had Vivian been the killer all along? Spending time with Tammy and Mama, mocking them? She'd wanted a big city detective to help find her dead nephew. Yeah right. Could she have killed her own nephew and made it appear to be a drug deal gone wrong? Tammy would say yes. That woman had been pure evil.

Acid sloshed a scorching trail the length of Tammy's throat as echoes of her failures overtook her mind. She was not the detective she thought she was. Maybe her encompassing desire to follow in Daddy's footsteps had ruined her life. So many clues had gone unnoticed ever since she'd been back home. It was time to change the path she'd taken. She had an opportunity to quit her job.

Uncle Ellis had seen to that when he left her everything he'd worked for.

She would be making a trip to Atlanta soon. To turn in her badge.

chapter seventy-two

The following day, Tammy woke to a headache and Mama staring a hole through her. She repositioned her leg on the hospital bed and licked her lips. "Hi, Mama. Where's Castle?"

"Castle is with Harry. Don't move too fast. Fred McCoy hit you so hard you've got a concussion." She put a straw in Tammy's mouth. "Sip on this, honey."

The cool water refreshed Tammy's throat as her mind worked to register what Mama said. Harry would take good care of Castle, but the rest of what Mama said made no sense. She rubbed her temples and closed her eyes. "What makes you think Fred McCoy hit me?"

"Well, didn't he?"

"No, I think it was Miss Vivian."

"Miss Vivian?" Mama rose out of her seat, her eyes bugged out. "Are you certain?"

"I believe so." Tammy turned her head to the right when the throbs intensified. "My head is killing me."

"Close your eyes. The doctor will be here shortly." Mama's lips lingered on Tammy's forehead.

"Okay, I think I will." Her eyes started to get heavy. Mama let out a sigh, and Tammy cracked her eyes open. "Mama?"

"I'm here, honey."

Heaviness threatened to take Tammy into a deep sleep, but she couldn't allow that to happen yet. "I'm sorry for denying you a grandchild. That was selfish of me."

Mama leaned close enough to Tammy that she could tell Mama had recently had a cup of coffee. "Don't worry about that. I'm just thankful you're okay. I love you."

"I love you, too."

An hour or so after the doctor left, a nurse wheeled Tammy out of the clinic and helped her inside Mama's car. Thankfully, Tammy's headache eased up a bit. On top of the concussion, she had a sprained knee. Considering what could've happened, she had no complaints.

Tammy ran the night's events over and over in her mind. "Why do you think Fred McCoy was there?"

"It's a long story. I only know it because Obie is staying on top of things from his hospital bed." Mama blew a long breath out. "You up to hearing it right now?"

"I may scream if you don't tell me." Tammy glanced at Mama before taking a pain pill out of the bottle. She hated taking medicine, but the pain in her knee, combined with her head, overruled that notion.

"Vivian isn't who she said she was. It turns out she's Constance McCoy."

The pill lodged in Tammy's throat. She gulped a few more drinks of water as her lashes flew high. "Douglas's mama?"

"Yes." She rubbed her neck, never taking her eyes off the road. "Remember, she left Fred a few weeks after Douglas was born, and as far as I know, she hasn't been back here since."

"But what motive could Fred and Constance McCoy have to grab me?" The struggle to keep her eyes open intensified. Her lids closed, and she leaned her head back.

When they turned down their street, rain pattered across the windshield. The sun shone brightly in the north, giving Tammy hope. *Things may seem dismal, but there's always a bright side to life.* They had leads, possibly the murderers, which was more than she had yesterday. She hated that Vivian lost her life, but it had been her decisions that caused her to get shot.

"It looks like they may be the ones who killed Ellis. Obie says this is an active investigation, so no arrests have been made, but I'm hoping."

That woke Tammy up. Her head whipped sideways, and she ignored the ache that came with the turn. "Have they declared Uncle Ellis's death a homicide?"

Mama glanced out the window and grabbed a rain jacket from the back seat. She handed it to Tammy. "Not yet, but I think they will."

She took the jacket and followed Mama inside. "Again, what motive could they have?"

"Jace and Obie think it was them messaging you about lost gold." She turned the thermostat up before heading to the kitchen.

Tammy's heart pitter-pattered like the rain hitting the window. "When did you talk to Jace?"

"When have I not?" She put on a pot of water to make sweet tea. "He's called me a hundred times since last night checking on you."

A familiar heat entered Tammy's chest, and her cheeks flamed. "Have they arrested Fred yet?"

"He's at the station for questioning. Last I heard, Douglas lawyered up." Mama put her hands on her hip. "You need to rest. Harry's bringing Castle home in a couple of hours, and I want you in bed until then."

After she curled up on the couch, Tammy closed her eyes. A picture of Lorene Pankey entered her mind. She'd been there. Tammy couldn't be sure, but it had to have been Lorene who shot Vivian and saved Tammy from who knows what. She'd fill Mama in on that piece of information after her nap. As her eyes drifted closed, she thought of what happened.

Maybe she'd found a killer. Or even two. If Tammy had to, she'd spend the rest of her life making sure Fred paid for what they did to Uncle Ellis. Since this was the last murder she'd solve, she had better do it right.

chapter seventy-three

Wariness crept into Tammy's bones as she left the police station. She paused a few feet away and looked back at the building. The meeting to identify Fred McCoy as her assailant left her feeling out of sorts.

"What's wrong?" Mama hovered worse than a car salesman needing one more sale to hit his bonus.

"I can't put my finger on it, but something is off." Tammy winced when she bent her knee. The brace helped some, but the pain had intensified over the past few days. "I don't trust Douglas McCoy, and I think it could've been him instead of his daddy."

"Well, you just confirmed it was Fred. Were you wrong?" Mama snorted and put her arm out. "Hold onto me."

"I said I thought it was his voice I heard, but I couldn't be positive." Tammy slid into the front seat of Mama's car, careful not to hit her knee on the dash. "I'd just been knocked in the head, so it's kinda hard to remember who threw me into the trunk."

"I guess Douglas could've been involved. Constance was his mama, after all," Mama said as she pulled out of the parking lot.

Tammy sipped her coffee and set the cup inside the cupholder. "It's hard for me to think of her as anything but Miss Vivian."

Mama nodded. "I just can't believe she had plastic surgery all those years ago to keep people from recognizing her."

A few of the cases Tammy had worked on over the years floated through her mind. One man killed his twin brother and assumed his identity. They'd fought over money, and it quickly escalated to murder. "People have done worse to keep from being charged with murder."

Her tone turned soft. "Tammy, I have to ask, what happened to make you so suspicious of men? Was it Jace leaving you for Una? You know he felt he had no choice."

A frown tugged at Tammy's lips. "I'm not any more suspicious of men than you are."

"Oh, really? What about Jace? You were suspicious of him. I also remember you saying you think Pat Woods is hiding something."

"That's just two men, Mama."

"I wasn't finished." Mama gave Tammy the side eye. "You thought Douglas McCoy was up to something that day at the bank. You think poor Erwin is a weasel, and I'd be willing to bet that Obie's name is at the top of your suspect list."

"I mean, it's not at the top..." Tammy stopped talking when she caught the look on Mama's face.

"So, his name *is* on your list?"

Heat ran up Tammy's neck. "Yes, Mama, it is."

Mama shook her head, and there was no mistaking of her sarcastic tone. "What about Gleason Murphy? Surely, he was up to something when he gave you and Jace jobs at the newspaper all those years ago. Do you think he had ill intentions when he picked up your boat and truck?"

"Okay, now you're going overboard." A sigh left Tammy.

"If you don't want to end up alone, you need to learn how to give people grace and stop treating everyone like they're a suspect or a criminal you're trying to take down."

"I get your point. Okay? I need to change my ways, or I'll end up a miserable human. Alone and full of suspicions."

"I hope you do. Now, are you sure you're up to going to Atlanta by yourself? I can always go with you."

"No, I'll only be there two nights. My testimony against Chip Reeker is part of the job." Tammy ran her teeth across her bottom lip. "Maybe the last part."

Mama gasped. "Are you saying what I think you are?"

"Yeah, I'm not a hundred percent sure, but I'm leaning toward moving home."

Mama squealed. "I'm so happy right now I can't stand it."

A grin tugged at Tammy's lips as Mama's happiness turned out to be contagious.

chapter seventy-four

THREE DAYS LATER, TAMMY sat at the airport in Atlanta, waiting to board the late flight to Memphis. Her testimony against Chip Reeker had been short and painless. He decided to take an offered plea deal. Chip agreed to plead guilty to the attempted murders of both Tammy and his grandmother for a shorter sentence.

Sadness crept into Tammy's bones. This young man had tried to kill his grandmother because she refused to give him money for video games. Tammy pitied him. He would have plenty of years to think about what he'd done. To consider how he'd allowed his gaming addiction to destroy his family. His soul, even.

She glanced at her watch and bit her lip. It was almost ten, and she couldn't wait to get home to see Mama. She needed a hug like never before. A few minutes later, she set her phone to airplane mode and boarded the plane.

The flight lasted around an hour and twenty minutes. Tammy used that time to reflect on the last few weeks. She'd learned a lot about herself. One thing was her lack of grace for mankind. She couldn't pinpoint when she'd turned so cynical, but she had to fix it. She'd already started by fully and truly forgiving Jace for marrying Una. When she thought of their past, the pain that usually hit her chest didn't come. In its place was peace like she'd never felt before.

As soon as she exited the plane in Memphis, she got her suitcase and hightailed it to the parking lot. She had a pep in her step that had been missing for years. Even the cold breeze frosting her cheeks and nose as she loaded her luggage couldn't take the smile off her face. She kept her coat on as she pumped the pedal to start the engine.

She turned airplane mode off her phone and rubbed her shoulders. Her phone pinged twice. When she picked it up, she stared at a message from Sheriff Obie. She frowned as she read that Fred McCoy had been released. Great.

When she clicked on the second message, a picture out of her most dreaded nightmare greeted her. Mama lay on a cot, her legs and hands tied together. Her curls had dried blood matted on the side of her head, and it looked like she had a black eye.

A burning sensation stormed through Tammy, over-taking every fiber of her body. She dialed the number. The line connected, but no one spoke. The churns of her stomach nearly overtook her thoughts as nausea begged to be released.

"Hello?" Tammy's tone came out even, calm, and col-lected.

A man's scratchy voice came on the line. "Hello, Detec-tive Sharp. Were you surprised by my message?"

"I want to see my mama."

"For now, you'll have to trust that she is alive."

"What do you want?"

"Are you so ignorant you still don't know? I want the gold Ellis stole from me."

"I told you I don't know about any gold."

"Pity. Because your pretty mama's life depends on it."

"I swear I will find you."

"Please do find me. As long as you have my gold, your mama will live." A pause. "And Detective Sharp, don't get the police involved. Not even Obie Wilson."

"I don't need the police."

"That's a girl. You have until dawn, or your mama will end up at the bottom of Black River."

The phone line disconnected.

She cried out, determined to push her emotions away. If Mama had a chance to live, Tammy had to flip a switch. She couldn't feel anything right now. She had to find a killer, or all would be lost.

Fred McCoy had no idea what he'd done. Tammy was coming for him, and he'd regret ever laying a hand on Mama.

chapter seventy-five

THE DRIVE OUT OF Memphis passed in a blur. As she sped toward the Marion exit, she dialed Harry's number. Please answer!

"Dr. Benson."

"Harry! It's Tammy Sharp. Mama's not home, and I have reason to believe Castle is there hurt. Please, will you go over there?" A sob left Tammy as she waited for him to answer.

"Of course." Ruffling, and then a door slammed. "I'm on my way there now. Can you stay on the line?"

"Yes. I'm driving down the interstate from Memphis." She wiped away the water that threatened to blur her vision.

"Tammy, please stay calm. You won't do Castle or anyone else any good if you lose control of the vehicle." Harry's smooth doctor voice seemed to calm her nerves at least a little bit.

She'd take a Valium if she didn't need to stay completely alert. "Thank you, Harry. I'll try."

"Where did you say Miss Ruby is?"

"Umm, I'm not sure."

Harry's labored breathing almost set Tammy off. "I located Castle. He's out back."

Moisture spilled from her eyes. "In the cold? Is he..."

"He's breathing. Tammy, I will have to put the phone in my pocket so I can carry him home. Is that okay?"

"Yes. Please, call me back as soon as you can."

By the time Tammy passed the Tyronza exit, her phone rang. "He's okay. Can you tell me why someone would lace a steak with a sedative?"

"I can't."

"All right. Listen, I'll keep him here tonight. You go home and get some rest. Did you find Miss Ruby?"

"I will." Tammy dried her eyes. "Harry, thank you."

With her mind at ease over Castle, she changed her course for Fred McCoy's house. Tammy sprang out of the truck as soon as it stopped. Her hands trembled as she banged on the screen door. Her fist knocked against the metal so hard it made her knuckles tingle. She opened the screen, intent on breaking into the house. Instead of breaking in, she laid eyes on a note taped to the door. Sloppy black letters stood out against the white paper.

STOP WASTING YOUR TIME AND FIND THE GOLD

She used her knife to shimmy the door open. As she stepped inside, she pulled her handgun. She would be ready, no matter what. As she made her way through every room, she found no one home.

Looked like her next order of business would be to take another look at Uncle Ellis's. His notebook said he'd be leaving her clues. So, where were they? What clues had she missed?

Her mind reviewed each suspect during the ride home. Fred McCoy had to be behind this. Now that his wife was dead, revenge very well could be the driving factor for each step he made.

Back at Uncle Ellis's, Tammy walked through each room. In the office, she picked up an old photo of Uncle Ellis and another soldier wearing uniforms. He'd served in the Vietnam War when he was a young man. Those days had impacted him, and he'd confessed to Tammy that his actions had been why he'd never had children of his own.

A drum-like rhythm rattled her heart as realization hit. The Vietnam War started in August of 1964. She almost tripped over her feet, getting to Uncle Ellis's bedroom. That had to be why he wrote 0864 in the notepad. She couldn't believe she'd missed it all this time. She pulled his uniform out of the back of the closet and laid it on the bed. A key and folded paper was tucked inside the coat pocket.

You'll find what you're looking for where fish sleep in tents and trees have holes.

She pressed the note to her chest as memories flooded her mind. One time, when Tammy was around six or seven, their entire family went camping at Davidsonville Historic State Park. Tammy had caught her first fish. A spotted little white crappie. She could still see its beady little eyes staring at her.

Uncle Ellis had told her to put it in their bucket for supper. She'd been so distraught thinking about that fish getting eaten that she snuck it back to camp and hid it underneath her sleeping bag. In her mind, she had been doing the right thing. By morning, their tent had smelled something awful. Uncle Ellis had never let her live that down. He'd joked with her about that every chance he got.

She dropped the key into her pocket and hastened to change into something more feasible for the task ahead. Her phone buzzed when she got on the road to Old Davidsonville. The name that flashed across the screen caused her veins to heat. "Hi, Jace."

"I'm at the airport. Is everyone okay? Harry told me Castle was given a sedative."

After she filled him in on the events, she sighed. "I'm on my way to Old Davidsonville now. Mama's getting away from that madman, no matter what."

"I'm so sorry I'm not there. I should be there."

"It's okay. Really, Jace. I want to tell you something that's long overdue."

"What?" His tone came out low, almost a whisper.

"I really do forgive you, and I hope we can try again."

"I've waited a long time to hear those words." His voice cracked. He cleared his throat before continuing. "Please stay safe. I'll be there as soon as I can."

"I will."

"Do me a favor and share your location with me. I'll be able to track you by your phone."

"Will do."

After Tammy hung up, she slipped a knife behind her knee brace. There's no way Fred McCoy would win this fight. Mama's life depended on it.

chapter seventy-six

A FEW STARS LITTERED the otherwise black sky as Tammy parked behind an abandoned house less than a mile from Old Davidsonville. She slipped on her night vision goggles and pulled the navy blue beanie over her ears as the cool night surrounded her. She wore the same outfit as when they'd broken into Lorene's house - all black, soft material other than the added beanie.

On the trek to the campground, cold, black darkness enveloped Tammy, and a shiver slid through her limbs. A frog croaked in the distance. Tammy's black hiking boots beat against scattered leaves as she broke into a run.

When she arrived, she went straight to the camp-grounds. A lone RV sat at the entrance. Thankfully, no one else was there. She had around three hours to find the gold and get Mama out of that man's clutches, so the fewer campers, the better.

When Uncle Ellis took her camping, he always picked spot number four or eight since those were his favorite numbers. She would focus her search near the vicinity of those two areas, starting with number four.

After an hour of sticking her hands up every hole in every tree she could find, she moved to the area around number eight. It had to be there. Uncle Ellis would not have sent her on a wild goose chase.

With less than two hours until dawn, Tammy spun around. She'd looked up every tree she could find but still had nothing to show for it. She closed her eyes and dragged in several slow, deep breaths.

As Tammy slowly opened her eyes, the first thing that caught her attention was a majestic oak tree standing tall a few feet away from her. Its large, gnarled limbs reached out in all directions, with a scattering of limbs and leaves piled up around its base. Intrigued, she made her way over to the tree and began clearing away the fallen limbs and leaves. As she did so, a sense of anticipation filled her, and she knew the gold would be there. Her efforts revealed a sizable opening in the tree, and as she reached inside, her hand brushed against a hard metal surface. She gasped when she pulled out a metal box wedged securely within the hollow of the tree.

She couldn't keep an ear-splitting grin off her face as she dug the key out of her pocket and opened the box. After pulling out a tattered pocket-sized notebook, an envelope, and a cloth bag that held a few gold pieces, she dialed the killer's number with less than an hour to spare.

"Have you found my gold, Detective Sharp?"

"Yes, but I won't show you where until I know Mama is okay."

Shuffling, and then Mama's voice came over the line. "Tammy Gail?"

"Mama!"

"Now that you know she's alive, let us set a meeting place. I warn you, come alone and unarmed, or there will be consequences."

"I understand," Tammy said as she moved deeper into the woods. She shoved the metal box into a hole in a different tree. "I'm at Old Davidsonville campgrounds. Meet me at number four."

By the time the Ford Taurus crept into the campground, rosy fingers seemed to make marks across the edge of the sky. Tammy's heart rate accelerated as a masked man got out of the car and opened the trunk.

He motioned for her to join him. Each step felt like she walked through cement that hardened the closer she got to the car. Mama lay inside the trunk, her hands and feet bound and a gag in her mouth. With one look at her, Tammy almost lost the calmness she'd worked so hard to maintain.

Mama's eyes glimmered with fear. Mama moaned twice and raised her brows. Tammy had no doubt the masked man would be in serious trouble if Mama had a gun. Even the more soft-spoken and easygoing southern women would go after people who threatened their offspring.

Just as Tammy worked out how to take him down in her mind, another masked man stepped out of the woods. He had a gun leveled at Tammy's chest. He turned it on Mama when he got near the car.

A chuckle left the man closer to Tammy. "You weren't expecting there to be two of us, huh? Surprise!"

Tammy frowned as her mind worked out every possible scenario. Things didn't look good, but her motivation had never been stronger. She'd found the killer. Now, she would do whatever it took to take him down.

Both of them.

chapter seventy-seven

TAMMY'S EYES ROVED OVER the man with the gun, and her gaze stopped at his left hand. A dark brown mole stood out like a shining light. Douglas McCoy had the same mole. "Do you want the gold or not?"

"Remove your jacket." He patted her down, lingering on her knee brace. Thankfully, she'd had enough sense to hide the knife in the woods earlier. "You will take me to it while my associate stays with Ruby. Try something, and she will die, Detective Sharp."

He snatched her phone out of her back pocket and powered it off. Even though he tried to change his tone, Tammy had no doubt the voice didn't belong to Fred McCoy.

Tammy met Mama's gaze and nodded. She did her best to let Mama know she'd get them out of this. No matter what she had to do, neither she nor Mama would be dying that night.

The killer pressed the barrel of his gun into Tammy's spine. She took a few faltering steps, focusing on following through with her plan. An owl hooted in the distance, singing an eerie tune with the crickets. She jumped and gasped. May as well make him think she was full of fear.

The killer made a bitter sound close to a laugh. "You're nothing but a scared little girl. I had such high hopes for you, Detective Sharp, but you're like my Constance was—nothing but a failure."

"You mean your wife?"

"No. Constance was never my wife. After she killed Dennis, she never could be. I would never marry someone with blood on their hands."

A zip passed through Tammy's heart, and she stopped walking. This man had to be a psychopath. "What do you mean?"

"I allowed her to leave town after she had our son. I love him, you know. Like I loved her." He pressed the gun hard into Tammy's spine. "She never should've come back."

Tammy took a step before she paused again. "Why did she kill Dennis?"

"She acted out of anger because he wouldn't tell us where he hid the gold. She was a stupid, impulsive woman." His voice raised an octave, and he became agitated. "Like you, she didn't know how to follow instructions."

"Instructions?"

He ignored Tammy. Instead of answering, he hummed the tune to Amazing Grace. "She never should've brought you to shore that night."

"Do you know who shot her?"

"That's not a question I will answer." The distinct click of his gun cocking caused Tammy's back to stiffen. As she turned and looked into his eyes, she had no doubt he planned to kill her, Mama, and probably even Douglas before the sun rose.

She took a tentative step, carefully stepping over a branch blocking her path. "Can you tell me what happened to Uncle Ellis? Why did you say he committed suicide?"

"He sealed his fate when he told me he found my gold."

"He found your gold? Where?"

The killer let out a swoosh of air, letting Tammy know he had very little patience. "If I knew that, I wouldn't have needed you, would I?"

Tammy ignored the question. Not that the killer would even expect an answer. "So you killed him over gold you didn't even know about?" Heat stormed throughout her blood.

"Why do you need everything spelled out for you?" He sighed. "I knew about it, Detective Sharp. I just hadn't located it yet."

"Then it wasn't your gold."

"It was the gold Dennis and I found. So, yes, it was mine. I already told you he hid it from the rest of us before he died." The pressure on her spine lessened as he pulled the gun back a smidge. "Detective Sharp, keep moving."

"What about Lorene Pankey?"

"What about her? She's another stupid woman." He shoved her, and she tripped, landing on the ground.

A pain shot through her already hurt knee. She sucked in a breath as she gained her feet. "Is she dead?"

"She will be soon." He shoved her again, but not as hard as last time. "Now, move."

This man was a lunatic if Tammy had ever met one. If she had any chance of surviving and saving Mama, she had to turn into something she was not. She added a tremble to her voice as she raised both hands. "Please don't hurt me. I'll do whatever you want."

"All I want is for you to find my gold. How many times do I have to tell you this?"

Tammy stayed quiet until they reached the tree where she'd hidden the box. "I think this is it, but let me make sure."

"Hurry up." He lingered close, keeping the gun pointed at her as she knelt on the ground.

She turned to motion for him to come near. He pulled the mask over his head, and she met the near-lifeless eyes of the bait shop owner, Lewis Carter. As he stuck the mask in his back pocket, Tammy's eyes widened to match the hole in the tree.

His laugh lacked humor as he hit her with a flattened stare. "That was your final surprise, Detective Sharp. You really thought Fred McCoy was smart enough to do what I've done? Foolish! I thought about allowing you to live, but I've changed my mind."

"Please, I have the gold here," Tammy said as she tugged at the box. With some determination, she added a tremor to her voice. "I'm having trouble getting it out. Can you help me?"

He stooped into a squat. The gun slackened in his hand as a joyful look slid across his face. "After all these years, I finally have my gold!"

In the blink of an eye, Tammy snatched the knife she'd hidden in the tree, turned the blade flat, and thrust it into the side of his throat. After a final yank of the knife, she kicked the gun from his hand, pushed him over, and skittered backward.

His eyes gaped as he landed against the tree trunk. He put his hand over the hole in his neck. Blood gushed in between his fingers as his eyes bore into hers. "I underestimated you, Detective Sharp." One side of his lips curved into a grin. "Well done."

She drilled her gaze into his. "If there's one thing I've learned the past few months, it's never hesitate when facing off with a killer."

chapter seventy-eight

JACE HID BEHIND AN RV. Tammy's location stopped here less than thirty minutes ago, so she had to be near.

His brow furrowed as he looked through his binoculars. Douglas McCoy leaned against a Ford Taurus. He lit a cigarette before he ran his left hand through his hair. He seemed to be watching the mist roll across the ground like a quilt draped across a cozy recliner.

He covered his mouth with his hands and made an owl sound. Hopefully, Tammy would hear it and know he was here.

A light popped on inside the RV. Jace's lips turned downward as he picked his way toward the woods. His Glock-19 pressed into his side as he slipped behind a tree.

Douglas McCoy continued staring into the woods. Jace darted to another tree and walked in the same direction Douglas looked, careful not to veer into his line of sight.

After several minutes, muffled voices came from a few yards away. A man leaned down beside Tammy. Jace's heart banged against his ribcage as he crept forward, careful to keep as silent as possible.

Tammy had her hand inside a hole in the tree. She said something to the man, and he lowered himself beside her. Jace's mouth fell open as Tammy yanked a knife out of the tree, turned the blade flat, and stabbed the man in the neck. Before Jace could get his legs to work, Tammy kicked the gun from the man's hand, knocked him over, and scooted away from him.

The man, whom Jace recognized as Lewis Carter, fell into the tree, which prompted Jace's legs to move. Tammy stooped into a squat beside Lewis and said something Jace couldn't make out.

"Tammy!" Jace called her name.

Her head cocked sideways, and they locked eyes. A look of pure relief crossed her face. She hoisted herself to her feet and staggered forward. Jace's legs jolted into motion, and she collapsed in his arms.

She retreated a step, grasping his hand in hers. "We have to get Mama away from Douglas McCoy."

Jace checked for a pulse and shook his head. "The best way to do that is if he thinks Lewis Carter is still alive." His gaze fell on the body. He removed Lewis's jacket, and Tammy grabbed the mask from his pocket. After he slipped the borrowed items on, he put his hand on Tammy's back like he had a gun on her.

They set out toward where Douglas McCoy waited with Miss Ruby. Along the way, Tammy filled him in on everything that had happened.

As soon as Douglas saw them, he stood up straight. "Did you find the gold?"

Jace leaned close to Tammy's ear. "Now."

She ducked to the ground.

A look of confusion crossed Douglas's face. His eyes narrowed as he unholstered his weapon.

Jace shot Douglas's hand.

Douglas cried out and dropped the gun. Blood trickled down his arm. "Why'd you shoot me, Pops?"

Jace kicked the gun out of Douglas's reach and pulled the mask off. "I ain't your pops." He pulled a zip tie from his pocket and secured Douglas's hands.

The trunk popped open. Tammy untied Miss Ruby and helped her out.

Jace dialed 911. When he hung up, he sought Tammy's gaze. "It's over."

She held her hand out to him. "Come here."

His heart slammed in his chest for the second time that night. He closed the space between them and put his arms around Tammy and Miss Ruby.

Douglas kicked the back tire when park rangers and police surrounded them. The local coroner nodded as he followed a detective into the woods.

A sigh left Tammy. She leaned her head on his shoulder and turned her face toward his. Her gaze burned into his and caused his legs to shake. "Thank you, Jace."

The cord in Jace's throat tightened as he fought to keep his emotions in check. So much had happened in his life over the past month that he could hardly believe was real.

The man accused of murdering Una was in jail, awaiting trial. Finally! A sense of weightlessness Jace hadn't felt since the day he found Una settled in his bones. And now that Lewis and Douglas had been caught, Ellis would also have his justice. Not only Ellis, but Jace figured they'd find out that Lewis Carter played a part in many, if not all, the deaths over the past few months. Sonny. Abigail. No telling who else.

Sorrow for the entire situation burst through Jace when the coroner wheeled the body away. But as he met Tammy's eyes, he couldn't help but be grateful it was finally over.

After medics treated Miss Ruby and Tammy, they loaded Douglas in the ambulance and zipped away with a policeman riding in the back with him.

An hour later, Jace gave his statement at the police station. He stood beside Miss Ruby and Tammy when the front door burst open.

Lorene Pankey placed her hands on her hips. "What are you all standing around like buffoons for? I'm here to confess to the murder of Constance McCoy. The woman y'all know as Vivian White."

chapter seventy-nine

THREE DAYS LATER, LORENE'S confession still had Tammy blinking. Tammy smoothed the front of her brown and black plaid blazer and met Lorene's gaze. "Where have you been all this time?"

Only one other person occupied the visitation room at the police station.

With tears misting in her eyes, Lorene sighed. "First, I owe you an apology. I should've told you everything when you came to town, but I was scared."

"I understand what fear can do. Are you up to telling me what happened?"

"Let me start at the beginning." Lorene closed her eyes before she took a sip of water. "Me and Constance were thick as thieves growing up. We both lost our parents at a young age, and I think we bonded over our loss."

Lorene swallowed and took another drink. "We could hardly believe our luck when Dennis Howard and Lewis Carter took a liking to us. Well, I couldn't. Constance was a rare beauty for such a small town. Anyway, the four of us became inseparable."

Tammy bit the side of her lip. "You and Dennis Howard were a couple then?"

"Oh yes. Things went well for a year or so." Her face took on a haggard look. "It took a turn when Dennis and

Lewis took me and Constance on a fishing trip. Dennis found a piece of gold, which prompted us to go on a treasure hunt that ended up costing Dennis his life."

"How so?"

"Well, it took us a few months, but we found a container of gold. Lewis took it home for safekeeping, but Dennis snuck into his bedroom and took it. Dennis said he had a map that would lead to enough gold that we'd never have to work again. But he wanted fame, not just the gold."

"Is that when he went to the newspaper about the gold?"

"It is. Oh, Lewis and Constance were furious. We argued on the boat, and Constance struck Dennis with a paddle. He fell over the side and sank. Lewis was so angry. I was petrified. In shock, really."

Tammy's eyes widened. "Did the paddle kill him?"

"I don't know." Her lips twitched downward, and she sobbed into the napkin she held. "We couldn't find him anywhere, so we went home and pretended like we hadn't been together that day. I was devastated, but Constance convinced me she didn't mean to kill Dennis. She only wanted to scare him. And her and Lewis said we'd all get in bad trouble if we said anything."

"I read a newspaper clipping where Dennis was missing a year."

A sad smile graced Lorene's lips. "Ellis always said you were a star detective. I guess he was right." She took another sip of water and exhaled. "Lewis and Constance parted ways. Constance struck up a relationship with Fred McCoy, and they married within weeks of their first date."

"Did you and Constance remain friends?"

"Yes, we knew it would look suspicious if we didn't. I left town for beauty school and stayed away until a couple of years ago. I still remember how Fred and Constance were the talk of the town when she had a baby eight months after they married. She told him she was early, and he believed her."

"That makes sense."

A police officer peeked through the glass. Tammy raised her hand, asking for five minutes. He nodded before he walked away.

"Three months after little Douglas was born, they found Dennis's body. Constance ran off and never came back. That is until I accidentally told her about Ellis knowing the truth."

Tammy's lips spread into a grim line. "Why would you do that? Did you want Uncle Ellis dead?"

"No! I thought Constance was my friend, and I wanted to warn her never to return to Pocahontas. That was all." A full-fledged sob shook Lorene's shoulders. "I loved Ellis. I just thought…"

Tammy could barely understand Lorene through her sobs. "Lorene. Please finish the story before they come for you. Did you tell Uncle Ellis the truth?"

"Not all of it, but I did tell him the part about Constance. I should've kept my mouth shut."

Tammy handed Lorene a box of napkins. "So why call Vivian or Constance rather?"

"I didn't. She called me once or twice a year to check in. She always asked about the gold, and the last time, she accused me of lying."

"Is that when you told her the truth?"

"I thought I owed it to Constance to tell her to stay away. But I let it slip that Ellis had found a map in Dennis's things."

"Did you know Vivian was really Constance?"

"I swear I didn't know. She changed her face completely."

"Did you know Lewis Carter killed Uncle Ellis?"

"Absolutely not. Lewis Carter has been an upstanding citizen for years. After his sister died, he raised her baby as his own. He gave to charities and worked hard in the community. I promise I thought he was a good man in a bad situation like me."

"Did you suspect someone?"

Lorene looked away. "I'm ashamed to say it, but I thought Obie had something to do with it."

"Are you the one who left the note at the newspaper?"

She shook her head. "I hoped Jace would investigate."

Officer Rayburn poked his head into the room. "Time's up, ladies."

A haggard Lorene Pankey stood and patted Tammy's hand. "Please forgive me. If you'll come back tomorrow, I'll tell you the rest of the story."

As Lorene left the room, Tammy shook her head at the senseless killings over gold.

chapter eighty

Within days, the story of Detective Sharp finding not one but two killers graced every news outlet in Arkansas and the surrounding states. Treasure hunters from all over traipsed around the area looking for the lost gold.

Nicole pinned a welcome home sign on the wall at Sheriff Obie's house. She stood back and glanced at Tammy. "I can't believe little Miss Vivian White was Constance McCoy."

Tammy looked up from the plate of vegetables she arranged on the table. "Me neither."

"I'm still mad you didn't tell me what you had going on." She narrowed her eyes, and her hand flew to her hip. "I mean, you were looking for a killer."

"I didn't want you in danger," Tammy said before she bit down on a carrot. "Then you and Harry had your problems to deal with, so I kept you out of the loop. I'm sorry."

"It's okay. I can't imagine how hard it was for you."

"I'm thankful you and Harry worked things out."

"Me, too." A grin the size of the sign she pinned to the wall graced Nicole's face.

"We've all had a lot to deal with over the past few months."

A dog barked in the distance. It must be Charlie. A family with a Golden Retriever moved into the empty house down the street from the sheriff the week before. Tammy propped the front door open in case Castle was ready to come inside.

"Miss Vivian, along with Lewis Carter, plotted to kill you, which is a lot crazier than Harry having a gambling addiction. Things like that don't happen in towns like ours."

Mama came out of the cozy living room and sighed when she heard what they talked about. "Unfortunately, many murderers hide in plain sight." She pressed her lips together. "It's hard to believe a man who was so close to your daddy was a lunatic. I didn't tell you this, but I took him a basket of muffins a few weeks ago."

"What?" Tammy's skin crawled. "You're lucky he didn't hurt you."

"I know it."

As Nicole and Mama continued talking about the murders, Tammy's mind wandered. The past few days had revealed a lot after she found the booklet in the tree. Uncle Ellis had hidden most of the gold in a secret compartment in his home, and the rest he'd put inside the tree. He had not known who the killers were before he died. It appeared he suspected Vivan of something, but he hadn't uncovered her true identity before he lost his life.

Tammy found a letter inside one of the containers about his plans to donate the gold to the town's museum, so she quietly did that.

After news of Lewis Carter's death spread, many citizens came forward, claiming that they always thought he had a mean streak. Anthony Carter and his family returned to town long enough to close the bait shop and finalize Lewis's affairs. They'd stopped by Mama's and profusely apologized for what Lewis had done.

Douglas McCoy confessed that Lewis had told him he was his biological father around the same time Tammy came back to Pocahontas. After secret blood tests, Douglas found it to be true. Instead of confronting Fred, he allowed his anger to seethe. Lewis pulled Douglas into the situation with Tammy by promising a considerable gold payout. Initially, he swore to Douglas that no one would get hurt.

Fred McCoy had been found tied up in Douglas's basement. Douglas planned to leave town with the gold before having someone release Fred. He hadn't been able to bring himself to kill Fred like Lewis had wanted. Fred raised Douglas, after all. Along with Fred, the stolen contents from Miss Howard's storage unit had been in the basement. Douglas would end up in prison, but Tammy suspected it would be a short sentence.

The history teacher, Patrick Wood, had been helping Uncle Ellis research the history of Pocahontas and Old Davidsonville. His interest in Tammy had been genuine, and she'd let him down as easily as possible.

Lorene told Tammy she'd never left town. Instead, she took a page out of Constance McCoy's book and changed her appearance to that of a homeless person. No one gave her a second glance except for Jace, who insisted on putting her up in a hotel when he met the person he thought was homeless. That thought made Tammy's heart go from fluttering to pounding.

Lorene had followed Constance to Black River when she and Lewis attempted to kidnap Tammy. That's when

Lorene shot Constance. Tammy was grateful, at least. From what the prosecutor told Tammy, Lorene would not be officially charged due to the circumstances surrounding Vivian's shooting.

"Tammy Gail." Mama shook Tammy's shoulder. "Are you listening to me?"

Tammy blinked several times. "I'm sorry, Mama. My mind is all over the place."

"Jace and Harry will be here with Obie any minute." Mama spun around. "Erwin, get over here and be quiet. I want Obie to be shocked."

Sheriff Obie had finally been released from the hospital, and Mama planned to surprise him with a welcome-home dinner. He and Erwin had a falling out several years ago, and Mama was determined to help them mend their relationship.

Castle trotted through the living room and nudged Erwin. He grinned as he scrubbed Castle's side. Tammy looked at Erwin and concluded he wasn't a weasel. He looked a bit mousy, but that was the extent of his weaseliness.

Later that night, Tammy stuffed her feet under the cover and picked up the notebook she'd found in the tree. Scribbles from the past lined Dennis Howard's pages. He seemed to be obsessed with a known killer named John Kizer. Very odd.

She'd have to talk to Nicole about learning more about this Kizer person. She had come home to Harry after he enrolled in counseling. So far, he had stayed away from gambling, and they were on the way to getting their finances straight.

She laid the notebook down and picked up the elusive letter with the instructions Lewis Carter had mentioned on more than one occasion.

Dear Detective Sharp,

I understand your need to bring Ellis Martin's killer to justice—truly, I do. But right now, you have a much more critical task. Your job is to find out where Ellis hid my gold. I've been informed he put the map somewhere only you can find, so you have a great responsibility. Once I have the gold, I will tell you what happened with Ellis, and I promise no one else will die. If you do not find my gold, there will be consequences.

I will be in touch soon.

When Dentmasters' owner fixed the hail damage on her Bronco, he dropped the key to the Bronco beside the seat. That's when he found a couple of mail pieces wedged between her seat and the console. If only she'd found the letter with the instructions earlier. Oh, how it would've saved her some heartache when she first arrived in Pocahontas.

The stillness of the wintry night was interrupted by the faint sound of pings skittering across her bedroom window. Tammy's heart raced with anticipation as she hesitantly pulled the curtain back. To her surprise, Jace stood outside, holding a dozen vibrant red roses in one hand and a bag of assorted candies in the other. A stark white sheet of snow blanketed the ground. Delicate snowflakes continued to fall from the sky, landing on his sleek black leather jacket. It was as if he was captured inside a perfect snow globe, creating a picturesque scene that took her breath away.

After she shoved her feet in a pair of boots, she stuck her foot out the window. Jace laid the roses and bag of candy on the snowy ground. He put his arm up to help Tammy down. She landed in the soft white snow with a crunch. The warmth that circled throughout her body overpowered her teeth chatters as snow littered her hair and face.

"Tammy," Jace said. His soft tone came out tender yet with an edge of excitement she hadn't heard in many years.

Tammy's hands burned to touch his face. To feel his hair. But she'd never get this moment back. She wanted to savor it. She needed to savor it. "Shhh. Let's take a minute just to be here."

"Together?" His glassy-eyed gaze clamped to hers.

"Yes. Together. Always." Rapid-fire heartbeats pattered against her ribcage.

Jace gently brushed a stray lock of hair behind Tammy's ear, his fingers leaving a lingering sensation that sent shivers down her spine. A radiant smile graced his lips as he held his jacket open, inviting her in.

Tammy moved forward, the world around her seeming to slow down as she slipped her arms into the warmth of the jacket. A wide, joyous smile illuminated her face. As their lips met in a tender kiss, a wave of affection washed over Tammy, carrying with it the promise of love, forgiveness, and new beginnings.

chapter eighty-one
two months later

TAMMY TRAIPSED INTO THE office at the newspaper. "If we're going to share this building, we need to lay some ground rules."

He tugged her onto his lap and spun the chair around. "What kind of ground rules?"

She squealed and held onto Jace until he stopped spinning. "For one, there can be no funny business when I'm working a case."

"Yes, ma'am, Miss Private Investigator. What else?"

She twirled a section of his hair. "You can't complain when I blast my rock music. It helps me think."

"No complaints here." He landed a kiss on her cheek. "What else?"

"Hmmm." She stared at the ceiling and tapped her chin. "I'll let you know as they develop."

He grabbed the hand she had used to tap her chin and pulled it away from her body like they were about to dance a tango in the chair. "So you get to make rules up along the way? I don't think that's too fair."

Laughter bubbled from her chest. "No, that's definitely fair."

"What if I have some rules of my own?"

"What kind of rules?"

"My first rule is I must be greeted with kisses every morning," he said as he brought the hand he held away from her close enough to kiss. "Number two is Bon Jovi must be included in the rock music playlist."

"Those are rules I can live with." She turned toward him and planted a kiss on his lips. "Have you heard from Leo today?"

"I have. She says hello." He kissed her nose. "I love you, Tammy."

Goosebumps overtook her entire body as she got lost in the warmth of his eyes. "I love you. So much."

Someone cleared their throat from the doorway. Tammy jumped off Jace's lap and met the shining eyes of Gleason Murphy. "Mr. Murphy, hi!"

"Hello, you two." He stepped inside and grasped Jace's outstretched hand. "It does my heart good to see you both here. I can remember how y'all used to run around the place making googoo eyes at one another."

"We can't express how much we appreciate you, Mr. Murphy," Jace said as he draped an arm around Tammy's shoulders. "You giving us both summer jobs brought us together."

"I'm happy to see the paper in such good hands." Gleason's gaze landed on the bookcase. "I see you found my book."

"You're the one who left that there?"

"I did. Something didn't sit well with me when Ellis drowned. I thought back to how Dennis also drowned on the Black River, and that got my wheels turning."

Tammy leaned into Jace. "What made you stop looking into it?"

"I hit a dead end and didn't know where else to look. When Jace bought the place, I knew he'd be all over it." Mr. Murphy nodded his head.

"Well, seems that things turned out like they were supposed to," Jace said.

"I agree. All right, I need to be on my way to the airport. I hope to see you two when I return from Honduras."

"Honduras? What will you be doing there?" Jace asked as he moved closer to where Mr. Murphy stood.

"I'll be teaching a semester of English at one of the schools."

"Look at you, living a life of adventure." Jace stuck his hand out. "Be safe and keep us posted."

"I sure will." He took Jace's hand before pulling Tammy into a hug. "I'm thankful I will have a good newspaper to read during my downtime."

Tammy met Jace's gaze as the door snapped shut behind Mr. Murphy. "I do believe you're right."

He jiggled his brows. "I like the sound of that. Right about what?"

"When you said things turned out the way they were supposed to. You were right. Life has taken us both down many crazy paths, but I love you now more than I could ever say."

"I love you, my Detective, Private Investigator Sharp."

He picked her up and spun around. Tammy felt certain her squeals of delight could be heard all over Pocahontas.

epilogue
six months later

TAMMY COUNTED EIGHT PEOPLE, including herself, plus Castle, inside Lorene's Love Locks. No matter how many times someone said her name, Tammy found it impossible to focus on anything other than the day ahead.

That is until a puff of smoke sizzled from the side of her head. She cut her eyes at Lorene. "You keep that up, and my hair will be fried."

"Be still." Lorene slapped the hand Tammy held midair. "You want to look good for your wedding, don't you?"

"Of course, but I don't think Jace cares about that."

"Baloney." Lorene tugged another section of hair around the curling wand. "He cares. All men do."

"You're wasting your breath, Lorene," Mama replied with a smirk. "Tammy Gail never has fussed much over her looks. She's so beautiful she hasn't needed to."

Lorene tipped her head to the side. "She does have natural beauty."

Sybil Riggs swiped mascara over her thick black lashes. She batted her hazel eyes and tossed the mascara into her makeup case. "When Tammy left Atlanta, she left a string of broken hearts."

Jace's mother, Inola, tucked black locks behind her ear. Her slim fingers held few wrinkles even though she was near seventy. "My Jace is a lucky man."

"I'd say Tammy is lucky to have Doda," Leo looked at her grandma before poking her tongue out at Tammy.

Tammy screwed her face up at Leo before they both broke into laughter. Thankfully, they'd bonded over the past few months. Leo had leaned on Tammy as they waited for the trial of Una's accused murderer, Slate Sanders.

"I'm lucky to have you both."

Giggles came from behind them. Alvie pressed her face to Castle's side. "I sure love you, boy." Castle wiggled away from Alvie long enough to lick her face.

Warmth spread through Tammy's heart. The moment she met Alvie at the park that day, she felt a connection to her. After she decided to settle in Pocahontas, she talked to Alvie about becoming a part of the family. She'd been living with Tammy and Mama for the past few months. Everything was set for her and Jace to adopt Alvie after they married.

As Tammy and Mama made their way toward the double doors, Tammy glanced at her bouquet and smiled. Mama had the florist build the flowers around pictures of Daddy and Uncle Ellis. Tammy couldn't have asked for a better or more thoughtful wedding present.

"I love you, Mama," Tammy whispered, "Thank you for walking me down the aisle."

"It's an honor. I love you, Tammy Gail." Mama cupped Tammy's cheek. "You're stunning."

A quick glance at the sparkly gown pooling around her ankles, and Tammy grinned. "I'm glad I let you talk me into going all out."

"I still can't believe it."

Mama put her arm around Alvie when the music started. "You ready to start?"

"I'm ready, Grandma," Alvie said as she glanced at Castle in his custom tuxedo top. She tugged on the leash, and her face lit up. "Come on, Castle. You ready to walk me down the aisle?"

Leo, Sybil, and Nicole, all wearing matching periwinkle gowns, lined up at the door behind Alvie and Castle,

Once Nicole got to the front of the auditorium, Tammy found herself locking eyes with Jace. His luscious, silky locks cascaded past his broad shoulders, effortlessly blending in with his black tuxedo. Yes, he had the looks to star in a commercial or movie. That man could go anywhere and do anything. He could have any woman he wanted. Despite this, he had chosen her. Tammy Gail Sharp. Every fiber of her being began to tingle, and she struggled to tear her gaze away from his captivating eyes. Her heart swelled with an unprecedented blend of joy and love.

A tremble shot up Tammy's spine as Jace pressed his lips to hers. The day she woke up in the hospital after getting shot, she would've never imagined things turning out like this.

The past year had taught her more than she could have expected. The main thing she'd learned was never to hesitate, not only when facing a killer but also when facing the love of her life.

Thank you for reading **To Find a Killer**. If you enjoyed this book, please consider leaving a review.

afterword

Want to stay updated with news about me and my books?

- Like my Facebook page: *@writingleahbrewer*

- Join my mailing list: *theleahjournal.com*

I hope you will leave a review. Your feedback on **To Find a Killer** is invaluable. It helps me improve and guides other readers who enjoy clean murder mysteries. I'm eager to hear your thoughts.

Thank you!

Leah

acknowledgements

I must start by acknowledging two extraordinary women who were pivotal in shaping this story: Vickie Mink and Patty Cooksey. Their distinctive contributions were crucial to the creation of this novel.

In 2023, we had a ladies' trip to Pocahontas and Davidsonville State Park. I needed to conduct further research, and several ladies joined me. While driving around, Patty recounted a childhood tale of camping and sneakily hiding a fish inside her tent. It was this very story that led to the discovery of the note Tammy found in Ellis's uniform. A special thanks to Patty for sharing!

Vickie Mink is the best "hole finder" a writer could hope for. She dedicated countless hours to meticulously reading and re-reading this story, offering advice, suggestions, and viewing things through the lens of a reader. Vickie, your assistance is immensely appreciated!

My daughters, Cassidy and Carissa, each assisted me in different ways. Carissa, thank you for enduring my endless discussions about my characters and story, and for accompanying me on numerous research trips. Cassidy, your insights on necessary changes and clarifications were invaluable.

To my sister-in-law, Brandie Hudson, your skill in reading and offering advice is exceptional. I'm grateful for your support as one of my readers and for your help in resolving so many outstanding issues!

Stephanie Taylor: Thank you for fearlessly editing and never hesitating to challenge me!

Regina Hagen, I want to express my sincere gratitude for meticulously analyzing this novel and providing me with exceptional feedback and suggestions that encompassed everything from the chemistry between characters to the cover design. Additionally, I am incredibly thankful to Regina's mother, Francis, whose exceptional proofreading skills greatly contributed to refining the final manuscript. Their insightful input has been invaluable.

My cover models, my husband Mark and Carlie Rich, are the true stars who made the cover exceptional from front to back. It is, in my opinion, the best cover ever! Thank you both for signing up. Mark, I know you didn't have much choice, but I appreciate you anyway. Haha! And Carlie, stepping in as the ultimate last-minute runner, you exceeded all expectations!

Much love,

Leah

about the author

LEAH BREWER IS A multi-genre author who focuses on writing clean books that anyone can read. She was born and raised in Des Arc, Arkansas, before moving to Northeast Arkansas when her children were young.

She spends her spare time with her husband, Mark, their grown children, and granddaughter, Charlotte. If she's not on a beach, she's dreaming about when she can be!

www.ingramcontent.com/pod-product-compliance
Lightning Source LLC
Chambersburg PA
CBHW062116290726
48975CB00001B/251